The powerful lights burned through the billowing dust. While Ross and Vic Dakin looked on, Big Ralph Veneker and Machen, his black body glistening with sweat shovelled brick dust from the opening. Pretty Billy Binns tore his fingers as he threw back solid chunks of masonry.

To Frank Ross it was the culmination of a year's planning; of a year spent laying out for specialized information, a year of meetings with city gentlemen who could convert the half a million pounds of marks, francs and guilders, a year of careful selection of his team.

Suddenly he heard the clatter of police boots, the triumphant voices of Bryce and Rimmer and he knew there and then in that cramped basement full of struggling figures that he had a debt to pay . . .

OUT

Max Austin

OUT

Based upon the exciting Thames Television
Drama series created by Trevor Preston

CORGI BOOKS
A DIVISION OF TRANSWORLD PUBLISHERS LTD

OUT

A CORGI BOOK
0 552 10821 9

First publication in Great Britain

PRINTING HISTORY
Corgi edition published 1978

Corgi Books are published by
Transworld Publishers Ltd.,
Century House, 61–63 Uxbridge Road,
Ealing, London W5 5SA
Made and printed in Great Britain by
Cox & Wyman Ltd., London, Reading and Fakenham

Out

OUT

Below the brick barrel-vaulted roof of the cellar the dust had begun to settle. In the powerful white glare of the storm lamp Frank Ross knelt forward to inspect the two holes drilled in the cellar wall. Outside the circle of light the figures of four men watched from the shadow.

Running his tongue over his dust-parched lips Ross probed the depth of the holes with a pink rubber gloved forefinger. Behind him Vic Lee came forward and knelt beside the younger man, silently handing him a plastic beaker of coffee.

'It looks good to me, Vic,' Ross said quietly. He moved aside. 'See what you think.'

Lee knelt and played the beam of an electrician's torch over the crumbling brickwork inside the first of the holes.

'Prima,' he said.

The standing men exchanged grins of relief.

He moved the beam to the second hole and the watching men tensed as a frown merged sweat and dust on his forehead. Pushing himself heavily to his feet he turned to Ross. 'To be safe that one needs another two inches. You're barely through the first skin there.'

Ross pushed down the pink rubber at his wrist and held his watch to the light. 'We're already running late, Vic.'

Lee shrugged. 'You're the boss, Frank. I'm only saying what I think.'

Ross nodded and picked up the hammer drill. 'Another two inches,' he said and pushed the bit into the hole.

The watching men tensed as the big drill thundered against the aged brickwork spewing dust and mortar chips back over the crouching figure of Frank Ross.

CHAPTER ONE

SWAYING with the motion of the train the man turned away from the buffet bar and carried the cardboard cup back to the seat where he had left his holdall.

He was surprised how he felt. After eight years he seemed to be without curiosity, without excitement, even without alarm. Somehow, after all he had heard, he had never expected this complete numbness.

He placed the cup on the yellow fold-down plastic table and took out his snout tin before sliding into his seat. He saw the man across the table eye the tin, its dented corners worn smooth as a gun-handle, then turn his eyes away. Perhaps he knew. Frank Ross swept condensation from the window with the palm of his hand. Perhaps the man knew. Perhaps he didn't.

Rolling a cigarette with a skill learnt in the dark Ross looked out over the monotonous November countryside. Ragged mist patches hung around stands of fir trees and gathered above junk filled ponds.

In corrugated iron farmyards men struggled with haltered animals or forked piles of steaming muck. Through the numbness a feeling rose, he knew he couldn't wait to get back to London.

'Ticket.'

Ross turned, in automatic obedience to the harsh tone of voice.

'Your ticket.' The Inspector looked down on him, enjoying his confusion as he quickly felt his pockets, the rolled cigarette dangling unlit between his lips.

'No ticket? You'll have to pay.' He flipped open a charge book.

'Just hold on, it's here somewhere,' Ross said, dropping the cigarette from his lips, conscious of the public humiliation. Four or five people were already watching curiously.

'What station you get on?' The pen was poised. Two or three more people, passing along towards the buffet car had stopped to watch.

'I tell you I've *got* a bloody ticket,' Ross hissed at the man.

The sharp edge of the ticket touched his searching fingers. He drew it from his top pocket. 'O.K.?'

The Inspector took the ticket without a word and clipped it. Ross picked up his cigarette and lifted a petrol lighter to it, his eyes never leaving the man's face.

The Inspector handed back the ticket and turned to move on. As Ross flicked the lighter, the Inspector stopped. Half turning he pointed to the 'No Smoking' sign. 'Can't you read, or what?'

The fury rose in Frank Ross. Then he quelled it. 'That's right' he said. 'Or what!' He drew on his roll-up. For a fraction of a second the Inspector hesitated. Then he turned away without a word.

The station terrified him. The moment the train stopped under the Victorian glass and cast-iron canopy the carriage doors swung open and the immensity of the noise rushed in upon him. Different, more varied than the prison clatter, these sounds were cheerful shouts of West Indian porters, the snarl of baggage trucks, the incomprehensible echo of loudspeaker announcements . . . and with the variety of sounds came a whole variety of sights. Through the window he sat watching, sweat breaking out on his forehead.

People were swarming from the train, shuffling slowly forward with their bags as they approached the bottleneck of the barrier. He looked down at the packed human mass struggling towards the barrier and involuntarily closed his eyes tight.

After a few seconds the moment of panic passed. He got up on unsteady legs, aware for the first time that he was the only one left in the train. As he reached the step down to the platform the cleaners were already pushing their way on to the train.

Moving through the barrier at the back of the crowd Ross tucked his holdall under one arm and headed for the row of black cabs at the rank. He felt better now, once out of the train, but he still found himself bumping into people, unaccustomed to the disorderly flow of passengers across the concourse.

The first cab in the rank was without a driver. But after a moment Ross saw a man of about his own age, big, a denim hat worn low on the forehead.

He opened the back door. 'Where to, Chief?'

'Tulse Hill,' Ross said and climbed in. 'I'll tell you where exactly when we get there.'

'Tulse Hill.' The driver got behind the wheel.

'That's a fair old way from here.'

In the back he heard his passenger grunt non-committally. He shrugged, switched on the engine and set the meter.

As the taxi pushed out of the station into the mass of noon traffic, Ross felt the panic return. But now it was mixed with anger. So much had changed, cheap boutiques, porn magazine shops, pizza parlours, screaming ads. and column after column of new brick and concrete. Even as they crossed Vauxhall Bridge and began to penetrate South London. Frank still felt strange, alien.

Suddenly with a screech of brakes the cab slowed violently, throwing Ross forward.

'Sorry, mate,' the cabbie called. 'You 'ave ter give way to royalty.'

Three young girls ran laughing past the bonnet of the cab, their hair green, their faces decorated with Swastika transfers.

'If the bleedin' Martians landed what *would* they think?' the driver said.

Ross sat staring at the three girls.

'What?' he said uncertainly.

The cabbie nodded at the girls as they disappeared down the road. 'What do they think they look like? A cross between old brass and an 'orror film.'

The cab began to pull forward again.

'It's changed,' Ross said almost to himself.

'You bin away?'

'Yeah.'

'Long?' The driver half-glanced over his shoulder.

'Too long.'

'Yeah. It's changed,' the cabbie conceded. 'You just have to look around you. So much bleedin' traffic you can't move. Why? Them juggernaughts . . . bleedin' monstrosities. How do they expect to keep traffic movin' with them cowsons stuck up every street. They're all bloody foreign. It's all wrong . . . England for the English, London for the Londoners. I know I've had enough, I'm gonna turn it in, go on the bleedin' dole, nineteen years I've bin drivin' one of these pigs, ain't worth a bleedin' carrot!'

In the back seat Frank Ross wasn't even listening. They were driving through the manor, through streets he knew, street corners he had stood on as a kid.

'First left,' he said, 'then sharp right.'

The cab was travelling down a tree-lined residential street.

Ross leaned forward. 'Three . . . just behind that Volvo.'

The cab pulled up. Ross got out and stood for a moment looking up at one of the houses. It stood apart from the others, peeling, uncared for, apparently abandoned.

'Call it four quid, gov,' the cabbie said after a glance at the meter.

'What?' Ross turned.

'Four quid . . . bleedin' robbery, ain't it?'

Ross took out his release money. 'I've only got three,' he said.

The cabbie's voice hardened.

'There's four-thirty-five on the clock . . . I'm doin' you a favour callin' it four.'

'I'll get it for you,' Ross said.

'None of my business, chief, but have you bin away, yer know, inside?'

Ross grinned. 'It must be the suit.'

For the first time a big smile creased the cabbie's lugubrious face. 'Bollocks . . . have it on the Guvnor. He can bleedin' afford it. You're gonna need that few quid, believe me.'

Ross looked at him, genuinely moved. 'Thanks.'

'Me bruvver, young David,' the driver said, 'he done three at Wandsworth.'

He revved the engine. 'Like we was saying – things have

changed out here, mate.' He nodded goodbye. 'Don't let the bastards wear you down, cock!'

Ross waved goodbye to the back of the cab and turned up the weed-grown garden path. From his pocket he took a key and, standing on the step, fitted it in the front door lock. He frowned as the key refused to turn.

On the other side of the road a middle-aged woman pulled back on her dog's lead and strained to see over the hedge. As Ross abandoned the attempt to enter by the front door and trampled a way through weeds to the back, she dragged the dog across the road to get a closer look. From her position slightly back from the garden gate she could see nothing. Then suddenly there was the distinct sound of smashing glass.

Pulling the dog behind her she hurried off down the road to the phone box on the corner.

Reaching through the broken pane to operate the catch Ross opened the french windows and stepped in. He was immediately overwhelmed by the sad abandoned air of the rooms, more poignant by far than the overgrown garden or the peeling exterior.

This, after all, was where they had lived together. Under those grey dust sheets was the furniture she had chosen.

He wandered through the house, his footsteps echoing where the carpets had been rolled up and wrapped in newspapers. On the upper floor he turned into the small bedroom on the left. A boy's bedroom. Time and the great patch of damp down one wall had disfigured almost beyond recognition the child's drawings of aeroplanes and houses.

Ross turned away abruptly and walked on to the bare-board landing. For a moment he hesitated, then crossed and pushed the door to the master bedroom.

Like the rest of the house it was cocooned in dust-sheets. He walked slowly across to the wardrobe and took down the heavy sheet covering the door. Opening it he saw four or five suits hanging there. He took one out and held it up to examine it. Then somewhere on the carpetless stair he heard a footfall. Dropping the suit on the bed he had just made it to behind the door when a step sounded outside on the landing.

As the door was flung open Ross jumped. The man that entered had no time to react to the apparently empty room as Ross grabbed his arm, twisting it high and hurling the man forward on to the bed.

'Take him, Len,' the man rolled across the bed and from the corner of his eye Ross just saw the uniformed figure before he was arm-locked painfully round the neck.

'What the hell . . .' Ross choked on the words.

The plain-clothes man scrambled to his feet and grabbed Ross's flailing arm, locking it in a breaking grip.

'This is my place, for Chrissake!' Ross twisted his head violently.

'This house has been empty for years, mate.' The plain-clothes man twisted him towards the door.

'It's my place, I tell you,' Ross said. 'Look in my bloody wallet.'

'Okay, I got him, Len,' the plain-clothes said. 'Take a look in his wallet.'

The uniformed officer fished the wallet out of Ross's pocket and flipped it open. Taking out the driving licence he read: 'Frank Ross: This address.'

The CID man released his grip. 'You broke in.'

'The front door was bolted from the inside,' Ross said angrily.

The CID shrugged then frowned towards Ross. 'Don't I know that name?'

'You're both trespassing!' Ross said. 'I want you out.'

'A forced entry was reported,' the uniformed man said. 'We found the broken window. Only doing our duty.'

They were moving towards the door. Suddenly the CID man stopped. 'You've been away.' He pointed.

'Sod off.' Ross exploded.

'We've got a celebrity here, Len,' the CID man said with a grin.

'A what?' The uniformed copper looked puzzled.

The CID man's grin widened. He turned towards Ross, nodding slowly, 'So . . . *you're* Frankie Ross!'

When his 'visitors' eventually left, Ross selected what had once been his tightest suit and put it on. But even that hung loosely about his waist – prison food had never exactly invited overindulgence.

Now, dressed in familiar clothes, Ross left the bedroom and wandered downstairs debating where he'd find the nearest telephone box – as the one in the house had been cut off – and what he'd say once he found one.

The two men stood opposite each other, red faced, the muscles of their necks corded in anger. Jerking his thumb at the loaded builder's van beside them Chris Cottle spat the words out: 'What you been doing to it, for Chrissake?'

The bigger man lapsed into surly defensiveness. 'It's done eighty thousand. It's clapped.'

'Because you drive it like a bleedin' tank,' Cottle said. 'Last month it was the gearbox – that cost me I don't know how much!'

The other man finished wiping oil from his hands and tossed the cloth aside. 'What you screaming about?' he said, the insolent menace in his voice evident to Cottle and the two other men who had just come into the yard, 'You ain't paid the geezer yet. Come to think of it – you ain't paid *no one* yet. I'm still waiting on my bonus money.' He looked round at the others and cocked an eyebrow in their direction. 'And far as I know I ain't the only one.'

Chris Cottle shot an anxious glance at the two other workmen. Then turning back to the van driver he said, 'You'll get your money. Everyone will.'

'How?' the other man sneered. 'A bob in the pound from some bankruptcy court?'

He had gone too far now, spurred on by the presence of his two mates. And both he and Cottle knew it.

'I don't have to take this from you, Alf,' Cottle said easily. 'You just slip along and collect your cards, right?'

'I'll collect my cards, mate, the moment you come across with my wages. *And* the rest.'

Somewhere behind them in the small builder's yard a door

opened and a girl with cropped punk hair, dyed pink and green, stood in the doorway. 'Phone for you, Mr. Cottle,' she shouted across the yard. Her vigorous chewing distorted the pillarbox-red lips against the shock white of her make-up.

'Take the number, tell 'em I'll ring back,' Cottle yelled across the bonnet of the old truck.

'It's nuffink nasty,' she called, unwilling to forsake what little shelter the doorway provided. 'Nobody dunning you,' she said to Alf's cackling enjoyment, 'it's personal.'

'Trudi?'

'No. Frank.'

Chris Cottle was already rounding the van. 'Frank?'

'Yeah,' she chewed, shivering, 'he just said tell him it's Frank.'

Cottle pushed past her into the office. She quickly closed the door and checked her face in the mirror as he picked up the phone.

'Frank, is that you?' His frown changed to a broad smile. 'For Chrissake mate, why didn't you let me know?' He listened, smiling. 'Okay, say no more. I'll be down there in five minutes.'

He put the phone down to see the girl staring at him.

'You got an appointment with the bank manager,' she reminded him.

'Screw the bank manager,' he said abstractedly.

'I'll choose me own friends, thanks, Mr. Cottle. What about the wages?'

'Yeah.' He thought for a moment. 'Look, Sandra, you slip across and see him. Tell him I'm sick. You know,' he said with a grin, 'use your charm on him.'

She snorted. 'He still won't let me draw no more money. Last week he said that. He meant it, Mr. Cottle.'

Cottle stood at the desk looking down at the toes of his expensive hand-made tan boots. Then he put his hand in his pocket and took out a bunch of keys. She watched him while he detached one from the ring and handed it to her. 'There goes me mad money,' he said. 'In the safe.' He pointed. 'Make up the wages. Alf's first *and* his bleedin' bonus. Tell Johnny to see him off the premises, make sure nothing don't stick to his fingers as he passes thru the portals. Pay yourself, love . . .' he winked, 'never know, it might be your last chance.'

She stood in the middle of the room. Beneath the grotesque make-up her face showed real concern. 'Things'll be okay, Mr. Cottle, won't they, if we get that Burnt Oak job?'

He put his hand on her shoulder. 'Things'll be better, Sandra, if we get the Burnt Oak job. But then I don't have to tell *you* that things couldn't be a lot worse. Right?'

'Right,' she grinned. ' 'Cause I sorta like workin' here. Work at a place where you can *rely* on your next week's wages and 'alf the fun'd go out of fings.'

'Cheeky little bitch,' he muttered. 'Anybody calls tell 'em it's my meals on wheels afternoon.'

Frank Ross stood at the gate to the unkempt front garden as Chris Cottle's red Jaguar swept into the quiet residential road and pulled to a halt in front of him. Stepping forward, Ross jerked open the door.

Without speaking Cottle tumbled out of the car and straightened up opposite Ross. For a moment neither man spoke.

'Don't know quite what to say, Frank. Welcome home. Something like that, I suppose.'

Ross nodded, swallowing. 'Yeah. Something like that'll do fine, Chris.' He reached out and hugged him. 'Come inside.'

Cottle followed him along the overgrown path. 'Why didn't you let me know, Frank? I'd 've come up and fetched you.'

They were entering the house now. Ross stopped to let Cottle go ahead. 'I needed a few hours to myself, Chris. I can tell you, the real world don't look like television at all.'

'Better?'

'Much.'

The hallway was dark and cold. Cottle shivered. 'Jesus, it's in a bit of a state.' He looked along the dusty hallway as if reluctant to go further, then leaned forward and poked his head round the living-room door. The carpets were rolled to one end of the room. Dust-sheets cocooned the furniture.

'You been lucky, you know, Frank. Empty all this time and nobody done it over.'

'I heard inside. Somebody put the word around whose place it was.'

Cottle looked at him. 'I don't like to say it, Frank. But that don't cut a lot of ice with the kids these days. You just been lucky.'

'If you say so, Chris.'

'Anyway,' Cottle rubbed his hands together, 'it's bloody freezing in here. Why don't you stay with me, Frank?'

'No thanks . . .'

'Not just for a few days while I send a couple of the lads round, give the place a lick a' paint, check over the heating?'

They moved through into the kitchen. Long forgotten shopping lists were scrawled on the reminder blackboard, plates begrimed with years of dust stood stacked in the sink rack.

'It's going to take time for me to sort myself out,' Ross said. 'I'd sooner be here.'

He stood silently looking down at the dust-covered formica surface of the kitchen table. 'How is she, Chris?'

'I went up to see her a week, ten days ago,' Cottle said slowly. 'Just to let her know it wouldn't be long.'

'You didn't answer, Chris. How is she?'

Cottle stood awkwardly. 'Up and down, Frank. Some days better than others.'

'I haven't had a letter since the summer.'

Cottle nodded. 'That's what I mean, Frank. She's not herself yet. We can go and see her tomorrow.'

Ross took a bottle of whisky from a paper bag on the worktop and found a couple of glasses in the cupboard. 'And young Paul? He must be going on sixteen.'

This was easier ground. Cottle puffed his chest. 'Big lad. Taller'n me now. The pictures I sent don't do him justice.' He paused. 'He really wanted to come and see you, Frank. Kept askin'. 'Specially early on.'

'Then stopped?'

'Don't blame him, Frank. The only answer he ever got was a "no", remember?'

'It wouldn't have helped him or me.'

'Your choice, Frank.'

Ross shook his head. 'You don't get a choice in there, Chris. You want – you can't have. There were days when I would have given anything to see him or Evie, you, anyone. But I could only play it one way.'

He poured some whisky for each of them. Ross lifted his glass. 'Thanks, Chris. For all you've done. Finding that place for Eve, getting Paul fostered out. I never have thanked you properly.'

'Don't be daft, Frank. I only wish I could have taken on young Paul myself. But my bit of bird fifteen years ago ruled that out.'

'They never forget.'

Ross wiped off a section of the table-top with a dusty cloth and perched on the edge. 'Okay, Chris – what about you? Regular girl around?'

'Very nice, Trudi.'

'Wedding bells?'

'I turn me duff ear.'

Ross laughed. 'You haven't changed. Still playing the field, eh?'

'I like to keep one hot favourite.'

'And the business, Chris? Doing all right?'

'Like most businesses these days.'

'Problems?'

'Not really.'

'I must owe you. How much is the hospital?'

Cottle swallowed his whisky. 'Forget it, Frank. Here, it's a cold old day inside. I'll have another of those and call it quits.'

'How much, Chris. That eleven grand I left for you didn't go that far, eh?'

'Things have changed, Frank.'

'They always do.'

'Prices, I mean. The hospital's near on five grand now.'

'Jesus Christ!'

'That's what I mean. When it's all tarted with rhubarb about the cost of living index it don't mean much. Bloody does when you're on the receiving end.'

'How much you laid out, Chris?'

'Look, mate, I'm not talking about Evie's hospital. I'm talking about running a bleedin' business. The hospital, forget Frank. You would have done the same for me, I know that.'

Ross poured himself a careful half-inch of Scotch. 'You're in trouble, aren't you, Chris?'

'Not if I cut down on the fags and sherbert.'

'It looked so good. The suit, the boots, the motor.'

Cottle smiled. 'The boots are mine. The motor's on the book. Okay, Frank, thing's ain't good – but they ain't hopeless either. Listen, you're going to need some ready.'

He pulled a wad of notes from his inside pocket and offered them across the table.

'No way, my son.' Ross shook his head.

'I shall be deeply offended,' Cottle grinned. He tucked the notes into Ross's top pocket. 'For Chrissake, it's only money.'

'Okay, Chris. Until I get something worked out.'

'What sort of something?'

Ross shrugged.

'How will it be now, Frank. Something straight?

'How much would this place fetch? Today's prices?'

'You can't, Frank.'

'A quick sale.'

Cottle shook his head. 'Frank, Evie loves this place.'

'It's Evie I'm thinking about,' Ross said stubbornly. 'What else do I do? Take a job? Put a tenner a week in the Post office?'

'And when you've sold up here, then what?'

Ross didn't answer. As Cottle watched he saw his jaw tighten, the muscles in his cheekbones flex. 'It won't come as any surprise to you, Chris. There's a few questions need answers. A few faces to see.'

'That's eight years ago, Frank. A hell of a long time.'

'Don't talk to me about time, Chris. I'm the expert, remember.'

Cottle shook his head. 'You used to be maybe. You don't have to be any longer. You've got the God-given chance of a fresh start, Frank. Use it, please!'

Ross smiled. 'That sounds like the routine gate spiel you

get from the Governor. "You've paid your debt to society . . . a new life . . . a second chance . . . an opportunity to contribute!" I'm lucky that I've got a house to sell. Most of them end up with a creased suit, a train ticket and just enough money to drink themselves senseless.'

'I know how you feel, Frank,' Cottle said.

'Do you, I wonder? Eight years, eight years of my life some grassing bastard's had – my wife in a mental hospital, my son not my son, living with strangers, my home turned into a mausoleum. Wouldn't you want to know who did that to you? Wouldn't you want to know every line on his face? Wouldn't you want to find out why?'

'No.' Cottle faced him. He had no experience of dealing with Frank Ross. Ever since he could remember Frank had been the big man in their area. He swallowed hard. 'No, Frank, I wouldn't. Leastways, I hope like hell I wouldn't.'

'You talk about a fresh start, Chris. Can't you see that until I've got this off my chest there's no fresh start for me.'

'Listen, Frank. I'm going to give it to you straight. It wasn't no grassing bastard that took eight years of your life. You handed those years over – on a plate.'

Ross's eyes hardened. 'I don't want to hear that kinda talk, Chris. Understand me?'

'So what you going to do when you find out who grassed on you? Break his back? Cut his tongue out? What good will that do Evie or young Paul? You, me, anyone?'

Ross stood silently watching him. 'I thought we were friends, Chris.'

'Jesus, I'm saying all this because we are friends. If you don't make the change now, Frank, you never will. You'll end up old and broken in some Victorian pigsty where all the doors open inwards . . . I'm saying this because I don't want it to happen to you, Frank. Forget about who grassed on you – or you won't make it next time. You'll end up like Vic Lee – finished!'

Ross crossed the kitchen and screwed the top on the Scotch bottle.

'I may be out of order, Frank,' Cottle said quietly. 'But I had to say it. It'll be the last time.'

Ross dropped the Scotch bottle into the brown paper bag. 'You've seen Vic Lee?'

'He looks a hundred years old. Got a job as a potman in the Admiral Nelson.'

'Langton Street?'

'Yes.'

'I got to have a word with him, Chris.'

A look of real pain shadowed Cottle's face. He nodded slowly. 'You ain't listened to a blind word I've said, have you, Frank?'

CHAPTER TWO

Lew Wilson was a man of regular habits. His mother had spent twenty-five years of her life in service with the Dukes of Devonshire before marrying a widowed shopkeeper in Catford. By the time their son, young Lew, was born she was nearing her mid-forties and set in her ways. There was a time, she proclaimed, and a place for everything, so that even now, ten years after her death, Lew Wilson's life was modelled in unconscious mimicry of the ducal life of long ago. He would rise early, bath, and breakfast well. From nine to twelve he would work on his accounts – a 'sleeping' interest in a chain of betting shops, four pubs and an afternoon drinking club. At midday he would walk briskly to the Admiral Nelson, two miles in just on half an hour, and occupy the corner table permanently reserved for him. Usually he was accompanied by his sidekick, Eddie Archer, but equally often his companions would be men in dark striped suits who unclipped bulging briefcases on to the scratched table. Lew Wilson was the sort of businessman who required that his solicitors and accountants came to him.

Today he sat with Eddie and a young architect, the gin and tonics holding down the edges of the coloured architectural drawing for a new Health Club that had been spread out in front of him.

'I've incorporated the saunas in the Church Street wing, Mr. Wilson, in order to group the plumbing and draining services in one area. This way we save money.'

'Good boy,' Wilson murmured but his attention was directed across the young architect's head to where Frank Ross and Chris Cottle had just entered the bar.

'For a roofing contractor my suggestion would be Myers and Gibbs . . .' the architect continued.

Wilson leaned across the drawings to Eddie Archer. 'Slip across to Frank Ross . . . my compliments, ask him if he'll have a drink with me to celebrate his return.'

'Do I get the message over on the way things are now?' Archer asked.

'He'll have to learn that soon enough, Eddie.'

Eddie Archer sauntered across to where Ross and Cottle had taken seats at the bar.

'Hullo there, Frank. Welcome back.'

Frank Ross turned on his bar stool. 'Eddie Archer. Last time I saw you, you were washing winkles down the fish market.'

Eddie grinned uneasily. 'That was a long time ago, Frank. I was only a kid at the time.'

'What is it, Eddie?'

'Mr. Wilson's inviting you for a drink.'

'*Mr.* Wilson?'

'That's the way things are, Frank.'

'Mr. Ross.'

The boy stood awkwardly. Then shook his head. 'That's the way things are, *Frank*,' he said. '*Mr.* Wilson's asking you over for a drink.'

Ross nodded to himself. 'You tell *Mr.* Wilson that if he wants to buy me a drink that bad he can come over here and do it. At which point I'll decide whether I feel like drinking it.'

Eddie Archer eased his big, weight-training shoulder muscles inside his jacket. 'I don't think you understand how things are in the manor nowadays, Frank. All this side of the road is Mr. Wilson – all the other side is Tony McGrath. No room for Mr. In-Between.'

Chris Cottle watched the anger rise in a red flush on his friend's cheeks. Eddie Archer stepped back half a pace. Then with what seemed an immense effort Ross inhaled sharply. He turned to Cottle. 'Get me half of lager and a sandwich, Chris. I'll go and have a word with Lew.'

Eddie Archer visibly relaxed.

Ross crossed to where Lew Wilson was sitting and extended his hand. 'I won't take you up on that drink just now, Lew.' He said without preliminaries. 'I'm here to see Vic Lee, Eddie tells me things have gone well for you.'

They shook hands across the table.

'That's right, Frank. Me and Tony McGrath have got things pretty well worked out between us. What're your plans?' he asked. 'I think Tony and me'd both be interested to hear.'

'I'm sure you would. When I've decided I'll let you know.'

'Okay, Frank. I'll buy you that drink some other time.'

'Sure.' He turned away to see Eddie Archer standing close behind him. Pausing, Ross wrinkled his nose. 'That winkle washing job you had, Eddie,' he frowned. 'How long ago you give it up?' And he walked across to join Cottle at the bar.

'I thought you were going to thump him,' Cottle said.

'Young Eddie? He wasn't a bad kid, was he?'

'Can't remember – but he's not up to much now. Throws his weight around ever since Lew Wilson took him on.'

Ross nodded and turned to see the familiar figure of Vic Lee standing in the passage that led to the Gents. As he slid to his feet Lee disappeared.

Ross took his sandwich in one hand and lager in the other. 'Hang about, Chris,' he said and crossed the bar to the entrance to the passage. At the far end a frosted glass swing-door gave on to a small yard. Ross walked past the door to the Gents. Out in the yard he could hear the sound of someone stacking beer crates.

He pushed the door and stood for a moment watching Vic Lee at work, limping across the yard, two full crates at a time, his breath billowing mist in the cold air.

'Can't even knock off for a minute to say hullo to an old mate, Vic,' Ross called across the yard to him. Lee let the last two crates thump and rattle into place on the stack and straightening up unhurriedly he rubbed the palms of his hands down his leather apron before limping across to where Ross was standing in the doorway.

'Hullo, Frank,' he said, 'you look as though you've lost a bit of weight.'

Ross waved the sandwich at Lee's injured leg.

'What happened to you?'

Lee leaned a hand against the wall.

'Fell off a roof. I was on farm detail, demolishing an outhouse . . . slate . . . like a poxy ice rink. Busted pelvis . . . got an infection in the bone. They reckon there's not much they can do.'

'It's there for good?'

'Looks like it. Still . . .' He smiled grimly. 'Got me an early parole, didn't it? When did you get out?'

'Today.'

Lee pursed his lips. 'You ain't wastin' much time.'

'You know why I'm here.'

'I reckon so. Can't let it go, uh?'

'You already have Vic, is that it?'

Lee shifted his weight to his good leg. 'I felt like you for the first year Frank . . . bitter . . . screwed up inside. I mean we was the only ones who knew exactly where and when – Billy, you, me, Bernie, Ralph . . . an' I mean, stands to reason it was none of us. I mean, no one's gonna give himself some, is he? As far as I was concerned it was the big one, the last one. My share would've bin around forty grand, I could've got lost, somewhere quiet, always fancied a little shot.' He looked round the yard. 'And I end up here.'

'Someone talked, Vic.'

Lee shook his head. 'It weren't none of us, Frank . . . you picked us careful enough. I never liked that big black sod but you could burn Bernie's hands off before he'd give you the time of day. Billy worshipped you. Ralph's like a stone . . . my old lady didn't even know I was into somethin' I was that careful. No, we all done like you said, went to work regular, everything normal, never two of us seen together. No snout could have picked up anything from watching us, Frank.'

'It wasn't a snout . . . it was someone close . . . it had to be.' He hurled his sandwich across the yard. Lee glanced idly over his shoulder to see where it had fallen then turned back to Ross. 'You want my advice, for what it's worth. Forget it, Frank. You've done your bird. You start nosing around you'll be in bother. Things have changed, Frank, in eight years things have changed a lot, it's all bloody violence now . . . no class . . .'

'Who's running things, Vic? Eddie Archer told me it's Lew Wilson and Tony McGrath, that right?'

'That's right, Frank,' Lee nodded. 'Evil slags . . . I don't know which of 'ems worse.'

'Still hate each other's guts?'

'Poison. You watch yourself, Frank, they ain't gonna take too kindly to you being back. Neither of them.'

'We'll see,' Ross said. He sipped his lager, grimaced and poured it slowly into the mouth of a drain.

'I know I don't want none of it, Frank.' Lee said slowly. 'I live in one room, work all hours, but I don't 'ave to look over me shoulder no more. An' I sleep nights. That last bit did me in, Frank, I can't take being banged up no more.'

Ross looked at the shaggy eyebrows, the grey stubble and the bubbles of saliva glistening in the corner of his mouth. They'd been close once. Not friends to meet and drink together – but a closeness based on a professional respect. He felt he had to probe the wound. 'You're asking me to believe that you really don't give a monkey's who put us away. You're asking me to believe that, Vic?'

Lee shook his head of thick grey matted hair. 'No, I'm not asking you to believe anything, Frank. I'm through. I'm sixty-one. And I've got nothing out of this poxy life but grief. That's the truth of it, Frank. My old lady died when I was inside – did you know that? I think that's what did it. The shame of that day – not for the neighbours, they knew I was inside anyway. Just for me. I was such a flaming great success that I couldn't even attend my old lady's funeral without a bleedin' escort!'

Ross watched him silently. 'I don't know why, Vic – but it's different with me. I have to know,' he said at length.

The other man had controlled the working of his mouth now. He drew the back of his hand across his lips. 'That's your cross, Frank, as the old chaplain used to say. But just don't expect me to give you a hand carrying it, right?'

Ross stood the beer glass on a pile of empty cases. 'Okay, Vic. Coupla questions and that's the lot.'

'I'll see what I can do.'

'Where are the others?'

'Ralph moved out of the manor.'

'Any idea where?'

'No.' His mouth twisted bitterly. 'Young Billy's on the trot.'

'What?'

'Done a screwer on a factory. The watchman caught him. Billy whacked him!'

'That's not Billy's way.'

Lee shrugged. 'The old boy's dead, Billy's way or not.'

'Dead!' Ross pushed himself off the doorjamb.

'Gave you quite a shock, eh? Billy Binns wanted for murder?'

Ross sucked in the cold misty air. 'As you say, quite a shock. Any idea where he might be?'

'I told you. I keep meself to meself Frank . . . best that way . . . they'll have him. Billy don't have the patience to stay loose for long.'

'And Bernie?'

'He's gone back to pimping . . . in Brixton . . . never did get on too well with that one.'

'Where in Brixton?'

Lee shuffled his feet. 'Stay away from him, Frank.'

'Why?'

'I don't reckon he's all there, is why.' He tapped the side of his head.

'But maybe he knows where Billy is?'

'Maybe.'

He took a stub of pencil from his pocket, then tore a strip from an old newspaper lying on a crate of beer. Licking the end of the pencil he bent over the crate and scribbled for a few seconds. Then, straightening, he handed the scrap of paper to Ross.

'Thanks, Vic. I'll come and see you again.' Ross turned back into the passage. Lee stopped him with a hand on his arm.

'Don't bother . . . nothin' personal, Frank . . . always got on good, you and me . . . respectful . . . but I just don't want to know no more.'

He stood awkwardly.

Ross put out his hand. 'Okay Vic.' They shook hands briefly and Ross turned back towards the bar.

Leaving the Admiral Nelson, Ross was silent. He found it hard to connect the prematurely old, grey-haired cellarman in the back yard with the Vic Lee he had known. Prison had done that. And the grass who had put them all inside. He stood beside Chris Cottle's car. Well, he'd get the bastard. He'd get him as much for Vic Lee as for himself.

Cottle was looking at him. 'Bit of a shock, eh? He's changed.'

Ross nodded. 'Can you fix me up with a car, Chris? Temporary.'

'Take this one,' Cottle nodded down at the Jaguar. 'Got a current licence?'

'I renewed before I came out. What about you then?'

'I got a van at the yard. Drop me off and the Jag's yours for as long as you need it.' He dropped the keys into Ross's hand.

Ross stood for a moment, the keys in the palm of his hand. 'You're quite something, Chris. I walk back into your life after eight years and you drop me money, a motor . . .'

Cottle dragged open the car door. 'You bring tears to me eyes, Frank. Listen, how about a couple of drinks tonight at my place. You can meet Trudi.'

'You're on.' Ross said and climbed into the car.

She was beautiful. Black, completely naked and beautiful. Bernie Machen led Ross into the room and clicked his fingers. 'Sonya,' he said, 'get the man a drink.'

She curled off the sofa and stood before him, lifting her chin in inquiry.

'A Scotch,' he said.

On bare tiptoe she moved across the floor, a parody of some ancestral memory, and poured the whisky.

'Talk.' Machen grinned his grin.

Ross shook his head. 'Only when we're alone, Bernie.'

'You don't like what you see?'

Ross watched the undulations of her body as she moved towards him. 'I like everything I see. Except the ears!'

Even the girl smiled.

'Frank baby, you crease me.' Machen turned to the girl. 'Get yourself ready for bed, Sonya. This here's a man of few words.'

When the girl slipped out Ross drew from his pocket the blue architect's drawing. 'On this one, Bernie,' he said, 'you'll make more than if you ran the best looking stable of black Toms in London.'

'I do that already, Frankie.'

'You'll still make more.'

Machen inclined his head, serious now.

CHAPTER THREE

TWENTY years ago it would have been fog. A thick warming dirty yellow blanket. Today the sulphurous skeins are still just apparent below the level of the street lamps or woven among the bare trees of Brockwell Park. But the body, the warmth has gone.

It was just after nine when Frank Ross pulled the Jaguar to a halt outside the large brick Victorian detached house where Chris Cottle leased the ground floor flat. Through the iron gate he could see the curtained windows of Cottle's living-room and with an effort he was able to remember the layout of the large rambling flat, the three big bedrooms, the french doors leading out from them on to the big back garden. He lit a cigarette with the lighter in the dash. It had already been a crowded day. Meeting up with Chris again, hearing about Eve, Lew Wilson, the pathetic broken figure of Vic Lee and then this afternoon, trailing around the Brixton afternoon clubs for a sniff of Bernie Machen.

Of course it was his white face. In eight years the barrier had gone up. Anybody who wasn't black was probably the law. The line of the lips had set, the eyes had tightened. Nobody on the door had heard of Machen. Or on the next door, or the next. At the Club Carib he had been luckier. The man on the door was an old Brixton figure, Tommy Yearly, off the boat from Trinidad in 1947 and still with the open easiness of the old West Indies in his smile. He had recognized Frank as soon as he had clattered down the basement steps.

'Bernie Machen? Yes, he used to get in here. Till the boss say that's it, no fights, I run a quiet place. Don't want to see you no more here, Bernie. That man he's . . .' and he made the same head-tapping gesture Vic Lee had used.

'So what's he do now. He's got a set of girls?'

'That's it, Frank. Ten, a dozen maybe. Nice business but he's hard, Frank . . .'

'On the girls?'

Tommy Yearly nodded. 'He got some big nigger sidekick. They gonna hurt one of those girls one day. Then we see trouble.' He shook his head. 'You coming in for a drink, Frank?'

'Later maybe, Tommy. Listen, do you know where I can get in touch with Bernie?'

Tommy Yearly shook his grey head. 'No . . . I hear he moved. No . . . sorry, Frank.'

'And the toms – where does he run them?'

'You know, Brixton Hill. Can't remember why but I think the girls round the Odeon is mostly his.'

Ross crushed the cigarette out in the car ashtray. He would stay an hour maybe with Chris and Trudi and push off.

He locked the car and crossed the pavement to open the rusting iron gate. Chris liked this place because it had a bit of old style about it. 'None of your biscuit-box rooms,' he always boasted. But then Chris Cottle was a pretty conservative guy altogether. Fifteen years ago he had done eighteen months for a breaking and entering and he had determined never to go back. At least, that was how Ross saw it.

Frank Ross rang the garden flat bell and watched the blurred outline of a girl's figure approach the frosted glass door. He knew before he opened the door that it was a good figure but he was even so, not prepared for the sheer blonde lushness of her body plainly evident under a thin pale blue dress that left her brown shoulders and an expanse of cleavage bare.

He smiled. 'You've just got to be Trudi,' he said.

She nodded, her blue eyes staring. She had heard so much about this man from Chris that she was at a loss for words.

'I'm Frank,' he said gently. 'How about if I come in out of the cold?'

'Sorry, yes.' She stepped back quickly almose tripping in her very high heels. 'It's just that Chris is still getting dressed.'

Ross stepped into the warm hall and closed the door behind

him. 'Fine. And you've finished.' He looked down at her. 'Or have you?'

She laughed for the first time, on familiar ground now. 'Come into the living-room.' She led the way. 'I forget you know this flat better than I do.'

Ross looked around the high-ceilinged room. The bright, thick carpet, the wallpaper, the inevitable tongue and groove bar in the corner were all new.

'What will you have to drink?' Trudi asked him.

'A beer, if you've got one cold.'

'A *beer*, you old bastard!' Chris Cottle's voice came from the kitchen. 'When the rest of us are on the champagne?' And led by Chris Cottle a mass of people surged into the room waving full champagne glasses.

The men were all eight years heavier, the women more carefully made up. Con Davies put one arm round Ross and hugged him. Dee Reynolds now fighting a desperate rear-guard action with middle age pushed Con aside and threw her arms round Ross's neck to plant a heavily lipsticked kiss full on his lips. 'The old place hasn't been the same without you, Frank.'

A huge hand gripped his. Quincy Reynolds, Dee's husband, blinked away the tears in his eyes. 'Don't go away again, boy,' he said and stepped aside to let Dave Mitchell detach Dee from round Ross's neck.

'Give someone else a chance to say welcome home,' he said. Ross took in the expensive blue suit, the heavy gold identity bracelet and the deep tan. 'The travel business doing okay, I see, Mitch.' They were the first words he managed to speak. Perhaps because he liked Dave Mitchell less than any of them he found it easier. He fingered Mitchell's lapel. 'Nice bit of schmutter.'

Mitchell grinned. 'I can do you a very nice fortnight in the Santa Ponso . . . Spanish decor . . . chips with everything. Just let me know, sir, when you feel you need a holiday . . .'

'Don't be daft,' Dee said. 'He's just had one, ain't he?'

Somebody pushed a glass of champagne into Ross's hand as Pete and Maggie Wilder pushed past Quincy's huge shoulder.

'Remember us, Frankie?' Maggie kissed him, ruffling the

back of his head. Pete shook his hand. 'Nice to have you back, son,' he said quietly.

Over Pete's shoulder Ross's eye caught, for the first time, the tall, dark-haired woman standing slightly apart from the press of people around him. About thirty, Anne Mitchell's clothes and looks were in restrained contrast to the rest of the women in the room. She lifted her glass. 'Hullo, Frank.'

As if in some unconscious deference to her looks or poise, Maggie stepped aside.

'How are you, Anne?' Ross said. 'You're looking well.'

'Thank you.'

Dave Mitchell gave his wife a tight look but Chris Cottle blunted the moment. Pushing forward into the middle of the group he raised his glass. 'Right now, this calls for a toast. To Frank. Welcome back, my old son.'

There was a chorus of voices and laughter. Then as the room went quiet, Frank Ross lifted his glass. 'To all of you . . . thanks for not forgetting.' His eyes met Anne's as he drank.

'God bless you, Frank,' Dee said, '. . . you and Evie.'

Quincy looked quickly at his wife who, already slightly high, shot Ross an exaggerated look of alarm.

'Thanks, Dee,' Ross reassured her with a smile. 'And thanks to old Chris here for laying all this on.'

As the champagne flowed the attention eased off Frank a little. Mitch and Dee were deep in an argument about immigration, with Dee vehemently supporting the right of the immigrants to a fair deal once here.

Quincy, Pete and Maggie played one of the new TV football games that Ross had never seen before.

Con and Anne stood talking in the far corner. But her eyes moved across the room, following Ross, resting for a moment as if willing him to look up.

'Now, ladies and gentlemen,' Chris Cottle clapped his hands, 'at Gawd knows what cripplin' expense, the management has provided some very fine nosh in the kitchen. You'll find Trudi in there ready to pander to your every wish. Make your way in and help yourselves – to the food I mean, gentlemen!'

As couples began to drift into the kitchen, the bell rang and

Trudi hurried through the sitting-room to get it. Frank Ross did not miss the nervous glance she shot at Cottle.

'What is it, Chris? You expecting some sort of trouble?'

'No ...' Cottle grinned uneasily. 'No ... I don't know Frank, if this is right outa line, just tell me. But I figured you just out today and Evie ... well not going to be well for sometime yet ...'

Ross frowned. 'What you talking about, Chris? What's out of line?' He turned as Trudi appeared at the door with a girl of about twenty-five, built on the same generous lines as Trudi herself, but dark-haired and under long lashes, dark eyed.

'Do you *want* to meet Hazel, Frank,' Chris Cottle underlined the question.

Ross looked at him and smiled. 'Why not, Chris,' he said and together they crossed to where Trudi was helping Hazel off with her coat.

'This is Hazel, Frank,' Trudi said nervously. 'My best friend. So be nice to her.'

'Hullo, Hazel,' Ross took her red-nailed hand. 'You're an hour or more behind everybody else – what can I get you to drink? Champagne?'

'Please, Frank ...' she stopped him with a hand on his arm. 'You don't mind me coming to your party? I mean I'm the outsider, the only one really ...'

'We'll soon put that right. First I get you a drink – then you come and meet some of the old gang.'

Anne Mitchell, Dee and Maggie had drifted together on their way to the kitchen.

Maggie looked across at Hazel with Frank. 'Who's the bit with the eyes and hot knickers?' she asked.

Dee pursed her lips, 'A friend of Trudi's. Must be. Out of the same stable, ain't they?'

'Frank's coming-out present?' Maggie said with a smile.

Anne stiffened. 'What? What d'you mean coming-out present?'

'You know Chris,' Maggie said, 'keeps his brains in his trousers.'

'Well . . . why not . . .' Dee's eyes were on Frank. 'Evie's not gonna be much use to 'im, is she? I could be though – couldn't you?'

'Twice on Sundays,' Maggie agreed.

Anne dropped back to let the others go on into the kitchen. She was unaware of her husband until he gripped her arm. 'What's up with you?' He kept his voice low.

'I've got a headache,' she said off-handedly.

'One of those, eh?'

'What's that supposed to mean?'

Anne took a gold cigarette case from her purse, opened it and put a menthol cigarette to her lips, waiting for Mitch to light it.

Irritably he took a gold Dunhill from his jacket pocket and lit Anne's cigarette.

'This is his first night out, for Chrissake!'

'What am I supposed to do about it?' She eyed him levelly.

'Just show a little enthusiasm, for a start.'

'What if I don't like cheap champagne?' She turned away from him abruptly and walked over to the bar. She was pouring herself a large brandy when Mitchell caught up with her.

'Don't start swilling that,' he said, in a tense whisper.

'Why don't you go and join the Frank Ross appreciation society?' Anne nodded across to the knot of men round Frank and Hazel.

'You can be a mean-mouthed bitch when you want to!' Anne took a large swallow of brandy. 'I didn't want to come.'

'A hundred quid dress,' he said sarcastically, 'half the afternoon gettin' ready. You *really* didn't want to come.'

The music was thumping now. After eight years of ordered quiet Ross found himself already exhausted by the drink, the sounds and even the sights of so much colour and variety. He'd heard about the reaction of course but had never imagined it would happen to him. His legs felt tired, his head ached. When Con Davies came to take Hazel for a dance he surrendered her gratefully.

'You okay, mate?' Chris Cottle was at his elbow.

'Just a bit over-ambitious, that's all, Chris. Inside you do your bit every day, work on the weights, keep in good shape. But it still hits you when you come out. I'll just get myself a breath of fresh air, right?'

'You do that, Frank. This is your night, mate. Play it any way you want to.'

Ross left the living-room and crossed the hall into the main bedroom. Opening the french doors he felt the cold cut of the November night on his face.

It was an old garden, thickly planted with shrubs, the paving cracked, the broken Victorian statuary moss grown. He descended four or five stone steps and followed the gravel path down to the fir trees, at the end of which filtered the yellow sodium lights from Brockwell Park.

He sat on a stone bench and lit a cigarette. Back in the world. After eight years he was back among people. Seeing women and kids for the first time. Hi-fi stores, supermarkets, pubs . . . Colour, that's what struck him most. Everything so high coloured. Bright paint, bright curtains, bright lights. Frank Ross was not a man to feel at a loss, but he recognized that tonight he'd come very close. Suddenly he thought of Chris Cottle and Vic Lee. Forget it, they both said. Forget whoever it was that put you inside. You can't re-live the past. But they didn't understand, either of them. For Frank Ross the dream of revenge had been the one thing which had driven him through those years. The motor fuel that had got him up two thousand nine hundred and twenty mornings, had propelled him through two thousand nine hundred and twenty bleak afternoons and two thousand nine hundred and twenty dreary evenings. Revenge had done that for him – kept his mind sharp, made him read, keep up with the news, take exercise and obliterated the appalling guilts and loneliness of the family man who has betrayed his family.

If Frank Ross abandoned revenge now he felt in some way it would be like another betrayal. Of himself mostly, of Vic Lee, Billy Binns, Big Ralph, even Bernie Machen. But most of all if he abandoned revenge now it would show him to himself as the phony he always feared he was. In some way that he would never understand, revenge to Frank Ross had become synonymous with a sense of security.

Detective Chief Inspector Christie Bryce sipped his mug of tea and surveyed his desk. He was slim, neatly dressed, with short hair brushed back in a way reminiscent of a thirties film star. He knew his whole appearance to be forty years out of style but it was a style he liked. Simpler, less pretentious than the affectations of today. It was a style too that was part and parcel of his own personality, his love of order, the neatness of his desk.

Unmarried, he normally worked late from choice, taking the last half-hour to drink his final mug of tea and consider the problems of the day.

Tonight, as he adjusted the pens in his presentation stand, his mind was working on only one problem. Frank Ross, he had heard less than an hour ago, was out.

He lit a cigarette and looked up over the lighter flame as the bulk of Detective Inspector Alec Rimmer filled the frosted glass door-pane.

He drew on the cigarette as Rimmer shambled into the room.

In almost every way he was a contrast to his boss. Long-haired, sloppily dressed, broad-shouldered and slow of speech, he was nobody's stereotype of a British copper, certainly not of a Detective Inspector marked down for rapid promotion.

'Thought you'd be interested, guv. Frank Ross. Out today.'

Bryce nodded. 'I know. Just heard.' He stood up. No point in staying any later. He took a bunch of keys from his pocket and crossed with his tea to his filing cabinet. 'He'll be back,' he said.

Rimmer shoved his hands deep into his pockets and stared down at his badly scuffed suède shoes. 'Maybe not,' he said slowly. 'Eight years. That's the longest he's ever done. I heard he didn't enjoy it.'

With his keys Christie Bryce tapped the filing cabinet decisively. 'He'll go back. And I only hope it's me who puts him there.'

Rimmer took one hand from his pocket and rubbed at his chin. 'What you got against him, guv?'

'Why should I have anything against someone like Frank Ross, Alec. After all he's the sort of man who makes our job worthwhile.'

Rimmer watched him as he locked his files. He had worked with Bryce for close on five years now and still Bryce had told him nothing about how he'd collected the tip that put Frank Ross away. Nothing about how – nothing about who from. Fair enough. Whoever it was had trusted Bryce with his life. And Rimmer was bound to admit that drunk or sober Christie Bryce was not the sort of copper to betray that trust.

'The trouble with the Frank Ross's of this world, Alec, is that they believe themselves to be much brighter than they are. There's no deprived childhood story here. There's no mum on the game and dad in the boozer. Frank Ross's parents were a nice orderly, quiet couple. Not very clever. Not very well off. Good people who just weren't good enough for their ever-loving son.'

'And you still say you've nothing special against him, guv?'

Bryce sipped his cup of tea. 'Old Mr. and Mrs. Ross . . . put him into grammar school, you know. *Tried.* Not good enough for Frankie Ross, though. He's got a grudge mentality, Alec. It's his Achilles heel. That's why they thieve – they're driven by the compulsion to take what they think of as their fair share. They're sick, Alec. On this patch Frank Ross is just the sickest. That's what I've got against him.'

'You knew his mum and dad then, did you?'

Bryce nodded. 'Met 'em once. I started here, you see. As a young D.C. One of my first numbers, Frankie Ross . . . second-hand jewellers had been done. Somebody recognized him running away. I went down to his house to nick him. Seventeen he was, and the apple of their eye. They just couldn't believe it when I came down from his bedroom with a handful of second-hand wedding rings.'

Rimmer shifted uneasily. 'Happens all the time though, guv. The old lady in tears, the kid giving you the lip, all full of bravado.'

Bryce shook his head. 'No, Frankie Ross isn't like that. He comes on that he cares. That's why I want him back where he belongs. Because he's one of those thieves who's in danger of making helping themselves out of other people's pockets, *respectable.*'

'That's the way it is now, guv. It's an upside down old world.'

Bryce nodded slowly. 'How's he spending his first day of freedom?'

'They're having a knees-up at Cottle's place.'

'Have you got someone on it?'

Rimmer looked at him in surprise.

'Well . . . no, guv . . . it was just a bit of local gossip from a D.S. I know over there.'

Bryce put his mug down hard on the filing cabinet. 'I want to know who's at the party. I want a list of his fan club.'

'He's too bright to get into anything for a long time yet,' Rimmer objected.

'He's broke . . . he's a grudge-bearer . . . he's an arrogant bastard. After eight years he's got to re-establish himself. But there's something else.' He paused. 'I wonder if Billy Binns knows he's out?'

'I never thought of that one.'

'Because when he does know there'll be a meet. We could pull Billy Binns before the end of the week.'

Ross had heard two or three steps behind him before fully registering that someone was crossing the garden. Turning on the stone bench he saw, half-way along the path, a woman's figure stop and bend forward peering into the darkness. Then Anne Mitchell's voice called softly. 'Frank . . . Frank . . .'

He stood up. 'Over here, Anne,' he said.

She gave a small gasp and with her heels clicking on the stone flags hurried to the end of the garden.

For a moment she stood in front of him.

'Why that way, Frank?'

He shrugged. 'There was no other way.'

'You could have answered my letters.'

'I thought about it . . . I wanted to . . . but . . .'

'You wanted to?'

He nodded. 'Of course.'

'One letter . . . one line on one page would have been something . . . enough,' she said.

He grimaced. 'You don't understand. I wrote that letter . . . fifty times . . . in my mind, Anne.'

'Say it again.'

'What?'

'My name. Say my name.'

Anne reached out and touched Frank's face with the tips of her fingers. 'What did you think I'd do, Frank,' she said. 'Stop loving you? Smile philosophically, shrug my shoulders, put it down to experience, just forget everything, flick a switch – on . . . off? Is that what you expected?'

He reached up and took her hand from his cheek.

'I didn't expect anything. When you've got years of the same faces, the same fear, the same anger, the same pointless longings, the same mindless routines, the same crippling nothingness day in day out, week in week out, months, years, you have to learn not to *expect* anything. You teach yourself to live without thinking, without caring, without wanting . . . because if you don't – you're finished!'

She shook her head slowly.

'I was twenty-two, Frank. Married three years and already knew I'd made a mistake, remember.'

'I remember.'

'Do you? Shall I tell you what *I*'ve been doing these last eight years?'

He was silent.

'No, you don't want to hear, do you, Frank? Because it might sound just a little like what you've been doing. And you couldn't stand that, could you? What Frank Ross does has got to be unique. Well it *was* unique, Frank Ross. And that's why eight years later I'm still making a fool of myself for someone who just may not be worth it!'

'You want a cigarette?'

'No.'

He took her arm. 'I'll take you in. You'll freeze out here.'

'I don't want to go in.'

He dropped his hand. She looked at him. Even in the filtered lights of the sodium lamps she could see new lines etched across his forehead and around the mouth. She knew she wanted him, not just as a physical thing, although the few times that it had happened it had been unforgettably good, but because she recognized some quality in him which matched her own restless ambitions for herself.

She came closer to him. 'You're going to need me, Frank. I'm the only one who really knows you . . .'

'Maybe.'

'Don't live in the past, Frank. Don't get dragged back in the sewer.'

They both at the same time, saw the light go on in the main bedroom. 'Looks like Chris is coming to fetch you,' she said. The french doors opened and Hazel stood uncertainly, a man's sheepksin coat draped over her shoulders.

'Wrong,' Anne said. 'Not Chris. Your welcome home present.'

She turned and walked quickly down the path. 'He's over here, dear,' she called to Hazel as she approached. 'I was just doing a little warm-up job on him for you,' she added as she walked past Hazel into the bedroom.

Hazel closed the french doors behind her and walked uncertainly down the steps and along the path. 'Frank . . .'

He lit a cigarette. 'Yes . . .'

'Chris asked me to come and fetch you,' she said as she reached his side.

'I won't be long.'

She looked up at him, uncertain about his tone of voice. She had heard a lot about Frank Ross from Chris and, second-hand from Trudi, enough to make her want to meet him. As for the rest she wasn't a professional but she sometimes picked up escort agency work from her cousin who provided girls for visiting firemen. So that when Chris Cottle had jokingly propositioned her about Frank Ross she had been more than willing to say yes.

'What you doing out here, Frank? It's not much of a night for a walk in the garden.'

He looked at her young face, drawn slightly by the cold air. 'You been around a lot, have you, Hazel?'

'A bit,' she laughed. 'Not too little, not too much.'

'I see. Is Chris paying you for this?'

'No!' she said indignantly. 'He told me that when someone comes out after a long stretch, his mates usually arrange someone for him. He asked me and I said yes – if I liked the look of you, like.'

'And do you?'

'Yes. Quite a bit.'

He reached out and pulled her towards him. Then kissed her hard, forcing her head back so that the coat fell to the ground. Slipping his hand between her legs he pressed her dress into her body.

She responded, shuddering, until he held her back at arm's length. His breathing was fast, billowing mist in the cold air.

'Chris said we can use the other bedroom,' she said. 'Trudi made the bed up before you arrived.'

He could almost *feel* being in bed with her, the soft arms round his neck, the warmth of her body. 'Not tonight, Hazel,' he said.

She looked at him in astonishment. 'Not tonight?'

'I've got things to do.' He knew that this moment was crucial. If he went with her, the momentum would have been lost. Tomorrow he might not still want to seek out Bernie Machen. It would be so easy to while away the day boozing or screwing – anything rather than pursue what he knew he had to pursue.

'You've got things to do?' she was tight-lipped. 'Like, for instance, that flashy piece who was giving you a warm-up job when I came out.'

She bent and picked up the sheepskin coat. 'Or is it something else,' she said at a safe distance over her shoulder. 'I've heard prison does one of two things for a man. Which did it do for you?'

He smiled to himself as she ran for the french doors. Hell

hath no fury, he thought. And lighting a cigarette, he turned through the trees for the back garden gate.

The Jaguar kerb-crawled slowly past the tall black girl and stopped about twenty yards farther on. In his wing-mirror Frank Ross could see that the black girl had stopped too and, cigarette to her lips, was affecting to examine the possibilities of custom from the other direction. He noticed that she was immensely long-legged, even taking into account her red ankle-strap shoes with the four and a half inch heels. He noticed too that her backside was a little too pronounced under her imitation fur coat and that the umbrella she carried had a ferrule sharpened to the status of a lethal weapon. He touched the horn once.

Immediately he saw the girl turn and begin a slow saunter towards the Jaguar. He rolled down the window. She stopped beside the car and leaned down, the cigarette drooping from her wide reddened lips, parodying herself.

'Got a light?'

He pushed the car lighter. 'Sure.'

'Nice car . . .' she waited for the customary inquiry.

The lighter popped. He pulled it out and lit her cigarette.

'Thanks . . .'

'Get in,' he said.

She ran quickly round the bonnet of the car, pulled open the door and climbed in. 'You do know it'll cost you,' she said, arranging her long legs.

'How much?' Ross said casually, driving off.

'Depends what you want, darling.' She'd made the sale now. She could afford to be offhand. This John with his expensive car wouldn't baulk at the extra few quid.

'What I want,' Ross said, 'is for you to take me straight to Bernie Machen's place.'

'Here, what is this?' she said warily. 'Who are you, the old Bill?'

'I'm an old friend of Bernie's – Frank Ross. Maybe he even mentioned me.'

'How could he if I've never even met Bernie Machen?' She let smoke curl from her wide nostrils.

Frank stopped the car. 'What's your name?'

'Gloria'll do. But that's all you're getting from me tonight.'

She already had the car door open and was swinging her legs out when she felt the ten pound note touch her lips.

'Now listen, Gloria. Run along to Bernie. Tell him Frank Ross is waiting here for him. Know the street, do you?'

'Arthur Street,' she said.

'Don't think this is the easiest tenner you ever made in your young life. If you don't come back with Bernie, it'll be the hardest. Don't you believe the story that all black toms look alike to us.'

She took the money and shoved it into her bag. 'I'll do what I can.'

'I'm sure you will, Gloria. I'll stay here for an hour. Should give you time.'

'I told you I'll do what I can. I can't say better than that.'

'One hour, Gloria. You or Bernie.'

She swung out of the car and hurried back to the High Street, her high heels clacking on the silent pavements.

The party was swinging, everybody present affecting not to notice the absence of the guest of honour. Chris Cottle had already spoken to Hazel.

'I've told you all I know. He grabbed me, touched me up. Then said something about having work to do. He didn't want to know, Chris.'

'It's still not like Frank, just to piss off like that.'

'I've heard it said before. In prison they think of nothing else, every night, year after year. Then they get it and they're dead scared. Don't know what to do with it, like they're fifteen year old kids again.'

'Calm down, Hazel, for Chrissake. You've got it wrong. A thing like that wouldn't throw Frank.'

She laughed. 'So much for the big man. Well, I'm pushing off.'

'Okay, Hazel. But don't take it personal, love.'

'Who's taking it personal. Shoving his hands up me crutch one moment and running for his life the next. It's not my problem.'

Chris Cottle watched her stomp into the bedroom and get her coat. Then he crossed the room to where Anne was helping herself to another brandy. 'What happened out there, Anne?' he asked quietly.

'Out where?'

'You were in the garden with Frank. I sent Hazel out to get him.'

'Did you now? Well then I've two suggestions for you, Chris. The first is to keep your bloody nose out of my business. And second is, if you want to know anything, ask that rubber tyre yourself.'

'She said Frank just pissed off. What did he say to you?'

She faced him, fuming. 'You've got a brass neck, Chris, asking me questions like that. I wish I'd never told you about Frank and me.' She laughed bitterly. 'No I don't, Chris, I had to tell someone. Even if you didn't approve.'

She put down her glass and lit a cigarette. 'So, Frank didn't want the little welcome home present you fixed. What's so worrying about that? I'm delighted.'

'He's after whoever it was who grassed on them, Anne. That's what's worrying.'

She shook her head incredulously. 'After all these years? After all these years he's going to start looking.'

'He started today. An hour after he got back. Before he saw Paul, before he went to visit Evie . . .'

'Before he even remembered how to spell my name . . .'

'I don't know about that, Anne. But I do know how I feel about Frank Ross. I think he's bleedin' obsessed. And if he ain't very careful it'll put him in one of two places – back in nick or in his box.'

She was sober now, momentarily perhaps, but enough to feel the sharp pangs of anxiety that Cottle communicated. 'I don't understand you, Chris. What can happen to him?'

'This whole manor's changed, you know that, Lew Wilson, Tony McGrath, they run the place. First, neither of them are going to take to Frank Ross being back, period. But second they're neither of them goin' to take to Frank Ross barrelling around, stirring things up, chasing some bloody eight year old shadow. You know how it is, the only people who want old stories told again is the law. 'Cause they hear slightly different angles.'

'So who did it, Chris. Who do *you* think turned Frank in?'

'Listen, we all sat around asking each other that question eight years ago, remember? We never got nowhere then, we won't now. Unless Christie Bryce writes his memoirs in the *News of the World* I doubt we'll ever know. And it's best like that. It could have been a slip of the tongue in a boozer, you know that. It could have been Evie even . . .'

'I always heard she never even knew.'

'Right. So she makes some innocent remark. But it gets back to Christie Bryce and he puts two and two together.'

'You believe that theory, Chris? That whoever put Frank away wasn't a grass. It was just someone close who didn't know what he was saying?'

Cottle poured himself a brandy, then waved the neck of the bottle at her glass. She shook her head.

'I'm not saying I believe that's what happened. I'm not saying I don't believe it . . . I'm saying that Frank thinks his only problem is to find out *who* it was. I'm saying it could be that's where his problems really start.'

She gave him a strange sideways look. 'Anyway,' she shrugged, 'wherever he is, at least at the moment he's not between some little tart's legs.'

'That's not like you, Anne. It's a bit crude for your style, an' it?'

'Like it or not, Chris, and some of the time I don't, that's my feelings about the man, crude, basic, animalistic. After eight years, Chris, I find I'm still completely crazy about him.'

A wide tan-coloured Buick turned slowly into Arthur Street and nosed along the kerbstone like a dog sniffing garbage. Behind Frank Ross's Jaguar it rocked to a stop. The driver's door opened and Bernie Machen got out, closed the door behind him and stood for a moment looking down at the Jaguar. Gold glowed dully in his wide smile of appreciation; gold glowed at his throat, a solid Peruvian dollar against his black skin; gold glowed as a thick-linked chain around his wrist. He buttoned the yellow pigskin jacket at his waist and walked round the bonnet of the Jaguar to open the passenger door. Bending down he flashed his predator's smile. 'Frankie Ross. How ya' doing, man.'

He extended the palm of his hand and Ross briefly palmed it.

'Sit in Bernie. You made good time.'

'Gloria called me from the box on the corner. When Frankie Ross calls – I come.'

'Bullshit,' Ross said.

Machen took out a Russian cigarette and hung it in his mouth unlit. Then he tapped the dash of the Jaguar approvingly. 'Nice bit of steel.'

'Belongs to a friend.'

'Too bad.'

'How did your bird go, Bernie?'

Machen turned slowly in his seat, his eyes clouded. 'Slow, man. Very, very slow. Six years, that's a lot of time to think.'

'About all the girls you weren't screwing?'

He shook his head violently. 'About all the air I wasn't breathing, man.'

Ross nodded. 'I saw Vic Lee earlier.'

Machen made a spitting gesture.

'He took it real bad. But he was older than us. A lot older.' He tell you about Billy Binns?'

'Yes. A real surprise,' Ross said.

'He didn't have your firm hand any more, Frank. Though exactly what it was holding I guess I was never that sure.'

'You're asking for a belt in the gold teeth, Bernie. You know where Billy's hiding up?'

'No, man.'

'Ralph Vereker?'

'Ralph, maybe.'

'Where?'

'Hey!' Machen grinned. 'You're really wired up, Frankie.'

'That's right.'

'Looking for the man with the big finger?'

'Any ideas?'

'If I did . . .' Machen said, 'he'd be dead already.'

Ross nodded. 'Yuh. I somehow don't see you gabbing all over.'

'You think it was *me*? You crazy?'

'You sure it wasn't, Bernie? By accident. In the sack with one of your Toms . . .?'

'No chance, Frank.'

'That's the way most pimps go, Bernie. Little domestic crisis and one of the girls shops him.'

Machen's hand came over and gripped Ross's wrist. 'I'm telling you, Frank, if I even half thought that was true I would've had her cut to pieces the day that judge passed sentence.' He paused. 'That what you wanted to see me about?'

'I've got to find out who it was, Bernie.'

'On the trail of the man with the big finger,' Machen laughed. 'After all these years! You must be crazy, Frank.'

'Why crazy?'

Machen shrugged. 'Unless of course it's your way of getting back to be the big man in your manor. You know, "Nobody screws with Frankie Ross." Even eight goddam years later he'll come at you with a meat hook.'

'That's not it, Bernie. I'm not bidding to get back. Just tell me – where's Vereker?'

'If you want to know where Big Ralph is . . . it's gonna cost you . . . call it . . . compensation,' Machen said slowly.

'Compensation?'

Machen took a Cartier gold lighter from his pocket and lit his Russian cigarette. Drawing on the cardboard tube he said, 'That's it, man. Compensation. And remember you're a long way from home.' He nodded towards the driver's window. Ross turned his head to see a wide-cheeked black face looking in at him. 'Meet Cliff, Frankie. I normally keep him on a lead.'

Ross glanced at the huge face at the window. 'That's a pretty public spirited thing to do. In the circumstances.'

At a sign from Machen, Cliff opened the car door and leaned over it, his long silver necklet swinging like a mesmerist's coin in front of Ross's eyes.

'I was telling Cliff how it is with us, Frank.'

'How is it with us, Bernie?' Ross said, not looking at him.

'You know, how you're the guy that owes me.'

'I owe you nothing, Bernie. Nothing I can remember.'

'You owe me six years, Frankie. That's a lot of debt and Cliff says it's time you settled.'

'If business is that bad, Bernie, maybe you should go out and get yourself a better looking set of Toms.'

'Business is okay, Frank. But Cliff here says a debt's a debt. So I'll just take the car.'

'You'll what?'

'I'll take the car.'

Ross looked from him to Cliff who watched him impassively. With a shrug Ross leaned forward and took the keys from the ignition. 'I'll be back for it, Bernie, you know that.' He was bouncing the keys in his hand.

'When you come I'll be waiting, Frank.' He flicked his fingers. 'Let's have the keys, man.'

Ross bounced the keys off the palm of his hand so that they slipped between Machen's knees to the carpeted floor of the car. As Machen bent to retrieve them Ross moved fast, his right hand reaching up for the thick silver chain around Cliff's neck, his left hand ramming Machen's face forward on to the dash. Throttled by his own weight pushing the top of the door into his neck Cliff's eyes bulged bloodshot as Ross gave an extra twist on the silver chain and then kicked hard on the driver's door hurling Cliff gasping and spluttering into the road.

Slamming Machen's face again hard on the dash, he reached past his blood-soaked cream jeans and grabbed the keys. Cliff, outside, began to scramble to his feet when Ross switched on the ignition and hit the accelerator.

The Jaguar left the kerb fast, snapping back Machen's head, then equally violently, hurling him forward again as Ross braked hard and spun the wheel to hurl the car across the corner of the pavement and into Jason Street.

On the corner Gloria and another Tom were both too absorbed in the Jaguar to think of customers. Wide-eyed they watched as Cliff stumbled into the Buick and pulled out after the Jaguar.

Spluttering blood and venom Bernie Machen clawed at the wheel as Ross threw the car round another corner to brake and U-turn in the narrow street into a space behind a parked van. Two seconds after he killed the lights the Buick powered down the street heading for Brixton Hill.

Inside the Jaguar Machen sat silent, a bunch of Kleenex held to his bleeding nose.

Ross lit two cigarettes and handed him one. 'Sorry, Bernie,' he said, 'but you come the old acid with me and that's the way it's got to be.'

Machen finished dabbing his nose and took the cigarette. When he turned to Ross his face wore his customary grin. 'Never say die, Frankie Ross. I'd forgotten.' He drew on the cigarette. 'Okay, Frankie,' he lifted the palm of his hand. 'No hard feelings. I asked you for the car – you said no. Let's leave it at that.'

As he moved to get out Ross stopped him. 'Just one more thing, Bernie.'

'Vereker's address?'

Ross nodded.

'He lives up Essex way. Hornchurch. You'll find him in the phone book.'

'How come you know that, Bernie?'

'He called me a couple of days ago. Asked me if you was out yet.'

'See you, Bernie. Sorry about the nose. But it never was much to write home about anyway.'

'Racist bastard,' Machen got out of the car. 'See you, Frankie. Never say die.'

CHAPTER FOUR

Carriston Lodge was a large white-columned country mansion approached by a drive lined with lime trees and set in the rolling Oxfordshire countryside just outside Woodstock. On the A40/M40 it was an easy hour and a half from Shepherd's Bush. To Frank Ross the fast-running Jaguar gave him an immense feeling of freedom but as they left the motorway and, at Chris Cottle's direction, took to the country roads a sense of impending gloom descended on him.

It was four years since he had seen his wife. Why he had refused her visits he couldn't clearly explain. The prison doctor had called in the psychiatrist and he had flatly refused to talk to either of them about it. Of course they couldn't force him to accept visits. And somehow it had been easier that way. One single event to look forward to. One single date to pace steadily towards. No interruptions, no deflections, his eyes firmly fixed on the day of his release.

She had taken it hard. From Chris's letters he had known that . . . With a sudden effort he blanked out his mind. 'About last night, Chris,' he said.

Chris Cottle shook his head. 'Forget it, Frank. It was your night. You don't have any explaining to do.'

Ross side-glanced him. 'You're a fantastic guy, Chris.'

'Balls. Everybody felt the same.'

Ross heard the hesitation as the sentence almost tailed away. 'Everybody?'

'Except Anne.'

The silence sat between them. 'She told me, Frank. Back five, six years ago. I think round that time, she came close to doing herself in. She was that desperate she had to talk to somebody.'

'I see.'

The black iron gates with elegant gold leafed tips stood open on to the drive.

'Straight ahead?'

Cottle nodded. 'It ain't none of my business, Frank, but of the two of 'em – it's Evie needs you more.'

Gravel spurted under the car's tyres. Ross gave him a single hard look and swung the Jaguar in a half-circle to park it beside the line of other cars outside the house.

Eve Ross sat at the dressing-table in her bedroom, the tears streaming down her cheeks carving runnels in the thick make-up she had already applied.

It was not difficult to see, even now, that she had once been an exceptionally attractive woman, a woman not perhaps with the mature good looks of Anne Mitchell but more pretty in the fashion of a fifties starlet.

The middle-aged nurse standing next to her offered her a Kleenex. 'Now we'll have to stop this, Mrs. Ross, your husband'll be here any minute now.' She had in fact already seen the Jaguar pull up and guessed that one of the two men was Frank Ross. God she was bored with the name. The hours she had spent nodding half asleep by Eve Ross's beside, grunting monosyllabically as Mrs. Ross rambled on and on, always over the same old ground. Why . . . why . . . why did he refuse to see me . . . Why had he turned away from me . . . Nurse Sackett had many times felt like suggesting her darling husband had simply turned queer while inside – but on reflection there was nothing queer about the tall lithe man that had climbed out of the driver's seat of the Jaguar.

The phone rang and Nurse Sackett picked it up and listened. 'Well we're not quite ready here yet, Doctor. Give us another five or six minutes, will you?'

On the other end of the phone a long-haired man in tinted glasses and striped collarless shirt said, 'No hurry, Nurse. Call me when you're ready.'

He looked across the strangely unoffice-like office to where Ross sat in a comfortable armchair. 'Some coffee, Mr. Ross?'

'No thank you, Doctor.' Ross watched the strange, wild-looking figure cross the room to open a cupboard and pour himself some coffee. He turned and looked over his tinted glasses. 'Something stronger.' He waved a brandy bottle. 'I often have one about this time. I'm afraid I've got all the vices.'

Ross nodded almost diffidently. 'Well, thank you.'

Pinching two glasses between thumb and index finger Dr. Whyte swung them off the cupboard shelf. 'Catch those.'

Ross took them and held them out for the doctor to fill. 'Now change your mind about the coffee.'

Ross hesitated. 'All right.'

'What dances we dancers dance,' Whyte said as he turned back to the coffee cupboard. 'Nervous?' he asked peering at the Cona machine.

'Yes. Very.'

'Me too,' said Dr. Whyte.

'You?'

The doctor poured coffee. 'Eve is one of my special people.'

Ross took the coffee from him. Whyte put his own coffee on on the cut down pine table between them and slid into a leather armchair. 'Well, let's see . . . where do we start?'

Ross looked at him slightly puzzled. 'Start?'

'Yes,' Whyte nodded. 'What can you tell me, how can you help?'

'Here, hold on. You're the doctor.'

'Mr. Ross . . . Mr. Ross, your wife's disease is not . . . self-contained. A virus dropped from the skies.'

'No, I see that. It's just that I suppose I expected you more to tell me than to be asking.'

'Tell you how she is?'

Ross nodded.

'Excited. Too excited. Not much help to you is it?'

'No.'

'What are you expecting, a diagnosis?'

'I thought that's what you got paid for.'

'*One* of the things . . . *one* of the things . . .' the doctor tossed back his brandy. 'Now how about another of those. Not finished yet?' He stood up and crossed to his cupboard. 'Your wife is evasive, Mr. Ross. Very evasive. Especially on one subject.'

'Me?'

'No,' Whyte pursed his lips, looking at Ross over the tinted glasses. 'Not you. Your criminality.'

Ross shrugged uncomfortably. 'Can you blame her?'

'Why do you say that?'

'If I hadn't been put away she wouldn't be here. The judge sentenced me . . . but I sentenced Evie.'

The doctor nodded, grimacing. 'Yes,' he said, 'you're all such terrible sentimentalists.'

Ross sat up. 'What the hell's that supposed to mean, Doctor?'

Whyte ignored the question. 'When did you start to blame yourself, Mr. Ross. Before or after you were caught.'

'I was put away. Grassed on.'

'You mean you *don't* blame yourself?'

'No. Not the way you mean it.'

Whyte nodded to himself. 'Now let's change the subject slightly. You were arrested previously?'

'Twice . . . and sent for trial.'

'You were innocent?'

Ross smiled grimly. 'They couldn't prove me guilty.'

'What was Eve's reaction then?'

'I sent her and the kid away.'

'Both times?'

'It was best.'

'She agreed to go?'

'I said . . . it was best.'

'For whom?'

'Both of us. The police can be evil. When they want you bad they'll get at you any way they can. They'll use your wife . . . your family . . . anything . . . anyone, to put pressure on you.'

'Quite, quite.'

'I promise you,' Ross said.

Whyte nodded his disinterest. 'The crux of your wife's problem, Mr. Ross, has to do with rejection. Your rejection of her. You refused to allow her to come and see you in prison. Why was that?'

'You don't understand what it's like in there . . .'

'Why was that?' Whyte repeated sharply.

'I felt I could handle things one way. My way.'

'At whatever cost to your wife?'

'Listen, Doctor, I didn't come here to be hammered.'

'I was only trying to elicit your attitude to your wife, Mr. Ross.'

'I . . . love my wife.'

The pale eyes examined him over the tinted glasses. 'I see,' Whyte said at length. He stood up. 'Go in and see her, Mr. Ross. I just hope you do a better job of persuading her than you have of convincing me.'

With a final glance at Eve's carefully restored make-up Nurse Sackett turned to answer the knock. As she opened the door she was pleased to see she had been right. The famous husband was the one she had decided. Tall, lean and good looking in a hard, restrained way. Quite a handful, Nurse Sackett decided, pulling wide the door. 'Come in, Mr. Ross,' she said.

He smiled, again the restraint. No easy effusion in his manner. She was sorry she had to step past him into the corridor and pull the door closed behind her.

Frank Ross stood opposite the stranger in the middle of the room. He was fighting to repress his sense of shock. Of course she was thirty-seven now. Of course she had been still in her late twenties when they had last stood freely together. Of course photographs had part prepared him, and his own common sense had told him what to expect. But the woman who faced him now was not just past her youth. She already had that pathetic quality of someone fighting to retain the irrevocably lost. Compared with Anne Mitchell's easy and elegant acceptance of the years, Eve stood breathless, tense, her face a hard mask of nervously applied make-up, like an actress direct from the footlights.

He put out both hands to her, unable to speak for the sheer pain of recognizing somewhere the shadow of the woman he had once loved. The woman whom he had reduced to this.

Unsteadily she took a step towards him.

'Eve . . . Evie . . .'

Her lips moved like rubber as she struggled to speak. 'Hullo, Frank.'

He took both her hands and pulled her towards him.

She stood stiffly against his body. 'It's good to see you again, Evie.'

'It's good to see you again, Frank,' she forced out the echo. 'You think I've changed?'

He shook his head.

'Frank . . .' She drew away from him. 'I'm sorry about the letters.'

She was apologizing to him. To him! Who had refused to see her for the last four years?

'Evie . . .' he said. 'Don't talk about being sorry. Let's both of us just forget the word.'

'I'm sorry about the letters, Frank,' she said again.

'I said forget it, love.'

They stood, hands clasped, opposite each other. 'It wasn't because I didn't *want* to write,' she said hesitantly.

'I know,' he said shortly.

'I just get depressed, Frank.'

'Yes.'

'But nothing's altered has it?'

He smiled with effort and touched her hair. 'Nothing, except maybe your hair. That's different.'

She flicked her hand through her hair. 'It's a mess.'

'Not what I meant, Evie.'

'Everything's a mess, Frank.' She half turned away.

'Look, Evie, how about a little drive. I'll talk to the doc, he'll let you come. It'll do you good.'

'When I leave here, Frank, it'll be to go home. But if you want some tea or coffee just pick up the phone. It's a private home – they rush.'

He walked over and lifted the phone. 'Anything for you, love?'

'Same as you.'

Nurse Sackett answered the phone.

'Can you arrange some tea in Room 22 please.'

'Of course, Mr. Ross,' she said. 'I'll bring it right away.'

He turned back to Eve. 'Coming up.'

She relaxed a little. 'When you met Dr. Whyte, what did you think?' she asked.

'A bit of a weirdo. You get on okay with him?'

She ignored his question. 'What did he have to say, Frank?'

'We just talked.'

'About me?'

'All sorts.'

'Tell me.'

'Tell you what, love?'

'What he said about me.'

'He was vague.'

'I want to know what he said, Frank. I have a right to know.'

Ross watched the compressed line of her lips. 'Tell me!' she almost spat out the words.

'We talked about . . . my being in prison.'

The anger flared uncontrollably. 'Me . . . me . . . Frank. What did he tell you about *me*?'

'Calm down, love.' He tried to take her hand again but she shrugged him off.

'Why won't you tell me?' she stood, her eyes bright, her breathing fast, in the middle of the room.

'I'm trying to tell you,' he said, 'but just calm down a bit, Evie.'

'I'm not an idiot, Frank. I'm not ga ga . . . my brain still functions. I'm not a cabbage. I do still comprehend basic English.'

'Evie . . .' he tried to stop the rush of words.

'Eight years . . . in eight years you haven't changed . . . not one iota . . . you're still talking to me like I'm a . . . a . . . a . . .'

'Evie . . .'

'My name's Eve . . . *Eve* . . . not "Evie" . . . *Eve*!'

He came forward fast grabbing her high on the arms but her head threshed from side to side.

'You keep away from me,' she screamed. 'You put me in here. But I don't have to stay. I don't have to . . . I'm not committed . . . I can walk out any time . . . any time I bloody well want!'

He released his grip.

'Sit down, Eve . . .'

She faced him, her face contorted. 'I hate you! I loathe the sight of your face! Look!' She held out her left hand. 'See! No wedding ring . . . no wedding ring!'

'What happened to it,' he asked quietly.

She smiled, her first triumph since he had arrived. 'I got rid of it . . . just like you got rid of me . . . flushed it down the lavatory. Instant divorce!'

She lashed out at him, the palm of her hand catching him flat and hard across the cheek. He stood, unmoving.

'Oh God, what you've done to me,' she snarled. Slowly, with deliberation she reached out and raked her red nails down his cheek.

The action seemed to jolt her out of the hysteria.

'Oh Christ, Frank . . . I'm sorry . . . I'm sorry . . I'm sorry I didn't mean it . . . I didn't mean it . . .'

He came forward and put his arms round her. 'It's all right, love. Just forget it.'

'Take me home, Frank . . . for God's sake take me away from this place . . . I'm dying in here!' Tears smudged the eye mascara and cut channels in the make-up.

'As soon as I can . . .' he promised.

'Today, Frank . . . now.' She was begging him.

'You know that's not possible, Eve.'

'Why not?'

'Soon, Eve . . . I promise you it'll be soon.'

She looked at him suspiciously, her head angled, 'You do want me still, don't you, Frank?'

'Of course I want you.'

She nodded as if confirming something to herself. 'I mean physically . . . sexually . . .'

'Eve . . .' he couldn't bear the pathos of the sudden angle of her hip, the rising breasts, the grotesque attempt at showgirl sexiness. 'Don't, Eve . . .'

'We always were good together . . . weren't we, Frank . . . remember . . . we always were . . . in bed?' She began to unzip her dress. 'Put the chair against the door, Frank.'

'Eve, love . . . please.'

She stood opposite him in bra and pants, slowly rotating her hips, her tongue moving across her upper lip.

'What's the matter?' One hand pushed his jacket from his shoulders. The other reached down.

'No, love . . . no . . . no, Evie!'

With a sudden movement she stepped back. 'No, Evie! No, Evie! *No, Evie!* Christ! God! Jesus!'

She began to scream totally unaware of Nurse Sackett entering with the tea. 'Wait outside, Mr. Ross,' she said crisply, 'leave her to me.'

The Jaguar swept through the gently undulating Buckinghamshire countryside with Chris Cottle at the wheel. Beside him Frank Ross sat in silence. He had hardly spoken since they had started the drive back.

'You feel like stopping for a drink? We can drive off the motorway at High Wycombe, couple of nice boozers there I know.'

'As you like,' Ross took a pack of cigarettes from his pocket, lit two and handed one of them to Cottle. 'Out there in the corridor, you heard her, did you.'

Cottle grunted. 'She's not always like that, Frank. Not like *that.*'

Ross lapsed back into silence, staring ahead at the ribbon of road. A few snowflakes flecked the windscreen as they reached higher ground.

'Snowing . . .' Cottle said.

But Ross was lost in the memory of the last hour. 'One minute . . . bit tense maybe but normal . . .' he seemed to be speaking almost to himself. 'The next . . . frightening.'

It was barely past midday but the heavy grey cloud sat low on a darkening countryside. Chris Cottle let the speedometer climb past ninety. He had no wish for this journey to go on for longer than necessary.

After a few minutes of impenetrable silence Frank Ross turned in his seat pivoting on his elbow on the arm-rest. 'Listen, Chris, is it possible that Evie ever knew anything about Anne and me?'

'Jesus, no,' Cottle said. 'Not from me.'

'Any other way you can think of.'

'Anne wouldn't. Never.'

'No,' Ross said reflectively. 'Just an idea. Something's got to account for the state she's in, Chris.'

Cottle's face flushed with barely perceptible anger. 'Come off it, Frank,' he said. 'You know why she's in that state.'

'Because I was put away, you mean.'

'Because you refused to see her for bleedin' years, that's why.'

He gunned the car forward until the indicator showed just over a hundred. 'Let's get a drink at Amy's place,' he said. 'I reckon we both need one.'

For the rest of the drive they sat in silence.

He had never heard Cottle burst out like that. And of course somehow it was pretty close to what that damned doctor had said. Well, they didn't understand. Not even Chris really understood. A long sentence was a desperate fight for survival. He'd done what he had to do.

'She still work in the same place, Amy?' Ross asked as they turned off the A40 at White City.

Cottle took the question as the peace-offering Ross intended it to be.

'No,' he said. 'Moved up in the world. Has her own drinker now. The Star and Garter. All the lads get in there, so it's full of Old Bill as well. Amy don't mind. They're good customers she says. Never knock the place about.'

They crossed the river at Battersea and were soon on familiar ground. The Star and Garter occupied a big corner site a few hundred yards from the end of Brixton Hill.

Inside, at the long Edwardian mahogany bar Amy Dickinson sat alone checking her order book for the coming afternoon's delivery. She was a somewhat over-blown woman in her fifties, apple cheeked and big breasted. To every regular customer of the Star and Garter she was known as someone to stay on the right side of.

Now as she heard the door swing open behind her, she kept the biro poised mid-way down the column of figures and called without turning her head. 'Sorry, love – the towels are up. Gone closing.'

Leaning over her figures she stopped frowning as she realized that the footsteps were continuing towards the bar.

'Now look . . .' she swung on her barstool. Then seeing Frank Ross she slipped nimbly despite her weight off the stool and into his arms.

'Frankie Ross . . .' She hugged him. 'You lovely man . . .'

Ross smiled 'Good to see you again, Amy.' He detached himself and gestured around. 'And I hear you're running your own ship.'

She nodded. 'Now let me look at you.' She walked round him grunting approvingly. 'Yes . . . yes, you're looking better than ever. When did they let you out of the queer place?'

'Yesterday.'

'Wonderful . . . like old times.' She hesitated.

'Have you been to see Evie yet?'

'Just got back,' Cottle said hurriedly. 'We could both use a drop of gargle.'

She caught his warning glance and moved back behind the bar and raised a glass to the whisky optic.

'And how's that boy of yorn, Frank, young Paul?' she asked over her shoulder.

'He's fifteen going on sixteen now, Amy.'

'Good Lord!'

Ross took out his wallet and opened it on the bar. 'Chris took this two months back.' He passed her a photograph.

Taking the picture she turned to Chris Cottle. 'He's goin' to be even better lookin' than his old fella. Break a few hearts he will. He reminds me of Pretty Billy when he was younger, Frank.'

She looked at Ross. 'You've heard of course.'

He took back the photograph and replaced it carefully in his wallet. 'Vic Lee told me. I couldn't believe it.'

Amy filled the last glass and handed them across the bar. Sipping her own whisky she said: 'He never was like that, Frank. Wouldn't hurt no one.'

'What happened?'

'Ask Lew Wilson,' she said shortly.

'Billy got caught up with him?'

'When he got out you weren't around. You know what he's like. Lew Wilson got his bloody hooks into him.'

She looked up towards the door and the two men half turned on their bar stools. Inspector Alec Rimmer let the swing-door bang closed behind him. Hands deep in his black raincoat pockets he walked across to the bar.

'I'm closed, Inspector.'

Rimmer ignored Ross and grinned at Amy. 'I could still do with a swift half.'

'Sorry. I didn't make the rules.'

'Come off it, Amy.'

'I'm closed,' she said firmly.

Ross deliberately raised his glass and sipped his drink. Cottle drained his and glance at Rimmer. 'We'd best be off, Frank.'

'What's the hurry?' Ross asked, eyeing Rimmer.

'He's worried that you might have a go at me,' Rimmer said.

'And he may be right.'

Rimmer smiled and shook his head. 'You've still got the stink of the nick on you ... the last thing you need is a run in with me.'

Ross nodded in apparent agreement. 'I read a lot ... in prison ... I had to learn to control my natural impulses. So I got books ... *Frustration and Conflict* ... *Human Aggression* ... *The Criminal Psychology*. You can learn a lot about yourself from books I don't suppose you get much time to read?'

'Not much.' Rimmer shook his head. 'I'm too busy protecting society from intellectuals like you.'

'You wanted a word with me?'

'Why should I want words with you, Ross?'

'Then this is purely a chance encounter?'

Rimmer shrugged. 'Amy is usually more obliging.'

'That all you're here for?' Ross said. 'Funny, I thought you might want to reminisce. I thought you might feel that eight years have added a certain perspective to our relationship.'

Rimmer picked up Ross's whisky and knocked it back. 'It's sad,' he said. 'You're a clever man. You could have been almost anything you wanted to be . . . but for one thing . . . one flaw in your make-up.'

'Come on, Frank,' Cottle said, sensing trouble.

Rimmer turned his shoulder to exclude Chris Cottle.

Facing Ross he said, 'You're corrupt . . . you can't help it, it's like an illness, a deformity . . . and you infect, you taint all those round you. That's why me and others like me have to separate you from decent . . . normal . . . healthy people.'

'Sort of . . . social surgery?' Ross mocked him.

'Facts, Frank . . . just facts. Oh, by the way . . .'

'Here comes the commercial,' Amy said from behind the bar.

'Mr. Bryce sends you his regards.'

'That's thoughtful of him,' Ross acknowledged.

'And he asked me to tell you,' Rimmer went on, 'if you should be foolish enough to have words with Pretty Billy . . . tell him it's only a matter of time. We're going to have him.' He paused. 'You too, first chance.'

The powerful lights burned through the billowing dust. While Ross and Vic Lee looked on, Big Ralph Veneker and Machen, his black body glistening with sweat, shovelled brick dust from the opening. Crouched between the gap in the bricks, his head shrouded like an Arab, Pretty Billy Binns tore his fingers as he threw back solid chunks of masonry.

In the heat and dust and exhaustion of the work all five men were buoyed by the presence of the smooth metal back of the safe exposed to them now through the gaping hole in the cellar wall.

To Frank Ross it was the culmination of a year's planning. Of a year spent laying out for specialized information; a year of meetings with city gentlemen who would convert the half a million pounds of marks and francs and guilders that lay on the other side of that steel barrier; a year of careful selection of the team – Lee as engineer, Ralph Veneker and Machen for muscle and sheer guts, Pretty Billy as a totally trustworthy peterman, the guy whose skill lay in his ability to crack any safe worth keeping money in.

Frank Ross watched the ton and a half of brickwork rattling aside.

When the first shouts were heard on the stairs above, the first clatter of police boots and the triumphant voices of Bryce and Rimmer, he had stood immobilized. Then watched the cramped basement fill with struggling figures in the swirling dust.

CHAPTER FIVE

FRANK ROSS moved around the room touching the items of furniture and decoration, struck by the restraint of the colours, the circumspection behind the choice of every chair, the positioning of every light. From the kitchen Anne called: 'I didn't ask you how much.'

'Drown it,' he said. 'I'll fall over if it's too strong.'

She appeared a moment later and extended a heavy tumbler towards him. 'There you are. One drowned whisky.'

He took it with a smile and gestured round the room. 'Some pad.'

'Nice, isn't it?'

'Very. Money and taste. Some combination. Who's is it?'

'Mitch's sleeping partner. The man who put up all the original money. He and his wife are sitting out the winter in Singapore. They asked me to look after the place.'

'Very convenient.'

She eyed him evenly. 'Very.'

He offered her a cigarette. She shook her head, her eyes never leaving his face.

'Does Mitch know about us?' he asked abruptly.

'No one knows.'

'Chris does.'

'Okay. I had to speak to someone. Nobody else.'

'Not Mitch?'

'No. Anyway . . . he wouldn't care . . .'

She reaches for the huge balloon of brandy on the piano and drinks a long draught. Ross watches her.

'No problems there, Frank. He wouldn't care.'

'He'd care . . . he'd care, so would I. I grew up with Mitch. I know him.'

She laughed. 'Then you've forgotten. Our marriage . . . is not what you might call . . . sacred . . . never really was.'

She reached for the glass of brandy. He picked it up, holding on to it.

'He doesn't know who to screw next! Business trips to Amsterdam, secretaries who can't type . . . he makes sure I know, that's half the fun.'

She went to take the glass of brandy from him. He swirled the liquid in the glass.

'This is heavy stuff to drink in half-pints.'

'It's an occasion.' She took the glass from him and drank. 'A special occasion.'

'And last night was too.'

'Last night too,' she said and walked across to the drinks table. She picked up a decanter and poured until the glass was half full.

'When did this start?' He pointed to the decanter.

'Don't pretend to be naïve, Frank, it demeans you.'

'Is it that bad?'

'What . . . the drinking or the reasons?'

'Both.'

'Did you think of me, Frank . . . in prison . . . I mean honestly think about *me* . . . about us . . . the way we were . . . what we did . . . said to each other . . . felt?'

'Often.'

She nodded thoughtfully. Her lower lip poised on the rim of the glass she asked: 'How often?'

He lifted his shoulders. 'Often.'

'How often . . . once a day . . . once a week . . . once a month . . . less and less until you'd almost forgotten me . . . forgotten the shape of my face . . . the colour of my eyes?'

'What do you want me to say, Anne?'

'The truth.'

He turned to her. 'Anne,' he said quietly, 'you know what happened to us.'

She shook her head. 'No. I know what happened to me, Frank. But I never really knew what happened to you. After all this time maybe you should try and tell me.'

He pointed to the drinks cabinet and she nodded. Crossing the room he poured whisky and water. 'You hit me at a special moment, Anne,' he said with his back still to her. He turned to face her and sipped his whisky. 'I'd been married to Evie seven years.'

'Oh, *that* special moment? The seven year itch.'

'Shut up, Anne,' he said quietly, 'you asked me to tell you.'

'Sorry. Go on.'

'You knew Evie in her early twenties.'

'Yes. Prettiest little thing in South London. All the guys after her.'

He nodded.

'So Frank Ross just had to be the one that got her.'

'Yes. Perhaps it's been like that all my life.' He shrugged. 'Anyway, I was just a kid myself. You know how the boys grow up here. A woman is a piece of decoration, a clothes horse, she's what she looks much more than what she is.'

'Evie was a sweet kid, Frank. You're not telling me any different.'

'No. She was a very pretty sweet kid. She liked children, clothes, a home . . .'

'So what are you holding against her?'

'You,' he said.

She inhaled quickly but remained silent.

'When I began to get to know you, when Evie and me, you and Mitch started going around a bit together . . . I found it tough. I found Evie was still the sweet, fluttery kid. I found you very different.'

'A new Everest to conquer, Colonel Ross?'

'Perhaps. You remember how it was those three, four months.'

'I remember, Frank.'

'The first night we spent together.'

She nodded briskly, on the point of tears. 'Yes, I remember.'

He sat on the arm of the sofa and drank whisky.

'If you hadn't been caught, Frank. If the next eight years hadn't been lost, what would have happened to us?'

He shook his head.

'You must have thought about it.'

'Of course.'

'Would we have stayed together?'

'God knows.'

'You must have thought, Frank,' she said, her voice rising. 'Or once you'd clambered to the top of this particular Everest were you already peering across to the next cloudy peak? Who would she have been Frank? The Lady Ursula Mustaffit-Quickly, or some shapely twenty-year-old Swedish starlet . . .'

'No,' he said, standing. 'It was Evie or you. That was the choice.'

'The choice that the judge made for you.'

He nodded.

'And now?'

'Now Evie's on the edge of being a mental cripple for the rest of her life.'

'So the choice has been made for you again.'

He finished his whisky without answering.

She put her glass down on the piano. 'Take me to bed, Frank.'

His head moved a millimetre either way in the faintest indication of refusal.

'Take me to bed, Frank,' she said again. 'I don't care why you do it, because you still love me or because coming out of prison you need a damn good screw. I'm not capable of being humiliated by you, Frank. You understand that that's how much I love you.'

He reached for her hand and drew her towards him. 'No,' he said, 'I don't understand it. But I value it.'

'You've the gift of tongues, Frank Ross,' she laughed only part bitterly.

Turning away from him she reached for her bag.

'Someone,' he said, 'called me "corrupt" today. He said that I infect the people close to me. I think he may be right. I haven't made the people I care most about very happy . . . have I?'

Anne opened her bag and took out an envelope and handed it

to him. He opened it. Inside was a wad of new twenty-pound notes.

'It's my money, nothing to do with Mitch,' she said.

Ross put the money back in the envelope and handed it back to Anne.

'No . . . but thanks.'

'No strings . . . no conditions.'

'No.'

'Don't you see? The police are just waiting for you to . . . what I mean is . . . it'll tide you over until you get something sorted out . . . I don't want you to . . .'

'I'm not going back inside . . . ever . . . don't worry.' He pointed to the money. 'Was that why you wanted to meet?'

'Only partly, I'm afraid.' She smiled. 'You see, Frank Ross, I'm a tryer. To get you into bed I'll try every which way. Seduction, rape, even bribery.'

He kissed her lightly on the lips. 'I've got to go, Anne.'

'Funny thing,' she said. 'I suddenly feel I'm nearer to success than I thought possible.'

He cupped one hand under her breast and with his thumb brushed the nipple. 'That,' he smiled, 'is exactly why I've got to go.'

Sitting on the edge of the bed, Eve Ross huddled miserably in her dressing-gown as Dr. Whyte leaned casually against the wall of her bedroom and lit a long thin cigar. 'I'm well enough to go, Doctor. What happened was just seeing Frank again. Just excitement. It won't happen again.'

He shrugged. 'Up to you, Eve, you know that. You can walk out of here the moment you want to.'

'But . . .?'

'But I wouldn't. I'd let Frank come down a couple of times in the next week or so . . . take you out for a drive . . . then bring Paul . . . you know, easy does it.'

Her mouth tightened. 'He hasn't had a woman for eight years, Doctor. I don't want it to be someone else.'

Whyte nodded. 'Good point. But then why not take a room at the pub this weekend?'

She shook her head. 'I've got to be at home. I've got to be *with* Frank.'

He pushed himself off the wall. 'Yup, I see the point. But I'd like you to take a couple of days to think about it. Maybe ask Frank down for tomorrow and we'll all three give it a going over.'

She shivered in the dressing-gown.

As he walked to the door he glanced towards the hand-basin. Four red pills stood in a medicine glass on the shelf above it. 'And, Eve, don't forget your tablets, okay?'

She nodded, still shivering as he left the room. Then she stood up, walked to the hand-basin and took the medicine glass from the shelf. Crossing to the window she opened it and shot the red tablets out into the bushes beyond. Then, without troubling to close the window she stripped off her dressing-gown and began to dress.

For a moment the big man held the rod delicately poised before a flick of his powerful wrists sent the line streaking out across the still water. As the float bobbed half-way across the stream, Ralph Veneker grunted his satisfaction. Without turning to Frank Ross who stood next to him watching the float ride the surface, he said, 'No bugger knows Frank. When I came out I put my hand on everybody. The lot. Anybody who owed me a favour, I called it in. And I got nowhere mate.'

'So you gave up?'

Ralph Veneker smiled, his huge leonine face creasing.

'We've all got a life to lead, Frankie. True enough if you'd come out here today with the bastard's name writ on a bit a' paper I'd be in there with you when we paid him a first and final. But it'd take the name to stir the guts again the way it used to. The way it did when I first come out. I'm not trying to get flash with you, Frank. But you'll learn. Ten to one you'll feel the same in a coupla months.'

Ross turned the collar of his topcoat up against the early evening chill. 'What you don't understand, Ralph,' he said quietly, 'is that I don't *want* to learn. I don't want to feel the same.'

Veneker began to reel in his line. 'I've known you a lotta years, Frank.'

'So . . .?'

'After eight years bird anybody's got problems. Cash, wife, kids . . .'

He reached out and caught the line. 'They're the big problems, Frank. They come first. Any other way of looking at it is out of order.'

'So are you, Ralph.'

Veneker inclined his huge head. 'Okay, mate, if you say so. But that still don't mean I ain't right. Now how about a tot or two to drive away some of this river mist.'

Veneker packed up his gear and together the two men set off along the darkening river bank to where a riverside pub already strung with Christmas lights, stood among the willows trailing in the mist laden stream.

On that same afternoon Chris Cottle had already decided he would call it a day. His secretary, Sandra, had left at lunchtime with a cold and with no work in the yard he'd seen no point in sitting by the phone waiting for the creditors to ring. Taking the van he had driven back to the flat, let himself in and had just poured himself a big whisky when the phone rang. As it always did these days the bloody thing caused his stomach to lurch. He picked up the receiver and listened to the pips. He wasn't expecting to hear from Trudi for a couple of days. Frank had gone off to see Ralph Veneker. He was still playing the guessing game when he heard the coin fall in the box and Anne's clear voice say, 'Chris . . . it's Anne here. Listen, you feel like giving me a drink.'

'Sure,' he said, puzzled. 'Nothing wrong, love, is there?'

'I'll be there in two minutes,' she said in answer. 'I'm at the call-box round the corner. You are alone there?'

'On me tod.'

'Okay. Two minutes.'

He heard the phone go down and slowly replaced his own receiver and took up his glass. Weird, that. Anne Mitchell and he hadn't really been that close except for the time she'd blurted about her and Frank. He liked her all right, liked her a lot. But she always had that slightly stuck up, upper crust atmosphere when other people were around.

He turned up the heating to top and strolled towards the door. Outside he could hear her heels clicking across the paving stones. Opening the door he saw her tall, fur-coated shape under the garden light. She reached the porch, shivering slightly.

'Come in, love.' He stepped aside and she smiled wanly and entered the hall. He took her coat and dropped it over a chair as she went on into the living-room.

'First things first,' he said following her in. 'What will it be.'

'You got some of that brandy left from the other night?'

'Let's have a look. Yes, half the bottle.' He poured and handed her a bulbous balloon, the brown spirit washing half-way up the glass.

'You're not expecting Frank,' she asked.

'No.'

'Or Trudi.'

'No.'

She nodded to herself and sat down.

He picked up his own glass. 'Bovver?'

'No. Nothing you don't know about. I just needed to talk. Like before, remember.'

'I remember. If it helps, love, just talk away. You've seen Frank, have you? Apart from the party, I mean?'

'Yes. For a couple of hours. He told me what you'd done. For Evie.' She looked at his blank face. 'The hospital money. The bills.'

'That.'

'Yes *that*. Why didn't you come to Mitch and Quincey and the rest. You know they would have kicked in.'

'It's past, Anne.' He paused. 'You talked to Frank. You found he's changed.'

'Too early to say. Too early for *me* to say.'

'You hope he hasn't.

'I want him, Chris.'

'And what happens to Evie? What happens to young Paul?'

'Divorces happen. Kids live with one parent or the other. It's not the end of the world.'

'For Evie it could be.'

'That's what you think.'

'And you should know I guess. More than anyone.'

His eyes narrowed. 'What's that mean?'

'Come off it, Chris. I know how you felt about Evie. Always did, didn't you?'

He reached for a cigarette box and took out a cigarette.

'Did it ever come to anything, Chris – between you and Evie?'

'Don't be bloody mad,' he said harshly.

'What's so mad about it. It happened to me and Frank. When he shut her off from him she only had you to lean on.'

'For Chrissake, Anne!'

'Listen, Chris. I gave you my secret and it helped me a lot. I gave it to you because I knew I could trust you. You can trust me, Chris.'

He drank some whisky and lit a cigarette without answering.

'I'm not asking just out of dirty minded curiosity, Chris. I've got reasons.' She watched him intently. 'Did anything come of it, Chris?'

He inhaled the cigarette deeply. 'No . . . never. Evie's life's always been enough of a mess without me buggering it up more.' He hesitated before deciding to go on. 'It was really rough on her, those first few months Frank was inside. Then, when he stopped her visits she didn't know where to turn. I wanted to help, would have done anything to save her from what she's gone through. She's a good kid, Anne, and maybe if I'd met her before Frank . . . well, who knows.' His voice trailed away, and it was a couple of minutes before he spoke again.

'Frank's the closest mate I ever had. I want to keep it that way. Okay?'

He stood and took her near empty glass. Crossing to the drinks cabinet he said. 'You want to redeal the cards, that it? You get Frank – and I get Evie.'

'Would that be so bad?'

'No. But it ain't going to happen Anne.' He poured her another brandy and handed it to her.

'Maybe,' she said, raising her glass. 'But let's drink to it all the same.'

As she drank, the phone rang. Chris Cottle moved across to pick up the receiver.

'If it's Frank,' Anne said, 'no need to mention I'm here.'

'Rely on it.' He picked up the phone and spoke the number. She watched his face as he frowned. 'Yeah,' he said, the worry in his voice evident. 'Yeah, I'll go over right away.'

He put down the phone and turned to Anne. 'That was the doctor from Evie's hospital. She ain't there. She's disappeared.'

CHAPTER SIX

As Eve Ross hurried down the familiar street she was unaware of the lifted net curtains, the pair of gossiping women who fell silent as she passed, the man on the milk-float nudging his mate as she turned into the bleak front garden.

It was over two years since she was last in the house and as she unlocked the front door the dank smell of disuse stung her nostrils. Panic flooded her. If Frank didn't live here – where did he live? She ran forward along the passage calling his name.

Indifferent to the front door swinging open behind her she ran up the stairs and flung open the door to the main bedroom. He'd spent at least one night there – that she could tell from the tangle of sheets and blankets and the plastic covered cleaning on hangers hooked over the wardrobe door.

Carefully she examined the bed for any sign of a woman's occupancy. No lipstick mark, no smudge of mascara, no stain . . . She spun round at the sound of a footstep in the hall below and moved quietly out of the room to the head of the stairs. A man, in his early forties, neatly dressed in a blue raincoat and carrying a black briefcase was pushing open the living-room door to peer inside.

'Yes?' she snapped, a sharp questioning note in her voice.

'May I speak with Mr. Ross?'

She was struck with the fear that he was from the police. 'Who wants him?'

'Mr. Ross . . . is he in?'

'No,' she said shortly.

'May I leave a message? My name is Hinde . . . I'm from the estate agents.'

'Estate agents?'

'Bellingham and Hinde.'

'I'm Mrs. Ross.'

'It's about the house, Mrs. Ross.'

'This house.' Her eyes narrowed. Under sedatives for the last three years she reacted slowly. 'What about this house?'

Hinde pulled down on the points of his waistcoat. 'Mr. Ross telephoned.'

'To say what?'

Any estate agent knows the signs. And retreats. Marriage breaks up. Husband decides to sell. Wife intends to stay put. The trade joke was that the lady always sat on her assets. Well, estate agency isn't a trade particularly known for its sense of humour.

'Mr. Ross telephoned,' Hinde said circumspectly 'to make certain preliminary inquiries.'

'Did he?' she said flatly. 'So what are you doing here?'

'Perhaps I'd better come back,' Hinde said.

'This is my house.'

Hinde sighed, bored with the old, old story. 'Yes, Mrs. Ross, I appreciate that.'

'This is *my* house!' Her voice rose. 'Is he trying to sell this house? Is he?'

'Perhaps you and Mr. Ross should discuss it,' he said briskly. He was already turning away.

She ran down the stairs after him. 'This house is not . . . *not* for sale. Do you understand?'

He was barely clear of the front step as she hurled the door closed behind him.

Chris Cottle knocked twice on the door, leaning back to scan the windows for any sign of movement. If Evie had come to London he couldn't imagine where else she would have gone.

After a moment or two he reached forward and tried the door. It was unlocked. Opening it he stepped into the darkened hall.

'Eve . . . Evie . . . it's Chris.' He moved to the bottom of the stairs. 'Eve . . .'

From above he thought he heard some faint sound. He stood listening. 'Eve . . .' He started up the stairs.

At the top he switched on the landing light. The door to the main bedroom was ajar and in the light thrown from the landing he could see inside an indescribable mess of torn sheets and rumpled clothing. A wave of frightened sickness engulfed him. He stumbled forward and pushed at the door.

She was lying on the bare mattress, the bedclothes having been stripped off and hurled in frenzy across the room. Photographs from old albums were torn and scattered across the carpet. He turned on the light. Like a rape victim she lifted her head from the pillow she was clutching. Her eyes were swollen red, her hair hanging, her shirt torn open to her waist. For a second it flashed across his mind that she really had been attacked.

'It's *my* house, Chris,' she breathed. 'He wanted to sell *my* house.'

'It was you he was thinking of, Evie. You and Paul.' He crossed the room and bent down to touch her shoulder. 'Come downstairs. I'll get you a drink.'

As his fingertips touched her she recoiled, her eyes blazing. 'Keep your bloody hands off me!'

'Okay, Evie . . . take it easy.'

He stepped towards her.

She pushed him violently aside and ran for the door. 'Get out,' she screamed at him from the landing. 'Get out. This is *my* house, d'you hear me. *My house.*'

Wheeling round she ran into the bathroom and slammed the door.

White-faced he approached the bathroom, hearing her shoot the bolt on the door. He leaned his forearm on the thin panelling and his head against his arm. 'Listen to me, Eve . . .' He made a massive effort to control his voice. 'You're upset, you don't know the whole story. If you come I'll give Frank a call and he will explain everything. Nobody's gonna' take your house away. Evie? . . . Evie, answer me!'

He fancied he could hear her breathing on the other side of the door. Then suddenly there was a violent shattering of glass and he recoiled shocked and immobile.

'Oh Jesus Christ . . .' He lifted his foot and kicked hard at the door. The thin panel wood bent and sprang back. Inside he could hear a horrifying wretching sob . . . He hurled all his weight at the door and the bolt gave. As the door sprang open he could see Eve half slumped against the blood-spattered basin, her wrists spurting blood as she sawed them back and forth on the jagged edges of the broken bathroom window.

In the long bedroom mirror Anne Mitchell examined herself critically. Long legs, a trim, well-controlled hipline, a smallish well-shaped bust. She had more than enough evidence that men wanted her. Not just the whistles of truck drivers as she walked down the road, or the appreciation of gas station attendants as she swung her legs out of her TR7, but more substantial offers. Tommy, Mitch's partner, had made it very clear on too many occasions. Even, surprise of all surprises, her staid bank manager, in the middle of a business lunch, had nervously mooted the possibility that they might meet sometime 'more informally'. No, the appreciation of men was there. Even of the only man she was really interested in. But then it didn't help to pull her out of the quagmire. She saw Frank Ross more clearly, she thought, than he saw himself. His peculiar sense of honour, more pride than honour, more ruthless than mere pride. That core of self which nobody had ever cracked, no woman, child, policeman, judge or prison sentence.

And yet she thought she could. Given time she could enter into Frank Ross, lock her life to his. She was a compassionate, sensitive woman. But in the last resort she was as ruthless as Frank himself. Eve had been sacrified once – by Frank. If she had to be sacrificed again, Anne was prepared to do it.

She turned as the bell rang and walked slowly through the furniture of Tommy Sloan's flat running her fingers across the carved backs of antique chairs. She was slightly high and suddenly happy. Frank had asked her for something. It was a beginning.

She opened the door and stood back gasping in laughing astonishment. 'Jesus Christ,' she said as he stepped into the hall resplendent in a well-cut dinner jacket, a red carnation in his lapel.

'If I'm not home by midnight,' he said. 'I turn back into a toad.'

'Did anybody ever tell you that you're a hell of a good looking man?'

She took his arm and together they walked into the sitting-room.

He turned, holding her at arm's length. 'I didn't want to ask you, Anne.'

'I bet you didn't,' she smiled at him. 'But I'm very glad you did.'

His face suddenly became grave. 'Evie left the nursing home today.'

She bit back telling him that she knew.

'She went to the house. As far as we can work out there was some cock-up with an estate agent. A guy I'd spoken to about a quick sale.'

'Did Evie know you were going to sell the house?'

He shook his head. 'After the agent had left she went berserk. Chris found her up in the bedroom. It was like she'd thrashed the place.'

'But she was okay?'

'When she saw him she just . . .' He shrugged. 'I don't know, she rushed into the bathroom. Broke the window.' He flinched. 'She tried to cut her wrists on the glass.'

'Oh Christ! I'm sorry, Frank.' Even as Anne said it, and meant it, a faint hope burned that this was the solution. 'How is she?'

'She'll be okay. Physically she'll be okay.'

She thought for a moment. 'This is why you're here?'

'Yes.'

'In fancy dress.'

'Yes.'

'You can't sell the house.'

'Not now. At least not yet.'

She turned away and picked up her bag. Opening it she took out the long white envelope and handed it to him.

'Twenty-four hours,' he said.

'I told you . . . keep it as long as you need it.'

'You'll have it back tomorrow.'

'Take care,' she said.

Frank Ross let the Jaguar carry him smoothly across Albert Bridge and the length of Oakley Street and turned left into King's Road. Chelsea was a bit out of his area – out of his class he would have *thought* but never said. It was a land of smart houses and smart-assed occupants. A land occupied by all the sorts of people that Frank Ross hated in this world – by the trendy, instant millionaire pop stars, or the trendy millionaire inheritors of Daddy's diamond fortune, or tea business or acres in North Wales. To Ross both sorts were parasites.

In Glebe Place he got out and checked the numbers and then climbed back in the car to drive a few houses further down to where a late eighteenth-century town house stood back off the road behind a set of high open gates. Swinging hard on the wheel he parked the Jaguar between a Maserati and a Rolls and got out to stand looking up at the house.

Only the faintest chinks of light split the heavy curtains. But above the door an iron coach lamp hung, throwing light on the softly worn stone steps and the clumps of rhododendrons on either side.

Frank crossed the gravel drive and mounted the steps. His quick eye took in the spy-hole which would reveal anybody, however positioned on the stone steps.

He rang. Inside he heard nothing but the faintest flicker of light telling him that he was being observed through the peep-hole. He turned his back casually and stamped his feet against the cold. After another moment or two the door opened.

The man standing in the carpeted, dimly lit hall was tall, blond and comfortably over six feet tall. His well-cut dinner jacket did nothing to disguise from Frank the width of his shoulders. He smiled pleasantly. 'Good evening, sir. Can I help you?' His voice was carefully modulated.

'I flew in from Sidney last night. One of my fellow-passengers mentioned this address.'

'But you're not a member, sir?'

'Not exactly.'

The big man moved to close the door. 'Then I'm sorry, sir . . .'

Ross already had his wallet in his hand. Opening it he revealed the wad of notes. The door stopped closing.

'Do step into the hall, sir.' He stood back and allowed Frank in. 'You're from Australia you say, sir?'

'My wife's here for an operation. Two to three weeks.' He grinned. 'In those circumstances a fella has to find himself a little entertainment.' He pulled out two twenty pound notes and handed them to the big man. 'That's why,' he said, 'I started up a few discreet inquiries on the plane over.'

'My name is Swann, sir. You understand we do have to be very . . . circumspect.'

'I bloody well hope so, Swann.'

Swann smiled. 'You're obviously the sort of gentleman . . .'

'Obviously,' Ross grinned at him.

'Perhaps you're someone's guest, sir?'

'Perhaps I am.'

'Mr. Jacobs?'

'Why not?'

'This way, sir. Your name is?'

'Stephens. Jack Stephens.'

'I think we have a chair free, Mr. Stephens. Let's have a look shall we?'

They walked together across the wide hallway, past an elegantly curving white staircase.

'Five card stud, sir . . . no limit . . . we're old-fashioned, we use real money on the table, there is no credit given, no markers taken, no cheques accepted. The game breaks for ten minutes in every hour.'

Swann opened a door and they entered a small room lined with dark Japanese wall-paper. Four men sat at a Sheraton card table in the middle. The house player was the only one to look up as Swann drew back a chair for Ross. 'Mr. Tony Rix is our house player,' Swann whispered. 'Enjoy your game, sir. You can sign the book later.'

Rix, dark-haired, in his early thirties, nodded briefly to Ross and turned back to the game.

'Fourth card,' he said. 'A ten to the seven eight. A queen to the tens . . . Another club to the dealer.'

Ross sat and took out his wallet.

In his office above the gaming room Richard Slater let the curtain drop back into place at the long window as Swann entered. He was a tall Etonian, as dark as Swann was blond. 'You've done it again,' he said.

'He's a guest,' Swann smiled.

'Mr. Jacobs? Again?'

'Mr. Jacobs has a lot of friends,' Swann said.

Slater pointed down through the floor. 'Who is he?'

'A punter.'

'Are you sure?'

'Am I usually wrong?'

'No. You do have a certain . . . instinct,' Slater admitted grudgingly.

'He was flashing his dummy.'

'At you? How much?'

'He slipped me forty.'

'So for forty quid you lifted the portcullis. It's crazy.'

'Forty quid and my hunch. He's okay . . . surrender without a fight.'

'How much does he have to surrender?' Slater asked, mollified by Swann's confidence.

'A spare thousand at least.'

Slater smiled. 'He shouldn't last too long.'

In the card room below, Ross's pile of notes was already seriously depleted. When Rix checked his watch and suggested a break the three other players happily agreed drifting off together towards the drink table. Ross followed Rix out across the hall.

'After you,' Rix pushed open the door of a luxuriously appointed cloakroom. He grinned. 'It's O.K., sir – there is room for two.'

Ross stepped past him. Three gold-topped basins were set in green marble. The walls were again Japanese papered in dark green.

'You've not had all the luck in the world this evening, sir,'

Rix said as they stood together at the elegant green wall urinals.

'Things are just about to look up,' Ross said.

They zipped themselves in unison and moved across to wash their hands.

'I hope they do, sir.'

Ross took one of the heated towels. 'Oh they will,' he said. 'Because you're going to make sure of it.'

Rix dried his hands slowly. 'I don't think I follow you, Mr. Stephens.'

'No . . .? Howard told me you could do anything with the cards.'

'Howard . . .?' His dark eyes watched Ross warily.

'Howard Cater. You remember . . .' He lifted up his hand, one finger held down by the thumb, '. . . lost his finger in a knife fight when you two were working the boats. Very talkative was Howard, liked to impress, be one of the chaps. I shared a peter with him for two years.'

'. . . What do you want?' Rix said anxiously.

'Nothing much. A few fat hands put my way. That'll do me.'

'I can't do that.'

'You do it for Slater . . . for the house . . . I watched you . . . impressive. I'm not greedy.'

'Slater'd know.'

'That's your problem.'

'If I call Swann, he can be rough.'

'So can I . . . take my word for it . . . but you won't.'

'Why not?'

'Easy. Because you're not Tony Rix.'

'What the hell has Cater been saying to you.'

'Tony Rix is buried somewhere near Johannesburg.'

The dark face drained pale. 'I had nothing to do with that.'

Ross nodded. 'That's what Howard Cater said. Or more or less nothing. But it seems that's not quite the way it'd look to the South African police if they started digging on a certain bit of riverbank near the church at Witzen.'

Ross turned to the door. 'A couple of rounds my way, okay. Then I go. You won't hear from me again, Tony – that's a promise.'

They rejoined the table and silently arranged money and cigarettes and drinks around them. Frank Ross and a large bald-headed man had lost the best part of a thousand each. Another player, an Argentinian was about breaking even. The third punter had been allowed to win a little.

When the game resumed, the pattern of play slowly began to change. Ross guessed that Rix had selected the Argentinian as the face and hand after hand came to him, tantalizing in its potential to judge from his betting, but finally disappointing in its result.

As the Argentinian lost and the fortunes of the other two fluctuated, Ross first recovered his position then began to build up a substantial lead. Swann entering discreetly to top up drinks, stood watching from the other side of the room for a few minutes before he left.

A few minutes later the door reopened and Swann crossed the room to lean over Rix's shoulder. As he whispered Rix's eyes flickered across to Frank Ross. Then he nodded. 'Sure, sure. Right after this hand.'

As Swann glided quietly from the room Rix flicked a card to Ross's opponent, the Argentinian. Last card . . . another king . . . two pairs showing . . . possible full house . . .

He flicked a card to Ross. 'Seven . . . three showing . . . possible four of a kind . . . seven's bet.'

Ross pushed a pile of notes forward. 'Three hundred.'

'Three hundred to the sevens,' Rix intoned then looking at the Argentinian 'Your bet, sir.'

The Argentinian glanced at Ross's face then down at his own cards. The skin just above his ears creased and the point of each ear waggled faintly. He threw down his cards.

'Fold,' Rix said impassively and pushed back his chair. 'Will you excuse me for a moment, gentlemen?'

Rix left the room and closed the door behind him. Swann waiting in the hall walked beside him up the stairs and opened the door to Richard Slater's first floor office.

Slater looked up from the desk as Swann closed the door.

'Swann says he's making you look like a cripple,' Slater said evenly.

'He's a class player, Mr. Slater.'

'So are you, Tony . . . and you have that little extra . . . that's why I employ you.'

'I'm not feeling too good tonight, Mr. Slater . . . it's not helping.'

'Oh . . . I am sorry.' Slater made his insincerity evident.

'I'd just as soon call it a night if that's okay with you, Mr. Slater.'

Slater watched him without answering.

'I mean I'd sooner not lose you any more.'

Slater nodded. 'Who is he, Tony. Who's your friend?'

In the warm carpeted hallway Swann came up behind Ross as he fumbled the door catches.

'Mr. Slater would like you to have a drink with him, sir.'

Ross turned slowly. 'Slater?'

'He owns the house, sir.'

As Swann gestured to the stairs Ross felt for the gun tucked into the back of his waistband, then stepped ahead of Swann to climb the stairs.

Ushered in to Slater's room Ross registered there was no sign of Rix. Slater rose from behind his desk, holding out his hand. 'Richard Slater,' he said genially.

'Jack Stephens,' Ross said shaking his hand.

'Sit down, Mr. Stephens. I hear you've had a *very* good night.'

'Not bad.'

'Over six thousand . . .' Slater said. 'I call that good. What will you take?'

He opened a drinks cupboard.

'Dry sherry.'

Slater poured him a sherry and closed the cupboard.

'Where are you from, Mr. Stephens? It's a small world, I haven't heard of you?'

Ross smiled and sipped his sherry.

'You are a professional?'

'I've been away.'

'Australia?'

Ross nodded and placed his half finished sherry on Slater's desk.

'Too dry?' Slater lifted his eyebrows.

'Too sweet.'

Slater took his meaning. He chose an armchair and dropped into it.

'How long have you known Tony Rix, Mr. Stephens?'

'About three hours.'

'Really.'

'Really.'

'He's the best stud player in London.'

Ross made a dismissive gesture. 'He's too sentimental . . . about money . . . you get that way when you're playing with House funds.'

Slater looked at Ross leaning casually on the edge of the desk. He was uncertain how to play it. If this man really was fresh in from Australia he probably carried no weight in London. He decided to risk it. 'You don't look like a violent man, Mr. Stephens.'

'What does a violent man look like?'

Slater shrugged. 'I myself abhor physical violence. I am a man of much gentler persuasions.'

'I can imagine.' He pushed himself off the desk. 'Thanks for the drink. I have to be getting along.'

Slater remained seated. 'Mr. Rix wasn't feeling well, you know. He's gone home to think about his future. If you would just place the money on the desk and then leave quietly . . .' He smiled apologetically.

'I beg your pardon?' Ross's mouth tightened.

'Mr. Rix couldn't be persuaded to tell me quite what your arrangement was. Frankly I don't care overmuch. The money . . . please.'

Ross said nothing. As he turned to leave, Swann stepped in front of him.

Half turning back to Slater Ross said: 'I've never met Mr. Rix before tonight. I don't know about any "arrangement" with Mr. Rix. I do know Mr. Rix carries a spooked deck.' He smiled, '. . . for emergencies. And I also know that if this gentleman insists on blocking my exit ... I'm going to break his arms!'

Swann stepped forward menacingly. But Slater motioned him aside with an almost imperceptible movement of his head.

Ross stepped past him to the door and let himself out without a word.

'Why?' Swann's face was flushed with anger. 'Break my arms! I could have taken him apart.'

'If you had,' Slater said brusquely, 'you would have found a gun tucked in his belt.'

Swann's head jerked up in alarm.

'Would he have used it, I wonder?' Slater mused to himself. 'Well, for six thousand it definitely wasn't worth finding out.' He got up and poured Swann a drink. 'So your *amour propre* has taken a bit of a beating. Let's hope your judgment about what is and isn't a real punter will be immensely improved by tonight's little experience.'

Crossing the gravel forecourt to the car, Frank Ross was aware that he had been more than a little lucky. The real gamble of the night had not been in the card room with Tony Rix. It had been upstairs with the public school hatchet man. And something had made Slater back down. Ross felt for his car keys – well, he knew and had banked on the fact that this sort of establishment couldn't afford trouble. He had even calculated that six grand was the optimum to take. It looked as if he had been about right. As he bent to fit the key in the car lock the fat wads of notes rustled in his pockets. He smiled to himself and pulled open the car door.

He was aware of no more than a huge self-enveloping thud. No pain, no real sensation of the blow as his legs gave way and he found himself, perhaps five or ten seconds later on his back on the gravel drive, the blurred figure of a man tearing at his jacket, delving into his pockets.

Then the pain hit him, sharp and icy in the back of his head ... and the panic that his skull had been split open by the blow ... and animal fury as he lashed out with his right foot to catch the man hard between the legs with the toe of his shoe.

There seemed to Ross's muddled mind no natural sequence to events. The man's scream, the second wild kick, the figure stumbling away, his own attempt to claw himself up into the driving seat of the car . . . everything happened instantaneously. Only when the car was moving, fishtailing backwards across the drive, only when he gunned it forward after the distant running figure did Frank Ross begin to think again.

The pain in his head was now frightening and he could feel the back of his collar soaked with blood. But at the same time he knew that most if not all of the money had been taken and despite the trembling sickness of shock he was obsessed with a determination to recover it.

Thumping his foot hard on the accelerator he propelled the Jaguar through the double lines of parked cars along Upper Cheney Row and as he reached the running man he saw the face, clearly now that of Tony Rix, turn in fear as Ross barrelled the car up the pavement and flung open the driving door.

Moving at ten miles an hour the door caught Rix in the legs and back and hurled him across the pavement. Braking hard Ross jumped from the car. Crouched on all fours, his head dropping with exhaustion Rix was in no shape to fight back. With his foot Ross pushed him, rolling him over on to his back. Then bending down he removed the money while Rix gasped out some incoherent plea.

Lights were flicking on in the bedroom windows around them now and Ross knew that in a neighbourhood like this four or five people would already be reaching for the phone to call the police. From his pocket he dragged out a bundle of notes, perhaps £500 in all and leaned over to shove them into Rix's pocket. 'From what I've seen of your boss, Slater, I have a feeling you're going to need money for a long journey,' he said. Then he dragged Rix to his feet, gave him a push off down the street and climbed back into the Jaguar.

Three minutes later he was crossing Albert Bridge as the first police cars swept down Oakly Street towards Upper Cheney Row.

CHAPTER SEVEN

At about the time Frank Ross reached the safe familiarity of Peckham, an ex-Post Office van, yellow and battered, an old sock for a petrol cap, windscreen and headlamps cracked and taped over, rattled at speed down a quiet suburban backstreet of sleeping semis.

Screeching to a halt in the middle of the road it stood for a moment silent, except for the shuddering. Then from inside came a shout of laughter and the back doors were flung open with a tinny crash.

A group of young people spilled out and with shouts of encouragement a boy of about fifteen staggered to the neat garden gate of number 86.

Paul Ross, his hair plastered wet, his overcoat wrongly buttoned, sputtered with laughter as the gate swung open under his weight and he fell on to his knees in the middle of the path in an attitude of prayer.

'Ere,' one of the boys said, 'you want to get up to them tricks, do it in the warm. It's as cold as church out here.'

The others burst into appreciative laughter. 'Night, Paul, see you tomorrer,' they shouted as they ran back and piled into the van.

As it rattled off down the street Paul scrambled to his feet and continued on the few paces to the porch. Alone, he suddenly felt vaguely sick and then just as suddenly overwhelmed by the fear that he was about to wet his pants. Unzipping himself he leaned one hand on the porch and sloshed urine wildly across the porch post and the door.

If he was aware of the lights flickering on the leaded windows on either side of the door it failed to penetrate his consciousness as alarm. When the door was pulled open a stream of urine passed the naked legs of the man standing in a dressing-gown in the hall.

'You filthy little sod!' Keith Andrews stepped back as Paul lifted his head.

'Sorry, Keith . . .' He smiled to himself. 'Just giving the milk bottles a wash down.'

Keith Andrews leaned out and grabbed him by the arm. 'Get in here. Get in here before I thump you back in the gutter.'

Pushing the boy hard enough to propel him to the bottom of the stairs Andrews slammed the door. His wife Lucy was standing at the top of the stairs. 'You see what he was doing?' Andrews exploded, 'All over the bloody door. Christ!'

'Paul,' Lucy Andrews came part way down the stairs, 'get up to bed right away. D'you need a hand?'

Paul stood white-faced, hanging on to the banister. 'No, no,' he repeated, 'I'm all right.'

He stumbled up the stairs. 'Sorry, Lucy,' he muttered as he passed her. 'Didn't think . . .' He reached the bathroom and staggered in.

She listened for a moment to his retching, then came down the stairs to where her husband was standing, fists clenched.

'I'll make you some coffee, Keith,' she said, leading the way into the kitchen. He nodded and with one final glance of antipathy up the stairs, he followed her.

Sitting in the kitchen, he stared fixedly at the row of plates in the dresser. 'I used to think you could break it, that criminal line, you know, like father, like son. But I'm not so sure now, Lucy.'

She spooned instant coffee into the two cups, hesitated about making a third one for Paul and decided against it. 'You've done a lot for him, Keith. Don't give up now.'

He shook his head. 'It's flogging a dead horse, love.'

'Look, he's just got in with the wrong lot, that's all.'

'No . . . if he was different,' he took a cup of coffee from her, 'if he was a different sort of lad, he wouldn't have got in with the wrong lot in the first place.'

She brought her cup and sat down beside him.

'When he did that, peed all over the door, even into the hall, when he did that he was showing what he thought of us. Couple of middle-aged squares. That's what he thinks of us.'

'Don't say that, Keith. He respects you.'

'You're wrong, Lucy. All he respects is his bank robber father who doesn't give tuppence for him.'

She trembled, trying to form the words to reject what he was saying.

'Okay,' Andrews said, 'how long has be been out. Two days is it? And did he rush straight round and see his son? Did he hell? He's probably been blind drunk himself in some boozer for the last forty-eight hours. Bloody wonder the two of them haven't met up somewhere.'

The November weather persisted across the low-lying areas of South East London, the morning fog rolled through the back streets and swirled through the market-places and broadways stirred only by the convoys of traffic chugging slowly to the South Coast ports.

At the newly demolished site which Lew Wilson had chosen for his Health Club, Frank Ross parked his Jaguar and sat watching the steel erectors in yellow hard hats bolting a section beam into place. Behind him he was unaware of a green Cortina which had slipped into a parking space between a van and a truck outside Harry's Hamburger Speciality Joint. The driver, a young man with giveaway short hair, stayed in the car.

Across the site Ross could see Lew Wilson flanked by Eddie Archer and the young architect he had seen in the pub yesterday. Getting out of the car he picked his way through the frozen puddles towards them.

'Good morning, Lew.' He ignored Eddie Archer and nodded briefly to the architect.

Lew Wilson, in a heavy camel coat, handed the architect the drawings he was holding. 'Okay, David,' he said dismissively, 'I'll have a word with you later.'

He turned to Ross and linked an arm through his. 'You got Eddie's message?'

Ross nodded. 'Chris Cottle told me you could have news for me.'

Wilson flicked his fingers to Eddie Archer who was walking a pace behind. 'Give it to him, Eddie.'

Archer came forward on the other side of Ross. 'A girl named Alison. *Very* tasty. Chertsey six double two nine. She's expecting you to call.'

'Six double two nine,' Ross repeated. 'Okay, Lew.'

'And, Frank . . .' Lew Wilson said, 'Tell Billy I'm sorting something out.'

Ross disengaged his arm. 'How long has he been on the trot?'

'Two months,' Eddie put in.

Ross stopped, turning to face Wilson. 'And you're sorting something out? Taking your time aren't you, Lew?'

Wilson said nothing, his forehead creasing in a frown.

'That's how it has to be, Frank . . .' Eddie Archer said, 'you know that. Wait till the scream's off.'

'One hasty move, one rick and I'm walking around minus laces.' Wilson walked on. 'Then what would happen to Billy . . . without me?'

'Without you? Without you Billy would never have been there, without *you* that old boy would never have got done.'

Wilson turned on him. 'You wanna take it to the grievance committee. You nause me, Frankie. You wanted Billy . . . you got Billy.'

Ross looked from one to the other. 'You know being around you two makes me feel honest.'

Eddie Archer stepped forward but Wilson shook his head. 'I don't need this, Frank,' he said. 'You come to me, stinking of the nick . . . shouting your crack off that I owe you ten years back . . . *ten years*! You wanted to know how to find Billy . . . I've arranged it . . . right . . . laid it on . . . all you've got to do is lift a phone . . . no sweat . . . right? Things have changed in the time you've been away, my son . . . if you want to find out the hard way you can. Take your choice, mate. But before you do, remember you're no longer the big man in *this* manor.'

'You don't mind, I won't stay for the lecture,' Ross turned away.

Across the broken ground they watched him climb into his car and make for the gate in a wide circle. As he drove he lifted his hand to wave to them but his eyes never left the driving mirror where the young man in the green Cortina was already preparing to pull out into the stream of traffic to follow him.

It was nine-fifteen on Tuesday. And at nine-fifteen on Tuesday for the last God knows how many years Lucy Andrews had started her washing. Today she sat with a cup of coffee in the kitchen staring at the big Bendix unable to gear herself to start filling it from the red plastic wickerwork basket full of dirty clothes.

She had decided on another cup of coffee before making the effort when the sound of a creaking footstep on the stair made her look up. She called, 'Paul, is that you, love?'

She waited but there was no answer. Then as she was about to get up to make her promised coffee the stair creaked again.

'Paul . . .' this time she went to the kitchen door. Paul Ross, already dressed in his overcoat was at the bottom of the stairs.

'How're you feeling? As bad as you look?'

'I'm all right.'

'Come and have some breakfast. They all say it helps.'

'No thanks. I'd better be off.'

'Off where?'

'School, of course.'

'What happened to your books?'

He glanced down at his own empty hands. 'I don't need none. Not today I don't.'

'I'm not sure I believe you, Paul.'

He shrugged. 'Your privilege, in'it?'

'Come on,' she said, 'Don't be like that. Come into the kitchen and have a cup of tea at least.'

'I haven't got time.'

'All right, Paul. But about last night . . .'

'Look, for goodness sake,' he said angrily. 'I was a bit pissed. Some bloke'd been feeding me those barley wines for a giggle. It's not the end of the world.'

'I tell you Keith nearly hit the roof.'

Paul smiled. 'He must've thought they'd moved a car wash into the front garden.'

'Very funny.'

'Well, I mean just a bit of a sense of humour sometimes wouldn't go amiss.'

'That'd be all right, Paul, if it was a two-way thing.'

'What's that mean?'

'It means it gets a bit much always having to be the ones who have to have the sense of humour. Ever *seen* your face in the mirror? Like to take a look at it now?'

'I've got to go,' he said shortly. 'I'll be late.'

'For school?'

'That's right.'

'You're lying,' she spoke quietly, 'I know when you're lying ... you're not going to school, are you ... are you? ... just more lies.'

She came out of the kitchen doorway and stood in front of him.

'What's this,' he said. 'Trying to stop me going?' There was an edge of contempt in his voice.

'That's right, Paul.'

'Get out of my way.'

'I want to know where you're going?'

'Out.'

'No you're not. Not until ...'

He shouldered her heavily to the side. As she came back off the wall she grabbed at his arm.

'Get out of my bloody way.' He swept her aside with his forearm, flinging her back into the banister.

As her head cracked against the banister upright he wrenched open the door. Behind him she rolled across the carpeted floor.

Frank Ross let the door of the phone-box bang behind him and glanced in the cracked mirror above the phone. The green Cortina had pulled up across the road and the young Detective Constable sat watching the phone-box.

He dialled and as the pips began pressed ten pence into the box. Ten pence! Christ when he was last using phones it had been three old pennies. A girl's voice spoke on the other end of the line.

'Frank Ross,' he said. 'Just tell me where.'

When Ross left the box a couple of minutes later he walked slowly towards his car. Then with a sudden movement he turned and ran straight across the road. Detective Constable Stiles saw him enter the launderette opposite as he struggled out of the Cortina and dashed across the road in pursuit.

As Stiles pushed open the swing-door he had already registered a passage leading out to the back. 'Man who came running in here,' he said to the old woman who was mopping the floor, 'did he go through the back?'

'Well he didn't come in for a quick wash and spin dry . . .' she cackled.

Stiles glowered at her and ran for the passage. As his footsteps receded, Frank Ross stepped from behind the big dry cleaning machine and patted her backside. 'Thanks, love.'

'Nice to see you back, Frankie.'

He stepped out into the street and, ignoring his parked car, swung himself on to a passing bus.

'What'll we do all day?' Mo Turner was fifteen, an exceptionally pretty girl despite the incongruity of a patched afghan dress under a torn school blazer.

'Do anything we like,' Paul said.

'We've got no money, no fags and I'm freezing cold,' she grinned at him, 'and you say we can do anything we like. You're an optimist.'

They were walking past Tulse Hill Post Office. 'Well, let's see what we feel like?' He had already spotted the two red Post Office bicycles leaning against the wall just inside the yard. 'How about a bike ride, just to warm us up a bit?'

'Okay. 'Cept we don't have any bikes it's a good idea.'

He skipped ahead of her. 'Who said we don't have any bikes?'

She watched in nervous amazement as he ran into the yard and grabbed one of the bikes.

'Here, cop this.'

'You can't, Paul . . .'

He pushed the machine at her and she caught it, laughing nervously.

'Jump on.' He was already climbing on to the other bike. 'Not exactly a pair of choppers but not bad . . .'

Together they rode out of the yard.

'Here,' he yelled above the traffic roar, 'ever see that picture 'Butch Cassidy and the Sundance Kid?' He started to swerve his upright handlebars from side to side, narrowly missing the oncoming cars.

'You'll get yourself killed,' she laughed. 'Here, let's go over the common and see if any of the kids've got a coupla spare fags.'

The old 2CV rattled through the country roads staying roughly parallel to the Thames. Alison Connors glanced sideways at the silent man beside her. 'Don't say much, do you?' She smiled her even-toothed smile.

Frank Ross shrugged. 'I haven't had much practice. Prison does that to a man.'

Alison nodded. 'Billy says some of 'em end up talking to walls. He knew a bloke on segregation who made a pack of cards by tearing holes in fifty-two sheets of toilet paper . . . a screw found 'em . . . took 'em . . . tore 'em up, bloody sadist.'

'Billy came through all right though?'

'Yes. He don't talk about it much . . . about prison . . . He says what good do it do, you can never explain what it's really like.'

'What's Billy going to do?' Ross asked.

'He thinks Lew Wilson's gonna sort somethin' out . . . get us abroad.'

'You don't sound convinced?'

'I would trust that septic pig as far as I could throw him. But he knows if Billy gets caught he goes down with him.'

'Billy wouldn't grass . . . it's not in him.'

She turned her head towards him, her eyes hard. 'Billy wouldn't . . . but I bloody would.'

The 2CV rattled up an unmade road full of junk and puddles, into a residential caravan site. Collarless dogs wandered about with snotty faced kids in hand-me-down clothes and shoes that were too big for them.

'Be it ever so humble . . .' Alison said bitterly.

She stopped the car beside a once white caravan and Ross caught a glimpse of someone watching from behind the net curtain. Together he and Alison got out of the car and picked their way across the mud and junk to the caravan. While they were still a few yards away the door opened and a young, good looking man in sweater and jeans stood grinning in the doorway.

'Frankie! Frankie! I can't believe it! Come in, mate.'

He dragged Ross inside. Smiling, Alison followed, closing the door behind them. Ross glanced quickly round the caravan. It was old, but well kept, the washing-up done, a pile of clean laundry on one of the formica tables. He looked at Billy, then noticed for the first time the dark smudges below the eyes. 'You look a bit rough, mate. Getting to you, is it?'

Billy Binns forced a grin. 'Nah,' he said. 'It's her. Gives me a right seeing to every night.' He stretched his arms wide. 'Got me where she wants me, ain't she? Bloody captive, ain't I?'

Alison smiled up at him then disengaged herself. 'Now you two might want to prance around like a pair of all-time pansies, but I feel like a stiff one.'

'There didn't I tell you, Frank boy, it's never out of her mind for a second.'

She pretended to swing at him and he caught her wrist and kissed her.

'Right, enough's enough,' she said. 'What'll you have to drink, Frank? Whisky and water, water and whisky or just plain whisky.'

'I'll have it with a drop of water,' Ross said dropping on to one of the narrow bench seats.

He took a cigarette from Billy and lit it while Alison poured the drinks. When all three had a glass in their hand Billy raised his. 'Here's to you, Frank . . . God bless.'

'And to you both, mate. You got a hard road ahead of you here.'

Billy glanced at Allison and nodded soberly. 'I appreciate you coming, Frank. I know anybody wanted for this ain't popular with the lads.'

'What happened, Billy? I couldn't believe it when they told me.'

'I never meant to hurt him, Frank. I swear it.'

'You never was a hammer.'

'He come up on me . . . I'd dropped me torch . . . pitch black . . . I tried to leg past . . . He grabbed at me, we fell, he was under me. I thought he was just out . . . I run . . . I mean . . . I didn't know.'

He downed his Scotch and stood up to pour himself another.

'I was at Ali's place . . . got a call from a mate, told me the old boy was dead and the scream was on for me.' He took a deep breath and drank.

'Who knows you're here, Billy?'

'Just Alison . . . you . . .'

'And Lew of course.'

'Right,' Alison said. 'He fixed it. Eddie drove us here.'

Ross nods thoughtfully.

'What's up, Frank?' Billy asked, looking down at him.

'How did you get mixed up with Lew?'

Billy sat down with a thump next to Alison. 'When I come out he had the lot stitched up . . . You couldn't ring a la-di without Lew taking his piece.'

'What Lew doesn't control, Tony McGrath does, and he's worse,' Alison said.

'You watch them, Frankie,' Billy said. 'Both of 'em . . . believe me . . . they're about as funny as a broken leg.'

Jimmy Young prattled away happily on the radio. The washing machine spun and foamed behind its glass front. As Keith Andrews came in the back door and saw Lucy bending over a cup of instant soup everything pointed to a normal Tuesday mid-morning.

'Hullo, love,' he bent over and hugged her. 'Slipped in for a quick cup of tea while the lads are finishing up at the depot.' He straightened up and saw for the first time her white, tear-stained face and the yellow and purple bruise spreading under her left eye. 'Jesus Christ – what happened?'

'It's not as bad as it looks, Keith. Black eyes never are. I tripped on the stair carpet and hit me head on the banister.'

He put his arm round her. 'You sure you're all right. Here, you're trembling . . .'

'Bit of shock, I expect,' she forced a smile. 'I'll make a pot of tea.'

'No I'll do it.' He filled the kettle and readied the tea cups without speaking. 'Young Paul still in bed I suppose. Sleeping it off aged fifteen.'

'No,' she said casually. 'He's at school.'

'School? That don't seem like him. He don't go when he's got no excuse. I don't see him going when he ain't feeling too hot.'

He made the tea and brought the pot to the table. 'What time did he go – late?'

'No,' she said uncomfortably, 'usual time.'

'Lucy, he wasn't there half an hour ago.'

'How do you know?'

'I rang the headmaster from work, I've got an appointment with him this afternoon at the school. We've got to get this nonsense sorted out. Half this term he hasn't been turning up. The teacher's got a whole stack of notes you're supposed to have written for him.'

He looked at her across the table. 'The boy's rubbish, Lucy.'

She shook her head violently. 'Don't talk like that, Keith, please.'

'I'm facing facts, love. We've done all we could. But we got him too late.'

'He's a bit wild, that's all.'

'He's a completely self-centred, selfish little sod.' He stopped, seeing her pained look. With an effort to control himself he said wearily: 'So what did happen this morning?'

'What do you mean?'

He was surprised at the alarm in her voice. He looked at her curiously for a moment. 'I was talking about Paul . . .' He looked at her bruised face. 'When exactly did that happen, Lucy. Before or after he left?'

'Before,' she said too quickly.

'You're keeping something from me. I want the truth, Lucy.'

'I told you . . .'

'Not all of it. Did Paul have anything to do with that?' The anger was boiling up inside him. 'Now listen, Lucy, I want the truth. I've got every right to know what goes on in my own bloody house.'

She nodded miserably. 'It *was* an accident, Keith. He didn't mean it. I fell, he pushed me and I fell. He doesn't even know . . . I was trying to stop him going out . . .'

'Out! So you knew he wasn't going to school. I never know when you're telling me the truth lately, you're almost as bad as he is! You see what happens – it's like he's got a disease . . . it infects everybody else.'

The small caravan rocked with their laughter. Half-way down the Scotch bottle Billy Binns, Alison and Ross had forgotten the grim world outside as they swopped stories of the past.

Billy wiped tears of laughter from his eyes. 'No, straight up, Ali, to go out with Frank and Colin some nights was to turn yourself straight into the bleedin' Marx Brothers.' He turned to Ross, 'Here, you remember that posh party you, me and Colin went to?'

'And Colin pulled that bird?'

Alison watched in amusement as the story got going.

'What was her name?' Ross frowned, 'Angela . . .? No, Abigail, that's it. What a name!'

Billy burst out laughing. 'Big built and randy as they come. All that horse-riding did it.'

'Get on with it,' Alison prodded him, laughing. 'What happened? Colin pulls this Abigail and . . .?'

'He's off upstairs with 'er. But what 'e don't know is that Frank an' me are up there before 'im.'

'Under the bed,' Ross put in.

'Off comes the bleedin' lot an' they're at it. Tick tock tick tock, half an hour goes by an' they're still rumpin' I mean, we thought it was down to a swift Donald . . .'

'By this time,' Ross topped up the glasses. 'We wanted to get back to the party.'

'So Frankie gives me the nod . . . takes out his fags . . . leans out, round the side of the bed, there they are on the vinegar stroke', he taps the bird on the arse an' says . . . all polite like . . .'

'S'cuse me . . . got a light?'

Alison screamed with laughter. Billy was almost in tears.

'You should . . . you should 'ave seen her boat . . . she can't believe it . . . Frankie looking as innocent as Jesus.'

Only gradually the laughter subsided. Billy wiped his eyes with the back of his hand. 'Yeah,' he said, 'Those were the days.'

Alison ruffled the back of his head. 'In the two years I've been with Billy I've never seen him laugh like that,' she said to Ross.

'Ain't much to laugh about lately.' Billy put his arm round her.

'Can't get any worse, luv,' she moved up close to him.

Ross looked at both of them. 'I'll see what I can do to get things moving, Billy.'

'You stay out of this, Frank,' Billy said. 'You shouldn't be 'ere now. You know that. If that bleeder Bryce finds out he'll have the skin off your feet.'

'I needed to see you, Billy, for my own sake,' Ross said.

'I know . . . I know, Frank, that bastard grass . . . he's due a spanking, whoever he is.'

'No one seems to know anything, Billy. Vic, Bernie, Big Ralph, it's like it never happened.'

'It happened all right,' Billy said. 'And nothing's gone right for me since.'

'But who . . . *who*, Billy.'

Binns shook his head slowly. Then lit a cigarette, thoughtfully drawing in the smoke. 'There's one thing I heard,' he said.

Ross's neck tingled. 'Something you heard? What's that, Billy?'

'Just recent . . .' he spoke slowly, frowning.

'Go on for Chrissake.'

'Do you remember that bird who kept coming to the trial . . . in the public gallery? Used to come from round our way.'

'Course I do. Short blonde hair, bit tarty, always wore junk ear-rings? Funny name she had.'

'That's the one,' Billy said. 'Cimmie Vincent, well . . . someone give it me that her and Ralph were like, very close.'

'I thought she was there for a cheap bang. You sure about this, Billy?'

'That's what I was told,' Binns said. 'No more than two month back, by a geezer she used to work for, in a spieler in Paddington.'

Ross looked totally bemused. 'But I don't get it. Ralph never said anything . . . right through the trial.'

'Not to no one,' Billy agreed. 'That's what's made me think. No, listen to this, straight after the trial she goes missin'. She does a runner . . . terrified of someone.'

'Who?'

Binns shrugged. 'Dunno, but I'm tellin' you, Frankie, I got this feelin'. Cimmie Vincent knew something. That's why they put the dogs on her.'

'I don't understand it . . . I was with Ralph Tuesday. He never mentioned it.'

'He never at the time, did he, Frank?'

On their bikes, Paul and Mo wove figure eights along the Common path. Most school days you would expect to see little groups of Tulse Hill fifth-formers bunking off from lessons but today, perhaps because of the iron cold the Common was deserted.

Swinging one leg off the bike Paul scooted down the path then jumped aside to let the bike shoot ahead deep into a clump of young fir trees. 'There you go,' he yelled, as the bike disappeared.

Mo got off her bicycle. 'Let's go down the café,' she said

giving the saddle a push. The bike toppled just short of cover and Paul picked it up and swung it by the crossbar over the green heads of the little pines and into the tangled shrubbery beyond.

He turned, put his arm around her and they walked off down the path. 'Brass monkey weather this is,' he said, shivering.

'What *does* that mean?'

'Ignorant little cow. Means it's cold enough to freeze the balls off a brass monkey.'

She laughed.

'Anyway,' he continued, 'I'll be going on holiday soon. Somewhere with white beaches and hot sun all day.'

'Spain?'

'Better than that. Not sure quite yet. Depends.'

'On your dad?'

'That's right. Depends where he happens to be.'

They headed towards the footbridge over the road that bordered the Common.

'Where is he now?'

'South Korea.'

'Funny . . .' she said, 'you don't ever think of places like that until someone else mentions them.'

'He's based in Japan, flies all over Asia,' Paul said casually.

'China?'

'He's been there.'

They began to mount the iron steps of the footbridge. Below them the traffic roared continuously.

'Do you think he'll ever get married again?' she asked above the noise.

'Married?' Paul looked surprised.

'Why not if your Mum's been dead all these years. Maybe he'll even bring back a geisha?'

Paul shrugged uncomfortably. 'Yeah . . . maybe.'

Frank Ross got out of the taxi and paid the driver, glancing across the road to where he had left the Jaguar opposite the phone-box. He guessed that the man in the green Cortina would be somewhere close, or a colleague maybe assigned to take over the watch. Well, he'd spot him soon enough.

He crossed the road and approached the car, taking the key from his pocket. As he bent to fit it in the lock Alec Rimmer and Stiles, his Detective Constable, stepped up close to him on either side. Ross took no notice.

Rimmer tapped him on the shoulder. 'Come on.'

Ross glanced up in mock surprise. 'We're bumping into each other all over the place these days, Rimmer. Could this be another of your carefully calculated coincidences?'

'Mr. Bryce wants to see you, Ross. No coincidence.'

Frank Ross believed he could tell a police station with his eyes closed. By the smell. Like you can a hospital or as he would have preferred to say – a public urinal. He stood alone now in the interview room listening to the footsteps approach along the corridor outside. Christie Bryce! He hadn't seen him for eight years but the hatred he felt for the man had not lessened. As the door opened he took a deep breath. He knew he needed to keep all the cool he possessed.

Detective Superintendent Bryce entered with Alec Rimmer a pace behind. For a moment or two he stood just inside the interview room staring at Ross. Then he gestured to Rimmer to close the door.

'What's the pull for?' Ross asked. 'I've only been out six days?'

'Six *busy* days, Ross.'

'Right. Lots of old friends to see.'

'But too busy even to see your boy.'

Ross winced.

Bryce nodded to Rimmer. Rimmer pulled one of the chairs from under the table and jerked a thumb at Ross. 'Sit down.'

Ross took the chair. 'Is anyone making coffee?'

Bryce pulled the other chair from under the table and sat opposite Frank. Rimmer remained standing deliberately positioning himself behind Ross.

'Where were you between eleven and two?' Bryce asked slowly.

'Walking.'

'Where?'

'Just walking about. Looking around.'

'Where?' Bryce echoed Rimmer's question.

'Anywhere. Fresh out of the nick, you want to see how things have changed.'

'You spent three hours just walking anywhere?' Bryce said incredulously.

'That's it. I couldn't have put it better myself.'

'Not much of an alibi, is it?' Rimmer said.

'Who needs an alibi?'

Bryce leaned forward. 'Let's cut the cat and mouse. Where's Billy Binns?'

'I have no idea,' Ross enunciated each word.

'You've just been to see him,' Bryce said.

'You're mistaken.'

'Lew Wilson told you where to find him.'

Ross smiled.

'You had a meet with him . . . twice.'

'He owes me money.'

'He put Billy on to that factory,' Rimmer said. 'We know that.'

'Then go and pull Lew Wilson for Chrissake.'

'This is murder, Ross,' Bryce said harshly.

'Not the way I heard it,' Ross said. 'The old boy was sick . . . dodgy pump.'

Bryce sat back letting Rimmer ask the questions from behind.

'Who told you that . . . Alison?'

'Who?' Ross turned to Rimmer, his back now to Bryce.

'Billy's grunt,' Rimmer put in.

'No. Ralph Veneker told me the old fella could have keeled over any time . . . natural causes.'

'Billy whacked him.'

'That's not Billy's game. You know that. He's never been violent.'

Bryce came back into the play.

'A man is dead, that's all I know, that's all I want to know.'

Ross turned back slowly towards him.

'I haven't seen Billy in eight years. I don't know where he is, and if I did I wouldn't go within ten miles of him.' He smiled. 'I wouldn't give you the satisfaction.'

'You're a bloody liar, Ross,' Rimmer exploded.

'You knew you were being obo'ed. You towed them round for nearly a week.'

'That gentleman in the Cortina?' Ross asked innocently. 'I thought a local fag had taken a fancy to me.'

'Today you had arrangements,' Rimmer said. 'So you slipped him.'

'Today I got bored with being followed. Fag or copper it's all the same.'

'You had to dump him to make the meet with Billy.'

Ross smiled, shaking his head. 'No . . . no . . . no . . .'

Bryce watched the confrontation between Rimmer and Ross.

'You're too calm, Ross,' Rimmer told him, 'too sure of yourself. You knew we had to pull you . . . you've been rehearsing.'

Bryce glanced up at Rimmer, signalling a takeover. 'I thought you might change,' he said quickly. 'But your sort never do.'

'My sort?' Ross bridled. 'What do you know about my sort?'

Bryce smiled contemptuously. 'All I need to . . . all I can stomach. I sometimes wonder how you can live with the smell you trail around.'

Frank Ross felt the anger rise inside him. In the cold, devoted person of Christie Bryce all his hatred and contempt for authority was personalized.

'Nothing,' he flared. 'Even in the nick with no visitors, even on segregation I wasn't as lonely, as isolated as you are. You've got no one, no wife, no kids, no family, no real friends, you've got nothing but the job. People aren't people to you, they're numbers, dates, times, places in diaries.'

Bryce eyed him coldly. 'I'll give you a few weeks,' he said quietly. 'Before you're back inside . . . or dead.'

'That's long enough.' Ross got to his feet.

'What for, Frank?' Rimmer opened the door. 'To find out who grassed on you?'

Ross nodded. 'That's it. To find the bastard.' He looked at Bryce. 'What did he say when you told him I was out . . *Mister* Bryce?'

Bryce looked at him. 'You really want to know?'

'Yes. And while you're about it I want to know what he said

when he first heard that my wife was in a mental home. Or when he heard she'd just tried to cut her wrists.'

'Same reaction,' Bryce said impassively.

'What was that?' Ross said.

Bryce looked at him, his lips pursed. 'Just laughed.'

CHAPTER EIGHT

CROSSING the hall towards the ringing phone Lucy Andrews was already praying it was Paul.

She picked up the phone. 'Four, two seven, three.' And listened a moment before her face tightened. 'Frank . . . Well of course we knew you were out . . . your letter . . .'

Her husband had come out of the kitchen and was standing beside her.

'He's . . . he's fine, Frank. Big lad now, of course . . .' She listened, looking troubled and uncertain. When she spoke again she forced the anxiety out of her voice. 'Well, Keith isn't back yet . . . but come when you like . . . about an hour? Fine . . . Good to hear you again, Frank. Bye . . .'

She replaced the receiver and turned slowly to her husband.

'Why did you say I wasn't in?' he asked.

'I don't know, Keith. I . . . couldn't think straight, I suppose I was trying to put him off . . . oh Christ!'

'There's no guarantee Paul'll be back in time. Or in any condition to see his old man.'

'I don't want him to see Paul,' she said flatly.

He stared at her and walked into the kitchen. She followed him in and he sat down heavily at the kitchen table.

'Now listen,' he said, 'Don't let's go through all that again, I'm not in the mood for your paranoia. Paul is *his son*, Lucy. Whatever we think about his behaviour.'

'My paranoia . . .' she exploded. 'What the hell are you on about. What has he ever done for Paul. He's got no bloody right just turning up after all these years, just ringing up and expecting us to . . . to jump. He's been out a week, a bloody week and this is the first time we've heard from him.'

'I am *not* defending him. But Paul's still his son.'

'He always was a selfish bastard. As long as everything is just so for Frank Ross.'

She picked up her mug of coffee and held it, trembling with anger.

'Easy, for Chrissake!'

'Easy, you say. Easy! Do you realize what effect it might have on Paul . . . what it might do to him, especially right now. Haven't we got enough problems without this?'

'We knew he would want to see Paul sometime . . .'

She was already crying, sniffing back the tears in half-strangled sobs. 'Take him you mean.'

'Not necessarily. If Eve was well it might be different.' He stood up next. 'Come on, Luce – how about a drink.'

'Eve's never going to be well.'

'So Paul'll have to stay with us.'

'Frank won't see it that way.' She shivered violently. 'He'll be here and take him. After eight years he'll just come and take him.'

'Let's wait till we talk to him before we start having hysterics.' He moved to put his arm round her but she pushed it away.

'Why don't you stop talking to me like I'm some sort of neurotic spinster, for Chrissake. I could hit you sometimes, you're so bloody patronizing. You don't really give a damn if he takes Paul . . . do you . . . do you! *Do you?*'

He stood there without answering.

'Well answer me!' she screamed. 'You don't care if he does take Paul, do you?'

With a sudden violent gesture she hurled her coffee into his face and ran from the room.

'No love,' he said to the empty room, wiping coffee from his face. 'I don't care. Fact is I'd be bloody glad to see the back of the little sod.'

Alison picked her way among the junk and mud of the caravan site to the communal standpipe. Hooking the red plastic bucket over the tap she turned on the water and cursed under her breath as the immediate strong flow dwindled to a trickle.

She straightened up to wait for the bucket to fill and watched three small kids come racing between the caravans.

'Promise you . . .!' one of them was saying. 'There's about four cars of 'em. One over there, one down the lane. We're surrounded!' he said gleefully.

At the word she stiffened. 'Here, come here, son,' she called.

The leading boy stopped reluctantly.

'What d'you mean, four cars. What sort of cars.'

'*Police* cars,' he said impatiently, hopping from foot to foot.

'Where?'

'One at the back, one down the lane, the other two's gone round the other side. Come on,' he said to his friends and together they raced away.

She ran. Leaving the bucket she slipped and slithered across the mud, ducked the washing lines and reached the caravan. No sign of anybody.

Letting herself in she crossed to the bench seat where Billy was stretched out sleeping off the effects of the whisky he had drunk with Frank. She pushed his shoulder urgently. 'Billy . . .!'

Binns' eyes opened.

'Get up, Billy!'

'What . . .' He stumbled to his feet. 'What is it?'

'They're here . . . the law! They're surrounding the site.'

He was suddenly wide awake. Reaching out he grabbed his boots and pulled them on. Then moving quickly to the back of the caravan he knelt and pushed the plywood wall back. Reaching in he pulled out a hand-gun. Alison grabbed his arm, white-faced with fear. 'Where did you get that from?'

Binns checked the gun without answering.

'You must be crazy,' she said.

He jerked free of her hand, and edged open the door.

'Leave the gun for God's sake,' she pleaded.

He gestured angrily. 'It'll be thirty years if they take me, Ali.'

'Please . . . please, Billy . . .'

He peered outside, then turned back to her. 'Are you comin'?'

Slowly she nodded. 'Yes, I'm coming.'

On the edge of the site Alec Rimmer hand-signalled to the

group of uniformed police at the far end of the track which bisected the field. As they moved forward he turned to Stiles and the two uniformed officers with him. 'Okay, let's go.'

They moved forward cautiously threading their way through the seedy caravans, ducking the washing lines but always keeping the edge of one caravan in sight. Passing the standpipe Rimmer vaguely noticed a spreading puddle from an overflowing red plastic bucket hooked across the still running tap. 'From here on,' he said, 'we're out in the open. We have no choice.'

He stepped from the cover of a big burnt-out caravan, Stiles and the two uniformed men beside him. Billy Binns' caravan was now in full view about forty yards away.

As the caravan door crashed open, the overflowing red bucket jumped into Rimmer's mind. As he broke into a run Billy Binns emerged from the caravan dragging Alison behind.

'Jack it in, Billy,' Rimmer roared, 'we've got men all round you.'

Then to his total astonishment he saw Binns swing round face them and two shots cracked and whined above their heads.

As they ducked for cover, Billy pulled Alison forward, slithering in the mud between two caravans they were momentarily lost from view.

'I don't bloody believe it,' Rimmer said to Stiles crouching beside him. 'Billy Binns with a shooter!'

Dragging Alison to her feet as she slipped to her knees on the mud and slime, Binns face was drawn with fear. 'Come on, love, for Chrissake.'

'Go on alone, Billy. Please.'

As he hesitated a uniformed figure from the other police group rounded the edge of a caravan. Binns jerked up the pistol and fired and as the man went down, he looked into the horrified face of Alison. 'Run,' she screamed, 'Run, you silly sod.'

His mouth opened and closed. Then he turned and raced between the caravans towards the lane on the edge of the site.

Clambering through the thin hedge he could hear the shouts of the police behind him. As the thorns tore at his shirt he jumped down into the darkness of the lane. He hit the squirting mud and scrambled to his feet. His throat was raw, the pulses thundering in his head. He had shot a copper! As he forced his legs to move again a beam of light hit his face and the waiting police car powered towards him. Lifting the gun in uncontrollable panic now he fired three shots until the chamber emptied, then stood paralysed as the car raced at him. He had no way of knowing that his last shot had shattered the windscreen.

Fifty yards away the car seemed to skid wildly, sloughing mud as it came at him broadside then tail-slipping as it crashed among the trees.

Billy Binns, released from paralysis by the noise of crushing metal, dropped the gun and ran.

Among the caravans Alison stood glaring at Stiles. Rimmer, kneeling over the wounded policeman, got to his feet. 'Carry him to one of the cars,' he said. 'It'll be quicker than an ambulance.' Then he turned and walked towards Alison and Stiles. Drawing level he said, 'Bring her along.' His face was hard as stone.

The Jaguar hissed to a halt outside the Andrews' house and Frank Ross juggled a bunch of flowers and a gift-wrapped parcel as he got out and locked the door.

Keith Andrews had seen the car pull up and had already opened the door to stand waiting in the hall. Week out of prison and he comes steaming up in a brand new Jaguar, Keith Andrews reflected bitterly. Crime, they say, doesn't pay! In twenty years of hard work at the depot he'd managed to rise to a three-year-old Ford Escort. And the insurance on that was killing him.

He felt a deep dislike for this man who was coming down the path now, a big smile on his face, flowers and presents in his hands. It was all very well for him hiding behind his well-deserved prison bars while his son turned into a tearaway and his wife, Lucy's half-sister, went into a home.

He extended his hand and forced a smile. 'Hullo, Frank, you're looking fit.'

'Hullo, Keith.' They shook hands.

'Come in then.' Andrews led the way into the kitchen. 'Sit down, mate.' He pulled out a chair.

Ross held out the bunch of flowers. 'I brought 'em for Lucy . . .'

'*Right royal generous of you,*' Keith Andrews thought. He took the flowers. 'I'll put 'em in water in a minute. I'm afraid Lucy had a bit of a fall today. She's upstairs having a lie-down.'

'I'm sorry to hear that. Nothing too serious?'

'No . . .' Andrews shook his head, 'I'm afraid young Paul ain't back either. Lucy got the nights a bit mixed on the phone. Apparently he could be back late.'

Ross nodded. 'Well, I brought him a present. I can leave it for him and drop in tomorrow.' He tapped the gift-wrap. 'I didn't know what to get him. Fifteen's an awkward age. I hope he hasn't got a camera?'

'Well, matter a' fact we bought him one for his last birthday.'

'Ah . . . yeah, really not my lucky day.'

They both turned at a creak on the stairs and a moment later Lucy stood in the doorway.

'Lucy . . .' Ross stood up and kissed her on the cheek. 'You shouldn't have got up, love.' He pointed to her other cheek. 'That looks very sore.'

'It's only a bruise,' she said dismissively. 'I'm sorry about Paul not being here, Frank. I didn't think until I'd put the phone down.'

He could feel the chill in her voice. 'Not to worry,' he said. 'We needed to talk anyway.'

'Yes'. Her manner was icy. 'Yes, I'd say it was high time.'

Ross glanced from her to her husband. Andrews' lips were compressed, an air of tension evident about the way he stood.

Lucy turned to him. 'Did you say anything yet.'

He shook his head. 'I was waiting for you to come down.'

'What did he tell you, Frank?' she asked. 'That I'd had a fall, was resting?'

Keith Andrews inhaled sharply.

'We had a row,' she said. 'Just after you phoned. We've had a lot of rows lately, most of them about Paul. I'll be honest with you, Frank, you're the last person I want to see!'

Ross looked from Lucy to her husband. 'I'm glad you come straight out with it, Luce,' he said slowly. 'Paul's causing you a lot a bother. Is that it?'

'That's it, Frank.'

'You and Keith don't always see eye to eye on what should be done.'

'That's natural enough, isn't it?' Andrews said, sitting down at the table.

'What's been happening then? I mean, what's Paul been up to?' He had to force himself to ask the question.

'Plenty I'm afraid,' Andrews said.

Lucy made an impatient gesture with her hand. 'Look, Frank, let's start at the beginning. All the time Paul's been here he's been a good lad. All right, a few dust-ups with Keith, you know, young stags, that sort of thing. But like I said we all got along fine, better than that even, till about a twelvemonth ago.'

'What happened then?'

'We took Paul, like we did every week, to see Eve. She was very strange . . . distant . . . she refused to see him.'

'We thought it was just one of her depressions,' Andrews got up and took a bottle of beer from the cupboard and a couple of glasses.

'We went the following week . . .' Lucy continued. 'This time she wouldn't even acknowledge she had a son.'

Keith Andrews put the glasses on the table and poured beer for himself and Ross. 'We showed her a photograph . . . she tore it up and stuffed the pieces in her mouth!'

'Go on,' Ross said, his stomach churning.

'Dr. Whyte took him in the third week.' Lucy looked at him. 'Well, you'd better hear it all. It'll help you understand. Right?'

'I'd sooner have it straight, Luce.'

'All right.' She sipped a drop of her husband's beer. 'This last time, Eve hit him. Hit him across the bridge of the nose. Then stood in a corner with her face pressed against a wall, just pouring out obscenities! It was . . . was horrible, Frank . . . Paul just . . . just stood there, his face . . . I shall never forget his face.'

'He hasn't seen her since . . . never mentions her,' Andrews said.

Ross wiped his mouth with his hand. 'And since then?'

Keith Andrews flushed angrily at the memory of the last months – why shouldn't Frank Ross hear the lot?

'At school they said he was certain for good 'O' levels. But since the business at the hospital he's been suspended twice, once for stealing, once for threatening a master.' He pointed to Lucy's bruised face. 'That was for trying to stop him going out. Two o'clock this morning he rolls in legless . . . pisses in the porch . . . it's the third time he's come home swearing drunk in a month. At home he's murder. That's giving it to you straight.'

Frank Ross drank his beer. He was afflicted with a more massive sense of failure than he could remember. Even in prison with less than half the sentence gone, he couldn't remember feeling like this. He knew somewhere that this was the price of his own survival. He wanted only to get up and walk out and pursue something that was clean and uncomplicated – and something he understood – like his own burning desire for revenge.

'What do you want me to do?' he asked. 'Do you want me to take him away tonight?'

'No!' Lucy's eyes were red with tears. 'No, Frank, don't take him now.'

Ross looked at Keith Andrews who said nothing. It didn't take a mind-reader to know what he was thinking.

And yet if he took Paul, what in hell's name would he do? Cart him around from place to place. Among people like Eddie Archer and Lew Wilson? Or dump him on Chris Cottle and Trudi – that's the way it'd probably be.

'Listen,' Lucy wiped her eyes with a Kleenex. 'Listen, I don't think taking him away would do any good right now. Like, it's not disturbance he needs. It's something, like solid . . . and all right . . . dependable.'

Again Keith Andrews sat, his face a cold, tense mask. Ross looked at him. 'What do you think, Keith?'

Andrews shrugged. After a moment he said, 'You probably know what I think. I think, beginning to end, you been a right shit. But if Lucy wants Paul to stay, that's all right with me.' He pushed his beer aside, stood up and walked out of the room.

Frank Ross had never felt so completely trapped in his life. No one like Keith Andrews had ever talked to him that way – and got away with it.

He turned to Lucy. 'What I'd like to do would be have a bit of time to think. A week or so maybe.' He knew he was lying. Even half-lying to himself. 'That all right with you, Luce?'

She nodded. ' 'Course.'

He stood up. 'Better not tell him I'm out just yet. Right?'

'All right, Frank. You got a number we can reach if we need to?'

He took a small sheet of paper from his pocket-book and wrote down his newly installed number. 'I'll phone you next week, Luce.'

She didn't look up. 'Yeah, you do that, Frank.'

With a final thrust he ejaculated inside her and collapsed panting on top of her.

Mo pushed at his head. 'Here,' she said, 'is that all?'

He rolled off her on to the ancient sofa, the only piece of furniture in the derelict, broken windowed room. 'What's wrong,' he said, offended. 'What different did you get from Tommy Arndale.'

She sat up and reached for her jeans. 'No different. Just a bit more of it.'

He grunted, zipping up his own jeans. 'Well, if you don't like it . . .' he said.

She laughed. 'Who said I didn't? Come on, don't be like that. Wasn't bad for a first try.'

His head jerked up. 'Who said it was a first try.'

'I did. Right?'

He shrugged. 'Maybe.'

'Come on,' she said. 'Give us a kiss. Nick and Boz and the others be down in a minute.'

He hesitated, then pulled her towards him and kissed her. 'That better?'

'Much.'

They lay back on the sofa, arms around each other.

'Bit of a dump this, an 'it?' she said. 'Wouldn't much like living here.'

'Well, they're squatting. They don't pay nothing and they've the whole place to themselves. Not bad. Boz goes down the Nab each Tuesday, picks up twelve quid. Nick, the same. Twenty-four quid a week. Not bad.'

She grimaced.

'Well, that's what they're taking us down the pub on tonight.'

Upstairs there was a shout of laughter and a clatter of footsteps on the bare stair-treads. A fist hammered on the door. 'Come on, you dirty bastard,' Boz's voice spluttered with laughter. 'You must have got it away by now.'

The Carriage Lamp was Lew Wilson's favourite restaurant. Not only because he owned forty per cent of it but also because Albert Rose, who ran it, served savouries and port with his Stilton and generally acted in a manner reminiscent of those butlers Wilson's old mother had always talked about.

But tonight as he sipped his port his mind was far from the smooth woody flavour of Albert's most expensive vintage. He was waiting for Eddie Archer to confirm what he had heard on the radio that afternoon. The police had traced the hide-out of William Binns wanted for murder of a nightwatchman last month.

The restaurant door swung open and Eddie Archer moved quickly to Lew Wilson's table.

'Well . . .?' Wilson put aside his port.

'The law was down the caravan site this afternoon. They got his bird but not Billy.'

'Billy had it away?'

'Looks like it.'

'They could 'ave him bolted up somewhere else.'

'He's away, Lew . . . don't worry.'

Wilson hit the table with the flat of his hand. 'Don't worry he says! If they have got Billy I could end up in the albums.

Bloody Ross! I knew it. I knew he was trouble. I bloody knew it.'

Eddie nodded thoughtfully. 'That rubbish, never thought he'd turn Billy in . . .'

Wilson's head jerked up. 'You think he did that?'

'Obvious . . . he done a deal with Brycc, scheming slag! Bryce gets Billy. Ross gets whoever grassed on him.'

'If he has . . . he's dead!' Wilson sat staring down at the table-cloth for a full minute.

'All right, I want to know, Eddie . . . I want you to find Billy before the law do.'

Eddie looked at him in total dismay. 'But he could be anywhere. If the law missed him at the caravan site he could have hopped a lift to anywhere in the country.'

Lew Wilson glared at him contemptuously. 'You're not thinking, Eddie. Billy Binns – until last month he'd never sniffed country air in his life. He's a Londoner – which means the first place he'll make for is London And he ain't got that much money, so it has to be somewhere he knows.'

'He's got a sister lives up New Cross.'

'Even Billy wouldn't be that dumb.' He shook his head. 'No, he's going to head for me, Eddie. He'll need money, passport, a motor. He'll come this way.'

'Tonight?'

'No telling. He could leave it a day or two. Or he *could* just have made it here already.'

'Jesus Christ!'

'Right.' Lew Wilson got to his feet. 'I'm going across to the Goat in Boots and have a long evening's drink in full view of fifty witnesses.'

'And me?'

'Visit all our places. Anywhere Billy Binns might come looking for me. Like I said, Eddie – get to him before the law do.'

Cruising in the Mercedes, Eddie Archer visited a succession of pubs and clubs in which Lew Wilson had an interest – or was widely known to use. But discreet inquiries of the landlords produced nothing. Everybody by now knew that Billy had been flushed out of hiding and Bryce's men were to be seen drinking half-pints of bitter in the corner of many of the bars. If Billy Binns showed his face in the manor tonight Eddie Archer could see that the police would have him so fast his feet wouldn't touch the ground.

But there was one place Eddie had been holding back on. Up in Battersea, way outside Lew Wilson's regular territory he owned a small garage workshop where Billy and Alison had in fact spent the night before Eddie had driven them out to the Chertsey caravan site. Now at just after ten o'clock Eddie Archer pointed the car towards the river and within fifteen minutes was running along Battersea High Street looking for the turn-off.

The garage was in a sidestreet not far from the river. Parking the Mercedes in the alley alongside Eddie let himself in and stood for a moment in the doorway peering into the darkness beyond. 'Billy . . .' he called softly. 'Billy . . . it's me . . .'

He got no further. The cold barrel of a gun pushed against the back of his neck. 'It's me! Eddie,' he said, too scared to turn his head.

The gun was removed. 'Shut the door and turn the lights on,' Billy Binns' voice said behind him.

Eddie stepped forward slowly and closed the door. Then fumbled for the switch to throw a pale yellow light over the oil-covered benches, the stained concrete floor and the two vans with their bonnets open. Billy Binns, white faced, his hair wild, stood on the other side of the door.

'You give me a nasty moment there, Billy.'

'Where's Lew?'

'He couldn't come himself, you know that. Half the cozzers in South London would have been outside by now.'

'I been phoning his place ever since I got here – where is he?'

'He's having a very public drink in the Goat and Boots. He's showing Bryce and Rimmer and the rest of them that he's got nothing to do with Billy Binns. But he sent me out looking all the same. Thank Christ I found you.'

'Somebody put it on me,' Binns said, his mouth working. 'When the law come they knew *exactly* where to look.'

'You're telling me you're surprised, are you? They knew where to look because they'd been *told* where to look, my son.'

'Told – who by?'

'Your old mate Frankie Ross, who else?'

Binns leapt forward and back-handed Archer across the mouth. 'You lying stump,' he hissed at him.

Archer recoiled holding his mouth. 'Okay then, Billy. You tell me a better story. Frankie Ross goes down to see you today, right. On his way back he gets picked up by Bryce.'

'Who told you that.'

'Lew Wilson's got one of the coppers on the bung. Frankie Ross was in with Bryce and Rimmer for the best part of an hour. Then they let him go.'

'So . . .?'

'So!'

Binns shook his head. 'Not Frank. He wouldn't. Nothing'd make him.'

'Something would, Billy. Something only Bryce has got. A name.'

'No!'

Eddie shrugged, relaxing now. He took out a packet of cigarettes. 'Okay, Billy, go ahead. Believe only what you want to. There's the phone – ring Frank Ross and tell him you're here. And ten minutes later the heavy mob'd have this place surrounded.'

He lit his cigarette watching Billy Binns' white face. Beneath the frowning forehead the suspicions grew like tumours. After a few moments he shoved the gun in his belt and turned for the door. 'Be here when I get back, Eddie.'

'When will that be?'

'As long as it bleedin' takes,' his voice rose almost to a child's scream.

'Sure mate,' Eddie Archer said as the door slammed in his face.

The new Ford Granada lay on its back among the stacks of sewer pipes, spotlit by the searchlight beams of two fire engines. As the firemen began to cut into the crushed door frames with their oxyacetylene cutters policemen were already taking statements under the flashing blue lights of the waiting ambulances. 'Came round the corner,' one shocked witness was saying, 'must have been doing sixty and crashed right through the Road Up sign, hit the pipes . . .' He stopped. 'I was just standing there. It flew straight up spinning over and over. I can't see anybody coming out of that alive.'

The first of the bloodied, unconscious passengers of the car was now being eased through the gaping hole cut in the side. Boz Clapton bubbled blood and alcohol fumes through his broken teeth.

CHAPTER NINE

THE bare corridors of the hospital echoed with their footsteps as Keith Andrews and the police sergeant made their way to the Casualty Reception area.

'How badly were the others hurt?' Andrews asked.

'The two boys and one of the girls got away lucky. They'll be out in a week. The other girl, Maureen Turner, she's being operated on now. You know her?'

'No.'

'Could very easily lose an eye, one of the doctors said.'

'God.'

'Your boy's been lucky. Very lucky.'

'He's not my boy,' Andrews said. 'I'm his guardian. And a bloody fine guardian I turned out to be.'

The Sergeant stopped before the door marked 'Casualty'.

'What will happen?' Andrews asked him.

'Well, sir, the boy was knowingly being driven in a stolen vehicle, the lad's in trouble . . .'

The Casualty door opened and Lucy and Paul came out. A wide scratch across his forehead was the only sign that he had been in the crash.

'All right, son?' the Sergeant asked him.

Paul nodded.

'Tomorrow morning you'll feel like someone run a steamroller over you, they always do.' He turned to Keith Andrews. 'You'd better take him home.'

The Sergeant nodded good night. On either side of Paul, the Andrews walked towards the swing-doors.

Suddenly the boy stopped.

'What's wrong, Paul?' Lucy was already reaching for the door handle.

'I want to see Mo.'

She opened the door. 'They told you . . . you can't. She's in the operating theatre.'

'Then I'll wait till I can.'

'Paul! For Chrissake.' Keith Andrews grabbed his arm.

'They said you can see her tomorrow,' Lucy said, placatingly. 'Tomorrow, Paul.'

The police sergeant watched them as Lucy crossed to Paul and with her arm round him led him back towards the swing-doors.

In the car they sat silently, Paul and Lucy in the back.

'Did you know the car was stolen?' Keith asked over his shoulder.

Paul didn't answer.

'You're all going to end up in court, you know that?'

'Big deal,' Paul said.

'Don't you talk to me like that,' Andrews' voice was spitting with anger.

'Jesus!' Paul said. 'I've just been in a car crash. My girl-friend's in the operating theatre . . .'

'Whose bloody fault is that?'

'Not mine,' Paul shouted.

'Yours and your lousy mates!'

'Leave it . . . just leave it . . .' he screamed from the back seat.

'Leave it, leave it . . . Somebody's got to knock sense into you!'

'Try . . . just try,' Paul was shaking the back of the driver's seat.

Suddenly the car skidded to a stop. Keith Andrews jumped out and wrenched open the back door. 'Out . . .!' he shouted. 'Leave it you said – well I've left this far too bloody long.'

He leaned in and wrenched Paul by the shoulder.

'Stop it,' Lucy was screaming from the seat beside Paul.

'You're not my bloody father,' Paul yelled, struggling to stay in the car.

'If I was I'd have done this long ago.' Open-handed he whacked Paul hard across the face and as the boy fell to the ground, half in, half out of the car, he stood over him. 'You're right,' he fumed, 'I'm not your bloody father. But just see how he takes it. Going to court with you. He'll enjoy that, just out of prison himself and his son up for car theft. He'll be very proud of you . . .'

Suddenly he realized what he had said. Paul looked up at him.

'Just out of prison?'

Andrew stood uncertainly.

'My dad's out of prison?'

'Get back in the car,' Lucy said. 'Yes, he's just out, Paul.' She was searching her bag. 'I'm going to phone him to come over straight away.'

She got out of the car and walked along the pavement to a phone box on the corner. After what had just happened she felt she had no choice.

When the phone rang Frank Ross walked from the kitchen still chewing a tuna sandwich. The tone of Lucy's voice immediately spelt trouble.

'You sound as if something's wrong, Luce. What happened?'

'It's Paul,' she said. 'He's been involved in an accident. He's not hurt.'

'What sort of accident?' He dropped the sandwich on the table.

'He's all right, just shaken up a bit. The thing is, Frank, he knows you're out.'

'I thought we decided it was best not to tell him yet.'

'Keith didn't mean to . . . it was just . . . well . . . there's been some trouble, Frank . . . the police.'

'Police?'

'He was in a stolen car . . .' she said flatly.

'I'm coming over. I'll be there in ten minutes, Lucy.'

Ross put down the phone and grabbed up the top coat hanging over a chair. Checking he had the key to the garage, he moved quickly through the kitchen and let himself out into the garden.

Letting himself through the garage back door he was fumbling for the light switch when a sound stopped him dead. 'Who the hell's that?' he said.

'It's Billy.' In the half-light Billy Binns' gaunt face rose above the height of the Jaguar. As he rested his arms on the top of the car Ross could see he was holding a gun.

'Billy! What the hell are you doing here?'

'He's got Ali,' Binns' voice was as expressionless as a drunk's.

'Who has?'

'Bryce.'

He pointed the gun.

'Lew's got one of Bryce's team on a pension. He says Bryce pulled you after our meet.'

Slowly Frank Ross began to understand.

'He did.'

'Eddie says you done a deal with Bryce, me an' Ali for the name of the grass.'

'You believe that, Billy?'

'He says eight years in stir has done you over, Frank,' Binns said.

'I'm asking you, Billy. Do you believe that?'

'They've got Ali . . . I don't know what to believe no more.'

Ross began to round the bonnet of the car. 'You've got a shake on, son, you're not thinking . . . give me the shooter.'

Binns shook his head. 'I'll take your face off, Frank.'

Ross stood his ground talking quickly. 'There was no deal with Bryce, Eddie cattled you. If you think I could do that you better pull that trigger now.'

He walked slowly forward.

'Frank!' It was a desperate plea. Then his hand dropped to his side, the gun dangling from his index finger.

Ross put his arm round him. 'Come on, son, you need a drink. Stick that in your pocket.' He pointed to the gun.

Binns nodded and together they walked back into the house.

In the sitting-room Frank took down a bottle of whisky. 'Pour us both a shot, Billy. I just got a call I must make first.'

He picked up the phone and dialled, speaking half over his shoulder.

'Someone put the whisper on you, Billy. It wasn't me, it

wasn't Alison. It was the last thing that Lew needed. That only leaves . . .'

'Eddie? But why, Frank, he's Lew's man. For Chrissake why?'

Ross turned his attention to the phone.

'Keith? Frank. Look, something's come up. Dead important I'll be a bit late . . .'

The lights sparkled on the river as Ross and Billy Binns climbed out of the car. Standing together under the street lamp Ross buttoned his coat. 'You think you can do it, Billy?'

The younger man nodded, shivering in Ross's borrowed car coat. 'I'll do it, Frank.'

They walked together across the road. 'It's here,' Billy said. 'He's got Lew Wilson's Mercedes parked up on the forecourt.'

'There you go then.' He touted Billy's arm.

Billy Binns moved forward, hesitated briefly and continued on down the road. Passing the parked Mercedes he walked down the side alley and hammered on the door. 'Eddie . . .'

Footsteps sounded across the concrete floor and the door opened. Binns stepped inside.

'Did you see him?' Eddie's voice had a ragged edge of anxiety.

'I saw him.'

'What did he say?'

'What did you expect him to say, "Yes, Billy, I shopped you"? The bastard denied it, of course.'

The relief spread on Eddie Archer's face. 'So? You didn't just turn round and come straight back here?'

'No.' Despite himself Billy Binns was beginning to enjoy it. 'Leave it, Eddie. It's all over. Just get on to Lew. Tell him I need money and a clean motor.'

'Now hold up, Billy.' Eddie Archer was baffled. 'All over? What happened?'

Billy Binns allowed a long dramatic pause. Timing, he'd heard it called by his cousin who worked the pubs as a blue comic. 'I'm the last bugger Frank Ross is ever gonna shop.'

Eddie Archer's eyes opened. 'Jesus . . .!'

'Why not?' Binns said. 'I'm up on the old fella's account. Probably another for the copper at the caravan site. What bleedin' difference does it make?'

'You killed him?' Archer's mouth sagged open.

'I only meant to give him a tooling . . .' Billy conceded. 'It was like . . . more or less an accident.'

Archer found it hard to conceal his excitement. 'He was a slag . . . a grass . . . he asked for it. Where is he?'

'In his garage. He was too heavy to move.'

'Okay I'll get someone to float him down to Tilbury. No sweat.'

'I'll need some dough . . . an' a motor.'

'Sure. We'll get you away. Lew's already got somethin' going for you.'

'What about Alison?'

'No way, Billy.'

'There must be something Lew can do.'

Archer pretended to think. He shrugged. 'I don't know. Maybe there is . . . look . . . I'll call Lew . . . he's at The Goat . . . tell 'im what's happened.'

He began to cross towards the workshop office. Then turned. 'You're sure he's dead?'

Binns nodded. 'You can't get deader.'

Closing the office door behind him Archer dialled and listened, a smile spreading on his face. When the receiver was picked up at the other end he said, 'Eddie here. It's worked out handsome, better than we thought. Frank Ross is dead, Billy offed 'im . . . He just told me here at the garage . . . yeah . . . It couldn't have worked out neater, it drops Lew right in it as well.' He listened. 'No, Billy won't grass on Lew but that poxy bird of his will. Lew's bleedin' feet won't touch.' He paused. 'Billy? He thinks I'm calling Lew at the club to sort out another flop . . .'

Suddenly, in mid-sentence, he spun round. Ross and Billy were already standing just inside the door.

'Who is it, Eddie?' Ross nodded to the phone. As Eddie Archer tried to slam down the receiver, Ross leapt across the room, catching him a blow which flung the phone from his hand. Grabbing up the receiver he listened but the line was already dead.

'Who were you phoning, Eddie?'

'It wasn't, Lew,' Billy Binns said, the gun on Archer.

'Who was it, Eddie?' Ross repeated. 'Lew wouldn't be too happy if he knew his boy grassed on Billy.'

'I didn't . . .' Archer said desperately.

'You lyin' dog . . . you told Bryce where me an' Ali was,' Binns came forward, gun in hand.

'No, Billy.' Archer backed away.

'Hold it, Billy,' Ross hooked his fingers into the heavy phone and moved between Archer and Billy Binns. 'Who are you *really* working for, Eddie?' As he spoke he swung the phone to deliver a crushing blow high on the side of Archer's face. Archer crashed back against the wall.

'I want to know who you're working for, Eddie.' He lifted the phone again and Eddie Archer groggily raised an arm to defend himself. But, a street-fighter since the age of fifteen, Eddie Archer knew all the tricks. Less groggy than he appeared he rocked forward. As Ross swung the phone, he reached up, grabbed and twisted his arm high behind his back.

As Billy Binns ran forward Eddie Archer kneed Ross viciously in the back, hurling him forward on to Binns.

Taking the wooden stairs behind him three at a time Archer hurled himself at a flimsy door and burst through it on to the roof parapet. A narrow track of guttering no more than eighteen inches wide led round the rusting corrugated iron roof of the workshop. Running along it, his coat tails flying, Archer took off at the end clearing the six foot gap on to the flat roof of a derelict factory.

Billy Binns, twenty paces behind him, hurtled across the gap, followed by Frank Ross. In the light from the street lamps they could see Archer climbing an iron fire-escape to a higher roof level.

'Get after him, Billy. I'll cut him off round the back,' Ross yelled and swerved right across the flat roof. Racing down the side of the raised roof section Ross knew that he had overtaken Eddie Archer on the level above.

At the far end a rotting set of wooden steps led upwards. Clambering up over the broken treads, Ross knew they had him. As he raised his head above roof level he could see Eddie Archer not fifty feet away picking his way across a badly holed asbestos roof. As it cracked like thin ice under Archer's weight Ross saw Billy Binns appear at the top of the fire-escape and start after Archer.

'Get back, Billy,' Ross yelled. 'It's cracking.'

As he spoke an asbestos panel gave way and his foot plunged into the hole.

'Get back, Billy!' Ross bawled across the roof. But ten yards away from Archer, Billy Binns was not prepared to turn back. With the roof cracking and splitting underfoot he hurled himself at Archer.

Frank Ross heard the shattered pieces of asbestos falling into the factory below. Then as he moved forward towards the two struggling men the whole panel gave way with a splitting crack and both men plunged through screaming to the concrete factory floor.

Sickened, stunned by the heavy thud of their bodies counterpointed by the thin clatter of the falling pieces of asbestos, Frank Ross turned and picked his way back across the roof. Jumping down the wooden steps he ran back along the lower roof level until he reached the fire-escape. Taking it down to ground level he jumped clear and ran through a gaping hole in the brickwork on to the main factory floor.

Eddie Archer seemed to have plunged head-first. He lay in a growing pool of blood on the surface of which factory oil floated. There was no sign of blood on Billy Binns' body. He lay across a concrete machine bed, face up staring at the sky through the gaping hole in the roof.

Turning away Ross ran for the nearest call-box and dialled 999. Even as he asked for the ambulance he knew it was useless.

CHAPTER TEN

THE pale November sun slanting across the floor of the hospital sun-room between Frank Ross and Eve seemed only to emphasize their isolation from each other. He had been shocked to see her, as he came into the room, seated with a blanket round her legs, her wrists still bandaged, her face drawn and without make-up, her blonde hair uncared for, hanging limp and pale like a white-haired old lady.

She had finally been persuaded to see him by Dr. Whyte. But as he sat opposite her now, the talk jerky and formal she seemed to Ross to be a picture of drugged indifference.

'I've been to see Paul . . .'

Eve scratched at the bandage on her left wrist.

'Hardly recognized him . . .' he went on, 'tall . . . tall as me nearly . . .'

Eve scratched the right wrist, her eyes wandering.

'He misses you, Eve, misses coming to see you . . .'

Eve lifted the edge of one of the bandages and looked underneath at the healing suicide scar.

'Keith told me about the upset you had with Paul. It must have been about the same time you stopped writing to me.'

Eve started to untie the bandage.

'You said you didn't want to see him any more, didn't want him to visit.'

Eve started to unwind the bandage from her wrist.

'Why, Evie . . . what happened . . . I mean, just suddenly like that . . .'

'You . . .,' she said tonelessly.

'I wasn't here, Eve,' he said gently.

She continued to unwind the bandage from her wrist. He watched her.

'You know what I mean,' she said.

'No . . . look, Eve, don't take it off.'

'Eyes . . . mouth . . . hands . . .' she intoned, removing the bandage and dropping it on the floor.

He picked it up and put it on the table between them. 'Try to explain, Eve,' he said.

She studied the scar on her wrist. 'I used to watch them.'

'Watch who?'

'Looking at you . . . standing close to you . . . smelling your body . . . wishing . . .'

'I don't understand, Eve.'

'Other women.' Eve began to untie the other bandage. 'You knew . . . enjoyed it . . . smiled back at them, that smile, his smile, your mouth, his mouth . . .'

She unwound the second bandage, quickly this time.

'Evie . . . I promise you, I don't know what you're trying to tell me.'

'Liar!' she laughed totally without warmth.

'I promise you, Evie . . .'

'Why didn't they leave me. Let me die? Help me . . . help me, Frank.'

'I want to, Evie . . . we all want to.'

She reached out to touch his face. 'It's all edges . . . your face, your face is all corners. Still love him, never stopped loving him, thinking about him . . .'

'Paul?'

Eve repeated the name as though trying to force herself to remember it.

'Paul . . . Paul . . . Paul . . . Paul . . . Kiss them better.' She held out her scarred wrists. He leant forward and gently kissed each scar.

'Every time he came it got worse,' she was looking out across the winter fields.

'*What* did? What got worse?'

'Every . . . every time I looked at him I saw . . . saw you . . .' She paused, a stricken furtive look on her face. 'Wanted . . . wanted you . . . kiss him, not like a mother . . . wanted him to love . . . him to love me, but not like a son . . . you . . . wanted you . . . he was you . . . then . . . your eyes . . . your mouth . . . hands . . . you, wanted you, him, you, him . . . frightening . . . secret . . . dirty . . . dirty . . . perverted.'

She dropped her head and began to sob. Ross moved towards her but suddenly he realized that the sobs had turned to laughter.

'Eve?'

She threw back her head and laughed.

'Eight years . . . eight years in prison. Guess who did that to you . . . guess who told the police? Guess who betrayed you Frank. Me . . . *me*, Frank . . . I told them . . . that policeman Bryce . . . told him . . . everything . . . he wrote it all down.'

He stood over her.

'Why? Why would you do that?'

'Why? Because . . . because I didn't want Paul to be like you, grow up like you . . . a criminal . . . a thief.'

He picked up the phone. 'Nurse Sackett. I think you should come in.'

Frank Ross walked through the littered entrance of the Bingo Hall. A man in a brown suit, fifty, balding was bending forward to talk to someone behind the cashier's grille. First house didn't open for another hour.

As Ross crossed the hall the man in the brown suit looked up and took a chewed cigar from his mouth.

'Sam Fine?' Ross asked.

'Might be . . . who wants to know?' He peered hard at Ross. Then screwed up his eyes. 'Hang about.'

He took a pair of thick-framed glasses from his top pocket and put them on. 'I remember that profile . . . Frank Ross.'

He led Ross out of earshot of the cashier.

'What can I do for you, Frank?'

'Billy Binns put me on to you,' Ross said.

At the mention of Binns' name, Sam looked nervous. 'You seen Billy then?'

Ross nodded crisply.

'I thought young Billy was on the trot . . . for brickin' an old fella.'

Frank shook his head. 'In hospital . . . broken back.'

'Jesus! What happened?'

Ross ignored the question.

'Listen,' he said. 'Billy told me what you told him.'

Sam Fine shifted furtively. 'What was that then?'

'About Big Ralph . . .'

'What about Big Ralph?'

'Cimmie Vincent,' Ross said hard-eyed.

Sam sucked on his cigar. 'We was just talking . . .'

'Talk to me. Same way.'

'If Billy's already told you . . .' Sam began.

'Tell me again.'

'Why don't you talk to Big Ralph?'

'It's important, Sam.'

'It would stay private like . . .? just between you and me?' Sam asked anxiously.

Ross nodded crisply. 'My word.'

'I'm sorry to hear about Billy . . . Nice boy . . . he done me one or two kind turns . . . what do you want to know Frank?'

'Anything you can remember about Cimmie Vincent.'

Sam Fine led him across to a plastic padded door. 'Come into the nerve centre of my financial empire . . .'

Opening the door he gestured Ross to go ahead.

The small office was completely chaotic – papers and files everywhere – cups with congealed coffee in them – cigar stubs left burning the edge of the desk.

Sam crossed to an old safe in one corner, opened it and took out a bottle of malt Scotch. 'The cleaner's a dipsomaniac,' he said with a smile.

He poured two large whiskies and held one out to Frank.

'There's not much to tell.' He sat in his swivel-chair. 'I used to run a spieler in Paddington . . . Cimmie worked for me . . . she was a good girl . . . Veneker used to pick her up . . . but once a week he'd collect her in a cab . . . She had a little place in Chelsea Bridge Road . . . opposite the barracks . . .'

'When was this?' Ross asked.

'As far as I know it started three . . . four months before your firm got done,' Sam said. 'They were very discreet, I suppose they had to be with Veneker's wife knowing so many of the same people. I reckon it was getting serious, then . . . Well . . . you know the rest . . .'

'Billy said someone put the frighteners on her?'

'It certainly looked like it,' Sam conceded. 'Just after your trial finished, she come in one night, terrible state, took her clobber and that's the last I saw of her.'

'What did she say?' Ross put down his untouched whisky. For the first time he really felt he was on to something.

'She wouldn't say nothing when I tried to talk to her . . . She was shakin' . . . I went to get her a brandy and she legged it.'

'Did she say anything to anyone?'

Sam shook his head. 'Don't think so. She give the key to her drum to one of the girls and asked her to pack her clothes, leave them at Victoria and post the ticket, but when the girl went over Cimmie's place was a right mess. Someone had really given it a spin, cut up all her clothes, left the taps runnin', paint all over the walls, there wasn't much point in packing what was left.'

'Any idea who it was, Sam?' Ross asked quietly.

'No . . .' Sam said flatly. 'If she'd come to me I might have been able to help . . . I mean a lot of useful people used my place. All I can tell you is the poor cow was terrified.'

He was bitterly disappointed. True enough he still had Veneker to talk to – but he'd hoped to get something solid from Sam Fine. He wracked his brains to open up a new line. 'Did anyone come to the club looking for her? Checking she'd gone?'

'Come off it, Frank,' Sam said. 'She was a good-looking girl. Never short of friends.' He sipped his malt reflectively, 'Good, ain't it?'

'Yeah.' Preoccupied, Ross picked up his whisky.

'For what it's worth,' Sam Fine said, relighting his cigar. 'Cimmie Vincent had more official visits the day she scarpered.'

'Who was that?' Ross asked eagerly.

'I wasn't there,' Sam said. 'And he didn't give no name, but one of the girls reckoned he was the law.'

'The law.'

'She reckoned she'd seen him before, in another manor.'

'This girl. What was her name?'

Sam smiled to himself. 'Yeah, that was Angela . . . A dancer, well, that's what she called herself. She'd go case for fifty . . . nice pair of scotches.'

'Angela what?'

'Rees, sort of Welsh, she an' Cimmie were close, shared a place at one time.'

'Where can I find her?' Ross asked.

'Long time ago, Frank. Last time I heard she was working the camps with a knife-thrower. No . . . hang about . . . she's back in the smoke . . .'

'How do you know?'

'Somebody came into the club a couple of years back. Used to be a regular punter when Angela was there. Told me he'd come down from Birmingham or wherever and fixed himself this girl with an escort agency. Turns out to be Angela.'

'An escort agency? You remember which one?'

'No chance, mate.'

Again the disappointment overwhelmed Ross. 'Try and think, Sam.'

'Won't do no good, Frank. Just an escort agency. That's all I remember.'

'The West End's stuffed with 'em.'

'Right. Looks as if you've hit a dead end, mate.'

'Nobody you can think of might be able to help?'

Sam reached across the piles of paper on his desk and extracted the phone. Dialling, he pursed his lips listening. 'Ah, Sandra,' he said after a moment. 'You remember that Angela used to dance at the club. You and 'er were a bit close just before she left. Any idea where she is?'

He listened nodding, then raised a thumb to Ross. 'Thanks, darlin',' he said. 'See you soon.'

He put down the phone and lifted his head to Ross. 'Your lucky day, Frank. This Sandra's run across her in the clip-joints in the last year. Angela's tried to get her on the agency books. It's called Mecklers. Run by some old bat named Mrs. Meckler.'

'Sam, I could kiss your bald head.'

Sam Fine stood up. 'Lovely thought, Frank. But I'll take a raincheck.'

'If you'd like to drop in, Mr. Stephens, we have photographs of all our girls,' Mrs. Meckler said. Careful make-up did not quite disguise her fifty-odd years but she had obviously once been a very attractive woman.

On the end of the line Frank Ross said with just a faint touch of Australian in his voice. 'But that wouldn't help a lot, Mrs. Meckler. You see, a fella on the plane coming over told me about her. Angela, I don't remember her last name. Said he had a *very* nice evening, if you get my meaning.'

She carefully ignored the innuendo. 'Angela . . . yes . . . could be Angela Rees.'

'Rees, that's the name,' he said. 'She wouldn't be free to-night, would she?'

'I could see and call you back.' She liked a punter who could make up his mind. 'Which hotel?'

He dropped his voice. 'I'm staying with friends. So when you call back, if I don't answer . . . a bit discreet, you know what I mean?'

'Of course, Mr. Stephens. Give me the number. I'll call you back in ten minutes.'

Ross gave her his number and went upstairs to run a bath. Less than five minutes later the phone rang.

'Mrs. Meckler here, Mr. Stephens. Yes, Angela's free to-night. Where would you like to meet?'

'Depends where she lives. I'll pick her up at her place if it's not too far out.'

'Not usual . . . but it's Victoria.'

'Fine.'

She gave him the address. Not before eight o'clock, Mr. Stephens.'

'Okay. And thanks for you help.'

'Not at all. I hope you have a . . . very nice evening.'

Ross replaced the phone and checked his watch. It was five o'clock. Too bad.

By six o'clock he was climbing the stairs of the small block of flats in Victoria. Ringing the bell he waited while the hall light went on and the door opened on a chain. A blonde head of hair above an unmade up face peered round the door. 'Yes . . .?' she said.

'Angela Rees?'

'Yes.'

He placed his knee against the door pulling it by the handle towards him and at the same time reaching round to unslip the chain. As he pushed the girl backwards with the door he said, 'They never fit these things properly. Get it fixed for next time.'

'Who the hell are you?' She was pressed back against the wall, scared now.

'I want a word with you. That's all.'

He took her arm and guided her into the over-furnished living-room. 'No trouble, Angela. Nothing to worry about. Just a little talk.'

'I've no time,' she said unconvincingly. 'I've got to get dressed. I'm expecting someone.'

'Your appointment's at eight.'

'Who the hell *are* you? If you're the guy I was expecting you're too bloody early.'

'I'm Frank Ross,' he said.

She stopped dead. 'When did you get out?'

'Few days.' He nodded towards the sofa. 'Sit down, Angela.'

She looked at him warily and taking a cigarette from a box on the coffee table she sat back on the sofa.

'Sam Fine tells me you were close to Cimmie Vincent,' Ross said.

'That old bit of sugar . . . is he still burning furniture with his cigars?'

He came forward and lit her cigarette. 'I know about Cimmie and Ralph.'

She frowned. 'That run she had with Ralph? That was years and years ago.'

'I haven't had the opportunity to ask you in the meantime.'

She shrugged. 'Only lasted a couple of months. Until he was put away.'

'Tell me about it.'

'It was nothing,' she said dismissively. 'Ralph was a married man. He just took a shine to Cimmie . . . bought her a few drinks . . . had a few laughs. Jumped into bed a few times.'

'She was at the trial. Every day.'

The girl nodded. 'So it was a bit more than nothing. On her side at least. She knew it was hopeless. She knew Ralph would never leave his family.'

For long seconds he sat staring at her until she shifted uncomfortably. 'Who put the frighteners on her?' he asked quietly.

'I don't know what you're talking about.'

'Sam said she was terrified.'

'Sam always did exaggerate.'

'She done a runner, left everything. It doesn't sound like Sam was exaggerating.'

She stood up. 'Look, if I'm not doing business tonight, I'm going out anyway. I'm not sitting around here watching telly. I'm getting dressed.' She stood up.

'Sit down.'

The rasp in his voice made her hesitate. She sat down again. 'All this is years ago, Frank.'

'Who was she running from, Angela?'

'I don't know. Truth.'

'Sam said a face came to the club asking after Cimmie.'

'Lot's did,' she agreed.

'No, this one was different. Sam said you thought he was the law.'

'Oh yes . . . that one.'

'How do you know?'

'Recognized him, seen him before. Maybe Cimmie was in trouble with the law. If she was she didn't tell me.'

Ross waved the idea aside. 'The filth don't make a habit of flooding flats, cutting up clothes, daubing walls, putting the fear of Christ up young birds.'

'She knew a few villains . . . I mean, like Ralph. Maybe one of them . . .'

'This copper that got a bit busy, what was his name?'

'Look,' she said irritably. 'I don't know his name. I'd seen him around. He was pointed out once by a fella I was entertaining. Listen . . . I haven't seen Cimmie in near on nine years. She went to Australia. She wrote a few times.' She stubbed out her cigarette. 'End of story.'

He stood up, looking out of the window. After a moment or two he turned back to her. She was already setting up a hand mirror against the cigarette box to start making up her face. 'You've no idea where she is now?'

She rummaged about in a make-up bag and brought out some foundation. 'Still over there, I suppose?' She smiled. 'If I know Cimmie she's shacked up with some over-sexed Aussie who's got more money than sense . . . She never was one to go short.'

'Okay.' He moved towards the door. 'Thanks anyway, Angela.'

'If you see Ralph say hullo for me,' she said, relieved.

'Sure. I'll let myself out.' He walked down the hall to the front door. He was aware that she had never once asked what all the questions were about.

When the door closed behind him Angela sat back on the sofa and whistled through pursed lips. Then pushing herself up she crossed to the phone and dialled.

'Can I speak to Kath . . . Angela.' She waited for a few moments. 'Kath . . . listen . . . I've just had a visit from Frank Ross. Yeah, he's out and he's looking for Cimmie Vincent.'

Thirty minutes later Angela emerged from the entrance to the block of flats and hailed a taxi. Frank Ross, watching from his parked car couldn't help smiling to himself at the transformation. The wan-faced little woman in the shapeless dressing-gown who had stood flat-footed before him in the flat was now a pert, high-heeled hooker in a fun fur and sharp parallel jeans. As the taxi drove off Ross got out of the car and walked quickly into the entrance of the block.

On the third floor he quickly slipped on a pair of driving-gloves and taking from his pocket a strip of celluloid with a garage calendar printed on it he inserted it in the door jamb. The tongue of the lock slipped back effortlessly. Entering the flat he closed the door behind him and moved into the living-room.

He was looking for letters, any letter from Cimmie Vincent. Any letter that mentioned her. On the sideboard was a large untidy pile of papers. He could see by the broken envelopes that most of them were bills but it seemed like a place to start. Carefully putting aside the bills he began to read through the two letters. One from a very indiscreet gentleman from Broadstairs described the night they'd spent together and arranged for another visit in December. The second, from Angela's mother in Wales, hoped she was getting on well with her dancing career and announced the death of old Uncle Tom.

Ross replaced the letters in the pack and put them back on the sideboard. The rest of the room looked bare of any interest. Quickly he moved into the bedroom.

Angela Rees was the sort of girl who'd never really lost the bed-sitter habit. All her most treasured possessions, everything that was closest to her, was kept in her bedroom – the huge pink nylon fur bear on the bed cover, the innumerable framed photographs of herself, all taken some five or six years ago. One of a man in a U.S. air force uniform and another of him standing in flying kit beside a Starfighter on a German airstrip were given pride of place. Frank Ross started on the chest of drawers.

From a tangle of bras and pants and suspender belts he drew a pack of photographs in an envelope. Riffling through them he saw they were mostly of Angela and the young American flyer, taken years back to judge by the brevity of her mini-skirt. Ross wondered idly whatever came of that affair. Was the Yank posted home, or decided to go back to his wife and six kids in Denver, Colorado, or did he maybe find out that sweet Angela was on the game. Then suddenly he stopped dead. In some sort of farmyard Angela stood beside an unknown man and Cimmie Vincent. He flipped over to the next picture. Farm, dogs, the man and Angela. Angela at the wheel of a landrover. Angela and Cimmie Vincent at a dinner table, paper hats, glasses being held up to toast the photographer. He removed the picture of Angela in the landrover and slipped it into his pocket. Replacing the rest of the photographs in the drawer he closed it carefully and left the flat.

At Mrs. Meckler's escort agency office Angela was working up to her finale. 'And if you ever give my home address to anyone again you can shove your job up your padded bra and find yourself another girl!'

'Listen, darling,' Mrs. Meckler tried to calm her, 'how was I to know you knew this whatever his name was . . .'

'It's not that I knew him, you stupid old bag,' she screamed, 'it's that he came looking for me. And you hand him the address on a plate. The last time, the last bleedin' time.'

She stormed out of the office leaving Mrs. Meckler white and shaking behind her desk. She particularly disliked that spiteful reference to the padded bra. She was in fact extremely proud of her bustline and had only in the last year resorted to a little discreet padding for support. How could the little Welsh bitch have known that. She picked up the phone and dialled. 'How much is it worth to you to know,' she said, when a man's voice answered, 'that Frank Ross is out.'

'Old chimes,' he said.

'Okay. How much is it worth to know that he's been round to see Angela Rees.'

'Jesus!'

She smiled. 'Next time I need a favour I'll expect you to be *very* quick off the mark.'

She replaced the phone, stood up and looked in the long mirror, inhaling deeply. Surely nobody could just *see* she wore a padded bra.

Stables of the gentry in the last century, a derelict hang-out for the late Edwardian poor, the mews was now a desirable property, painted in white and pink, with fast growing creeper clambering across trelliswork and expensive cars parked the length of the cobbled roadway.

Detective Chief Inspector Bryce's own private Ford looked modest among the Rolls and Jaguars. As he rang the bell and waited he pursed his lips, eyeing the restrained opulence of the housefronts.

The door was opened by Roy Hallam, a man in his early forties. Towards Bryce he exhibited the sort of aggressive deference which marked him as a one-time subordinate. He smiled grimly, 'Thanks for coming.'

Bryce nodded dismissively and stepped past him into the narrow hall. 'Straight up?'

'And on the left.'

Bryce climbed the stairs and entered the minute but well-furnished room. 'Used to be the old coachman's quarters I suppose,' he said to Hallam entering behind him.

'Times have changed. Can't buy one of these places now for love nor money.'

'You managed.'

'Yes . . .' Hallam hesitated and indicated the cupboard of drinks. 'Same old poison.'

'No thanks.'

'For old times' sake.'

'I'd rather forget the "old times". What do you want, Roy?'

'I've been hearing about Frank Ross.'

'I thought that was it.' Bryce shrugged. 'He had to come out some time.'

'He's got his nose up everyone.'

'Is that all you dragged me over here for?'

'You know what a cunning bastard he is.'

'He's just another thief with form, that's all.'

'He's gonna sniff out something.'

Bryce shook his head slowly from side to side.

'Unless someone stops him, he will.'

Bryce lifted his eyebrows. 'What sort of talk is that?'

'You know what he's after don'tcha?'

'Yes. He wants to know who grassed him. Are you surprised?'

'Of course not but . . .'

'What did you expect him to do, Roy, swallow it? Frank Ross?'

'He's only been out two weeks. Eddie Archer's dead, Lew Wilson's on remand, Pretty Billy's in intensive care . . .'

'Precisely.'

'What's that suppose to mean?'

'You're an ex-copper, a smart one, too smart. Think it out. I've pulled Ross for questioning twice already. On the street he's caused a lot of aggravation in a very short time . . .'

'Piggy in the middle, caught between the law and the chaps, not a very healthy place to be. I see what you mean.'

'The way he's going,' Bryce said easily, 'Frank Ross is going to be back in stir by Christmas, or he'll end up in an alleyway with a white chalk line drawn round him.'

Tony McGrath's apartment missed none of the finer points of luxury. Designed by a young fag and over-ambitious interior decorator it looked like a cross between a film set for *Cleopatra* and a regency maison de rendezvous. Tony McGrath was delighted with it.

A small, sallow Geordie, he had left the North forty years ago when his mother had brought him to London in pursuit of a sailor who was the father of her second son. Dragged through a series of Salvation Army Hostels, only seldom with an abode sufficiently fixed to necessitate a month or two at the local school, Tony McGrath had developed a predator's instinct for survival. He had fought and bullied on the streets, working first as runner and then tic-tac man for a dozen bookies until one day Alf Torrence's clerk fell ill. And Tony McGrath, virtually unschooled, discovered, because he had to, that he could stand up in the wind and add a sheet of figures faster than the next man, calculate the bets and show the win or loss on the four dogs at a moment's notice. From that day he was made. Every bookmaker in the area used his stand-in services and two years later McGrath was making a book of his own.

But the profits of Catford dog track weren't enough for Tony McGrath and over the years he extended his petty empire to bingo halls and escort agencies until now he and Lew Wilson could divide the patch. And Lew Wilson was remanded in custody on a charge of aiding Billy Binns' escape.

All in all, until Anna Meckler had called this evening, things seemed to be going particularly well for Tony McGrath. Now with a worried looking Roy Hallam hunched over the Scotch bottle opposite him, he wasn't so sure.

'What did Bryce say then?' he said, looking down at the top of Hallam's already balding head.

'He reckons Ross will be back inside by Christmas . . . or dead.' Hallam didn't look up.

'He could be right,' McGrath said casually.

Hallam's head came up fast. 'Look, Tony . . . I'm having no part of . . .'

'Shut your mouth,' McGrath said icily.

'He's pulled Ross for questioning twice already. He reckons he was on that roof with Eddie Archer and Pretty Billy.'

'I *know* he was.'

'How?' Hallam asked, astonished.

'Eddie was *my* man.'

'*Your* man? He was Lew's man.'

McGrath laughed. 'He was on the phone to me when Ross turned up with Billy.'

He looked at Hallam's set face. 'Don't you think it's funny.'

'I don't have your weird sense of humour.'

'Well here's something that should crack that face. Frank Ross is on to Cimmie Vincent.'

'Oh Christ.' The colour drained from Hallam's face.

'I thought that might amuse you.'

'Are you sure?' Hallam said. He fingered his mouth.

'He's just been chatting that old friend of hers, remember, slag named Angela Rees.'

'Angela Rees,' Hallam frowned.

'Right . . . Friend of Cimmie's way back. Remember?'

Hallam nodded. 'She knows nothing.'

'How do you know . . .? They were girly, girly at the time. Chances are Cimmie told her the lot.'

'Cimmie Vincent went to Australia.'

'Did she come back?'

'She wouldn't.'

'Let's hope you're right . . . but I think just to make sure, you better take it on your arches and go and have a little heart to heart with Miss Bangor.'

It was a small stone village, fog wrapped in a valley between the Welsh hills. Frank Ross had enjoyed the drive from London. Along the motorway he had sat back while the Jaguar took itself along at a silent, comfortable seventy, giving him plenty of time to think. He had forced himself to think about Evie. After the last visit to the hospital he had talked to Dr. Whyte. Eve had a long, long road to travel, Whyte had told him, and it was far from certain at the moment what part of the journey Ross could take with her. He hadn't pulled any punches. Eve had had problems all her life but meeting and marrying Frank Ross he'd said was the toughest problem she'd had to face. 'In simple terms,' the doctor had said, adjusting his goddam shades and sipping his brandy, 'in simple terms, Mr. Ross – a girl with an abnormally developed need for security and reassurance had married someone even more essentially insecure than herself.'

That had stuck in Frank Ross's throat.

'You're a weak man, Mr. Ross,' the damned doctor had said smiling. 'Just think about it. Have you ever really done anything important in your life for any other reason?'

'If you weren't Eve's doctor I'd hook you one now,' Ross had said, furious.

'Yes,' Whyte had agreed. 'That's why I'm taking such outrageous advantage of my position.'

The Jaguar swerved round a Ford Transit and continued down the ribbon of road. That damned doctor had the ability to probe a finger into Ross's gut. Weakness? Was it weakness to pursue the grass that had put him away for eight years? Of course not. Or was it?

He turned off the motorway and headed north-west across Wales. In these narrow roads, sometimes amounting to no more than lanes he was forced to concentrate more on his driving, and think less about Whyte's insolent analysis.

The fog, thickening in the bottom of the valleys, hung heavily over the stone houses arranged in a small village square.

Ross parked the car outside the Three Feathers and smiled to himself at the sign: 'No singing or dancing' nailed to an old elm. He looked along the bleak stone house fronts. It had been a long time since an excess of singing and dancing had worried the inhabitants of this little township.

Next to the pub, the lights of a village shop sparkled through the mist. On an impulse he decided to try there instead of the Three Feathers. In the small, deaf person of Miss Phipps, he was amply rewarded.

'Good afternoon,' Ross greeted the round bundle of beige cardigan and grey hair.

'Yes . . .' Miss Phipps answered meditatively, 'yes . . .'

Ross hesitated. 'I said good afternoon,' he felt he was already explaining himself badly.

'Yes,' she agreed in her lilting voice. 'It's often the case.' She smiled an overful set of dentures at him. Ross noticed disconcertedly that they slipped a fraction at the apogee of her smile. He also noticed she was wearing an incredibly ancient hearing aid.

He pitched his voice up. 'I'm looking for Round Oak Farm.'

'That's right,' she agreed.

'Round Oak,' he said at a volume just short of a shout.

'You're well past it.'

'I'm well past it?'

'Pardon?' Miss Phipps cocked an eager hearing aid.

'It's back to the crossroads, is it?' he shouted.

'No, no . . . you have to go back to the crossroads . . . then left . . . then bear right into Round Oak Lane. The farm's about a mile and a bit farther . . . down an unmade track . . . it is marked, Rhys put it up himself.'

'You know Mr. Upcott?'

'Pardon?' her smile clicked across the counter.

'Rhys Upcott. You know him?' Ross enunciated.

'Who?' Miss Phipps looked genuinely baffled.

'Mr. Upcott.'

'Knew his mother . . . went to school with his father . . . used to smell . . . put lard on his hair he did, couldn't afford hair oil.'

'What about his wife?'

'Whose wife?'

'Mr. Upcott's?'

'Dyes her hair, y'know. Got a boy they have ... nice little thing ... got her looks. She's from London, you can tell ... don't talk much but when she does you can tell ...'

Frank Ross thanked the old lady, a difficult operation in itself, and left the shop. Regaining his car he drove through the village towards Round Oak Farm ... back to the crossroads, left and bear right. As he made the final turn he saw bumping towards him down an unmade track an open-sided landrover. As it turned on to the road and sped past him he saw that it was driven by a thirty-year-old woman, her face partly obscured by the upturned collar of a sheepskin coat, her blonde hair pulled back and held with a band.

As the landrover disappeared round the bend behind him, Ross spun the Jaguar in a U-turn and followed.

He recognized immediately the road she was taking. She was heading for the village.

Cruising comfortably behind the landrover he followed through the square and out to a village school on the far side. He saw now the reason for the landrover's speed. She was late. Already children were pouring through the gate.

Braking the landrover, the woman jumped down and headed into the school playground. Ross pulled his own car in behind the landrover and got out in time to see her emerge from the school hand in hand with a small boy of six or seven.

Ross stepped forward. It was her without any doubt, eight years and a change of name to Kath Upcott in between. 'Hullo, Cimmie,' he said.

She stopped dead, the little boy continuing a pace then swinging on her arm.

'I think ...' she swallowed, 'I think you've made a mistake.'

Ross shook his head. 'No.'

She pushed the boy gently towards the landrover. 'Get in, Jimmy ... I won't be a minute.'

As the boy climbed into the landrover Ross said, 'I just want to talk. No trouble.'

'I don't know who you are but my name is Katharine

Upcott,' she managed a cold, haughty look as if he were trying to pick her up.

'No one knows I'm here . . . not even Angela.'

She shook her head irritably. 'I'm sorry . . . but I don't know you at all.'

She moved to get into the landrover. But he barred her way. From his pocket he took the picture he stole from Angela's flat.

'Let's talk, Cimmie.'

'You step aside,' she said, 'or I start yelling for help.'

He glanced involuntarily along the road. Most of the children were being picked up by young Mums. But there were enough broad-shouldered Welsh young Dads milling about to make things uncomfortable.

Ross stepped aside. 'I'm sorry, Cimmie, but I'm going to talk to you, whichever way you play it.'

She climbed into the landrover without looking back at him.

She drove fast, watching the mirror but there was no sign of Frank Ross's Jaguar behind her. As she turned into the lane she realized that Jimmy had been chattering on about his day at school as usual but she had heard nothing. Now, as the comparative safety of the jumbled farm buildings appeared round the bend in the lane other feelings mingled with her fear – feelings of anger and self-pity that after all these years with Rhys Upcott, all these years as a Welsh hill-farmer's wife, her lousy past should rear up and hit her again.

The wheels spun in the mud pockmarked with cattle hooves as she brought the landrover to a halt outside the door of the stone farmhouse. Jimmy jumped down asking if he could get to see the pigs before tea. Abstractedly she nodded and walked into the big open kitchen.

Rhys Upcott, in his late thirties, tall, boney and already balding looked up from the kitchen table.

'Where's Jimmy?' he asked amiably.

'Gone to see the pigs,' she said shortly. Then stared at the mud on the floor. 'You can clean that up.'

'It's only a bit of mud, love.'

'You might as well move the pigs in *here*.'

He watched her banging about the kitchen.

'What's up, Kath?'

'Nothing.'

'Don't look like it. You've got a face like a fox-trap.'

The phone rang.

'Jimmy'll be looking for you,' she said.

He got up and jerked his thumb towards the phone. 'Aren't you going to answer it?'

He moved towards the ringing phone but she crossed the room quickly and snatched it from him.

'Two six eight,' she said into the receiver. She recognized Frank Ross's voice immediately.

'You've got the wrong number.'

Rhys Upcott looked on with mild interest.

'Couldn't we meet somewhere?' Ross asked.

She felt his voice was carrying across the room. 'No,' she snapped. Then looking at Rhys, 'this is two six eight. Not six, six, eight.'

She slammed the receiver down and turned on her husband. 'Haven't you got anything to do? Jimmy'll be *in* with them pigs by now.'

In the phone-box Frank Ross replaced the receiver and went back to the Jaguar. For a few minutes he sat there smoking. If Cimmie Vincent had made a new life for herself the chances were her old man, Rhys Upcott, knew nothing of her past. In which case he didn't want to upset the applecart for her. At least, not until he had reason to think she had played any part in informing to Bryce.

He wheeled down the window and flipped out his cigarette. It arced across the front of an old man pushing an empty pram. 'Visitors,' the old man said contemptuously to himself.

Ross turned on the engine and drove slowly down to the beginning the lane. He felt he had to put pressure on Cimmie now or he'd get nowhere.

At the end of the lane he saw the farmhouse, a low stone building with a corrugated iron barn on one side and a pigsty on the other. He grimaced at the smell as he got out of the car.

Rhys Upcott leaving the piggery with Jimmy looked with surprise at the posh car pulled up in the yard.

His wife, crossing in front of the window, saw it at almost exactly the same second. In total horror she watched as Frank Ross crossed to her husband and began to speak.

After a few moments while she stood unable to move, Ross stepped back waving a casual arm towards Rhys. Then the Jaguar spurted mud from its tyres, circled the yard and was gone.

She was just leaving the window when Rhys entered. He looked quickly at her white, drawn face and crossed to shovel some more coal on the kitchen fire.

'Who was that?' she asked, finding it hard to control her voice.

'From London,' he said, still shovelling coal.

'What did he want?'

'What did you think? The way of course.'

'Of course,' she said and began laying the tea.

Tony McGrath looked at Hallam as he stood, still in his top coat in the middle of the room. 'Was she telling you the truth.'

Hallam nodded as much to himself as to McGrath. 'She says Ross came and went. She says she told him nothing because she had nothing to tell him. As far as she knows Cimmie Vincent's still in Australia.'

'You believe her?'

'Yeah . . . I think so.'

'You *think* so,' McGrath exploded.

'You never know with that sort.'

'You were a copper for twelve years . . . And you don't know when someone's lying to you.'

'I couldn't kick her door in and bounce her around, that's the only way I can be sure of getting it straight from a slag like that.'

'You listen to me, Roy. If Cimmie Vincent is around and Frankie Ross finds her . . . your mate Bryce is going to start counting bodies.'

She knew he would not give up. She had heard enough about him in the old days to be sure of that. She sat there now in the old stone kitchen, with Jimmy playing by the fire, and felt relief whenever Rhys went outside. Behind her the telephone crouched like a fat green toad.

She started involuntarily when it rang and went to answer it, her heart pounding.

Outside in the yard Rhys Upcott had also heard the phone. Twice, he thought, in one evening. Strange when most times they hardly got two calls a week. He crossed the yard.

In the kitchen she held the receiver tight to her ear, her eyes on the door for Rhys to enter. 'For God's sake,' she said, 'why don't you leave me alone.'

'Meet me there, or I come back up to the farm,' Ross's voice said.

She could hear her husband's footsteps. 'I'll see you there in twenty minutes,' she said desperately.

Rhys entered as she put the phone down. 'Another call?' he said. 'We must be getting popular.'

'Mr. Davis. I'm just going down to the village,' she said.

'What for?'

'I forgot to pick up a prescription.'

'They'll be closing.'

'He said not if I hurry . . . I'll take the van.'

He waited until the door slammed then crossed to the telephone. Dialling, he waited until the number answered. 'It's Rhys Upcott here. My wife left a prescription with you.' He listened. 'Then I must have got it wrong . . . thank you, Mr. Davis.'

He dropped the receiver and pulled on his coat. 'Jimmy,' he called. 'Jimmy . . . you sit tight . . . I'm just going out for a few minutes . . .'

Going quickly to the cupboard he took out his twelve bore, broke it and took down a handful of shells. Pushing two into the chamber he dropped the rest into his pocket, snapped the gun shut and made quickly for the door.

Mrs. Meckler, her bustline profile to the young man on the other side of the desk, said into the phone. 'Angela, there is definitely no need to get your knickers in a twist, my love. I haven't given any address.' She winked up at the sharply dressed man. 'And I won't unless you want me to.'

She listened for a moment rolling her eyes at the man. 'He's waiting in the outer office,' she said. 'He's about thirty, not short of a few bob. *Very* good looking – could almost fancy him myself . . .' The young man gave her a V-sign . . . 'Name's John, John Pavey. Recommended by another client. Up to you, dear.'

She listened for a few moments longer. 'Now remember,' she said at last. 'It was *your* choice.'

She put down the phone and looked up at John Pavey. 'My goodness,' she said, 'the things I do for your boss. You can go round to her place in half an hour.'

The Jaguar followed the woodland track and stopped when the van in front drew to a halt. Frank Ross sat tight while the van lights were cut and the figure of Cimmie Vincent got out and hurried towards the Jaguar. Then he killed his own lights.

She opened the passenger door and climbed in. 'I've only got a few minutes,' she said. 'Ten, not more.'

He nodded, handing her a cigarette. 'I'm sorry to put the thumb on you, Cimmie. But there's no way I'm going to let this one go. Understand that and I'll do my best for you.'

'How did you find me?' she asked flatly. 'Through Angela?'

He shook his head. 'She told me nothing. I picked up some pictures in her place. You, her. One of them had the landrover. Mate of mine blew up the photo and we got the number. After that it's easy.'

She accepted the light he held out for her. She lifted her head and blew smoke. 'Rhys, Jimmy's Dad, he knows nothing.'

'That's all right with me.'

'Okay,' she said, 'for the rest I don't have a choice. From what Ralph always said, you're a straight sort of guy. I'll take me chances with you.'

'Let's have it then, Cimmie.'

She took a deep breath. 'Ralph Veneker. 'Cept to Angela I haven't mentioned that name in eight years.'

'You were seeing him.'

She nodded. 'I loved Ralph . . . maybe still do a bit. But what with Marge and his kids, I knew there was no chance.' She shrugged. 'Still . . . once a week I could forget all the sweaty hands . . . the whisky mouths, all those nasty bastards that think because you work in a club you're rubbish.'

Sitting next to her, Ross realized suddenly how desperate she was to talk.

'Ralph is a big, hard man, cross him and he'd break your arms without thinking . . . but with me he was gentle.' She looked at Ross. 'He was always on about you. The only time he ever hit me was when I said something silly about you.'

On the lower road the landrover squealed to a stop behind the old man as he wheeled his pram, now piled high with a tangle of dead branches, towards the village.

Rhys Upcott looked down from the driving seat. 'Sorry to startle you, Jacob. Seen anything of Kath, she's got the van.'

'Up the wood road,' the old man said.

'You sure?'

'Course I'm sure.' He didn't mention she was nose to tail with the big posh visitor's car.

Upcott swung the landrover in a tight U-turn and powered off down the road. Swerving into the wood path he cut the lights and bounced along for a few minutes until he reached the trees. Then drawing the landrover into the side, he got out, taking the shotgun in one hand and a heavy rubber torch in the other. About a hundred yards up ahead he thought he saw the dim outline of a parked car.

In the Jaguar Cimmie Vincent had exhausted her first burst of relief in talking again. Now her face was drawn, her mouth difficult to control as she sniffed back the tears. 'I swear,' she said, 'Ralph was one hundred per cent loyal to you . . . he would have killed me if he knew . . . I was too frightened to say anything . . . frightened of them . . . frightened of him . . . but I swear Ralph knew nothing about it.'

'About *what*. You keep on about *it*, about *what*?'

Neither saw the shadowy figure step forward. Then suddenly the whole car was filled with a bright white light.

'Get out of that car, Kath,' Upcott's voice shouted.

'It's Rhys. Oh my God . . .' Her hands flew to her face.

'You sit tight, mister . . .' Upcott bent close to the window, 'or you'll get both barrels from this.' He tapped the driving window with the barrel of the shotgun.

'For Chrissake do as he says,' she hissed at Ross. Then raised her voice. 'It's not what you think, Rhys.'

She reached for the door, opened it and climbed out of the car.

On the other side Ross opened his door. 'Listen to her.'

Upcott jabbed the shotgun at him. 'Stay in the car.'

'Please, Frank,' she said, rounding the bonnet.

'Frank is it?' Upcott said, his hands trembling on the gun.

'Put that gun down, Rhys, and listen to me.'

'Who is he?' Upcott ignored her.

'He's a friend of a friend from a long time ago.'

'If he's a friend why did he come sneaking up to the house like that, pretending to be lost. And all those phone calls . . . wrong numbers – that was him.'

'Put the gun down, Rhys, and I'll try to explain,' she begged him.

'You must think I'm a bloody idiot.'

He jerked the gun up as Ross got slowly from the car. 'Get back in.'

Ross shook his head. 'You won't use that.'

'Try me.'

Ross walked slowly towards him. 'That's exactly what I'm doing.'

He continued forward until the barrels touched his chest. 'I've known too many faces who use shooters, there's something about their voice. It's not there in yours.' He slowly pushed the shotgun aside.

'Is this the sort of man you knew before you came here, Kath?' Upcott let the gun point down.

'Rhys . . .' She tried to take his arm but he shook her away.

'Big car . . . fancy clothes . . . what else . . . what else, Kath?'

He turned and began to walk slowly. She ran forward. 'Wait for God's sake. Give me a chance to explain.'

He stopped and looked at her. Then past her to Ross. 'Jimmy's by himself . . .' he said and turned.

'I'm coming with you,' she said.

'You please yourself.' He looked up to see that Ross had come forward.

'I'm coming too, Upcott. I'll give Cimmie . . . Kath half an hour alone with you then I'll join you.'

'You bloody won't . . .'

'Listen,' Ross said, 'nobody could blame you for thinking what you did – but only a real mug would refuse to hear the explanation. And only a right bastard wouldn't give you one.'

Upcott stood uncertainly. 'We'll see,' he said gruffly, 'when I've talked to Kath . . .'

In the passenger seat of the White 3-litre BMW as it nosed its way through the West End traffic, Angela Rees was thinking that for once old Mother Meckler had come up trumps. The good looking guy next to her was certainly not one of your regular punters. The sort of evening, she reflected to herself, that you'd almost take on for free. Free! That reminded her. She turned in her seat. 'Mrs. Meckler did explain the financial arrangements?' she said sweetly.

Pavey grinned. 'I gave her fifteen pounds introduction fee . . . and for you it's . . .'

'Fifty,' she said.

'Fair enough.'

She smiled. 'Sorry to sound so mercenary, it just saves any misunderstanding later on. Some of them think that just because they take you out to dinner they're going to get the lot for fifteen quid.'

He shrugged. 'It all goes down to expenses. Personal expenses.' He leaned forward and thumbed the cassette radio. Suddenly the car was filled with an explosion of martial music.

She clapped her hands over her ears.

'D'you like brass bands?' she asked, laughing.

'That's a military band.'

'They all sound the same to me.'

He turned the volume down. 'They do to most people.'

'I like soul . . . do you like soul?' she said then noticed that they had turned off the road into a narrow alley.

'Where are we going? Is this the restaurant.'

He said nothing, stopping the car in front of a metal ride-over garage gate. Almost immediately the gate rolled up and with a jerk that threw her back in her seat he gunned the car forward down a ramp into an underground car park.

'What are we doing down here?' She was alarmed now.

He braked and switched off the engine. 'Get out,' he said without looking at her.

'I'm not getting out.' She grabbed the seat below her.

He leaned casually across and opened her door. Then with one violent shove he pushed her out on to the oil-stained concrete.

From a big American car parked in the deep shadows of the underground car park, Tony McGrath watched impassively as Pavey got out of the car and stood menacingly over her.

'All I want,' Pavey said easily, 'is the answer to one simple question . . . and you can go home. With your fifty quid.'

She began to get to her feet. 'What question?'

'Where's Cimmie Vincent?'

She stopped, looking up at him. 'Who are you? Did Frank Ross send you?'

Pavey grinned. 'Yeah . . . that's right . . . Frankie.'

'I told him . . . Australia,' she was reaching for her bag which had fallen from the car.

'You're lying.'

'She's in Australia.'

He leaned towards her and placed his shoe on her backside, rolling her back on the concrete.

'Just watch this,' he said, taking something from his inside pocket. 'And just think about your face.'

He leaned over and slipped something into her bag. Then straightened up and stamped hard on it. Angela watched with horror as the open mouth of the bag began to emit acid fumes and the imitation leather buckled and distorted and finally burst like some erupting clutch of skin boils.

'Oh Christ,' she said. 'Please no . . .'

His face like iron, he took another phial from his jacket. 'Your choice, darling. This stuff makes you the Phantom of the Opera in five seconds flat . . . or are you going to tell me where I find Cimmie Vincent?'

Standing together near the fire both men could hear the sounds of Jimmy being put to bed in the room above. Rhys Upcott leaned one arm on the mantelshelf and looked down into the flames. 'Kath's given me her word,' he said, 'that there's nothing going on between you two. And that there never was.'

'Do you accept it?' Ross asked.

'Aye,' he said, looking up. 'Whether I can accept some of the other muck she's got to tell you I don't know.'

'It was all a long time ago,' Ross said.

Upcott nodded. 'I'm what they call a simple country fella, Mr. Ross. But I'll be straight with you. I'm not so simple as not to know muck when I sniff it.' He looked straight at Ross. 'I'll tell you I was for calling the police. Kath said no.' He shrugged, 'All right, no. But the moment you've heard what you want, I'm expecting you to walk out of here. And to never come back.'

He bent and shovelled coal on to the fire. 'You were dead right about that shotgun up in the wood.' He stood up, tall, boney. 'Next time you'd be wrong, Mr. Ross. Is that an understanding?'

Cimmie's footsteps sounded on the wooden stair.

'That's understood,' Ross said.

She came into the kitchen, her face still stained with tears. Crossing to a cupboard she took out a half bottle of whisky and without asking poured three glasses and handed them round.

'Water in the tap,' she said to Ross.

He shook his head.

She sat down at the kitchen table and for a moment stared into her glass. 'One night,' she said without introduction, 'Ralph drove me home and left me at the door. Can't remember now but I suppose he had to get back to Marge. I went up, let myself in – and Tony McGrath was standing there.'

The hair on the back of Frank Ross's neck tingled.

'There was another man with him, about twenty-two, good-looking.' She shivered. 'I've met nuts, Frank, but this one . . .'

'You get his name?'

'John, that's all. McGrath called him John. Anyway I walk in and they're both there. And in the bedroom this terrible noise . . .'

Upcott looked up from the fire.

'My cat, Frank, you never heard a noise like it, McGrath steps aside and says take a look. And I go into the bedroom . . .' She banged her fist on the table with the effort of getting it out. 'The cat's face, Frank . . .' She burst into tears. 'McGrath said that was what this John was called – the acid man.'

She lifted her glass and took an enormous gulp of whisky. 'It died while I stood there – I couldn't touch it, help it in any way. Then McGrath slammed the bedroom door and pushed me into a chair.'

Ross glanced once at Upcott. His face was like stone, the whisky glass hanging loose in his hand sloping spirit over his shoes.

'Well,' she said, 'no prizes for guessing the acid was for me too if I refused to help.'

'What did he want exactly?'

'He knew Ralph was into something big.'

'How?' Ross asked sharply.

'He said he'd heard you and Ralph were tapping people for a price on a very big chunk of foreign currency. By luck, my bad luck, he got to hear about it.'

'I see,' Ross said slowly. 'But he knew nothing concrete.'

'No. He knew you were the leader of the team. That's all, nothing else. He wanted me to supply the details.'

'You were to get them from Ralph?' Ross said slowly.

She shook her head violently.

'Ralph never mentioned the job, not once, I swear it, Frank. I wouldn't have ever known about it but for Tony McGrath telling me.'

She refilled her glass and drank.

'One night . . . Ralph had fallen asleep. I was looking for his lighter in his jacket pocket. I found a drawing . . . sort of map . . . roads . . . and a diagram . . .'

'I told him to burn that,' Ross exploded.

'I took it to Tony McGrath,' she went on. 'I didn't know what he was going to do . . . I was so frightened.'

She sucked on a cigarette, found it still unlit and flicked a lighter at it. 'Then . . . I couldn't stand it anymore. I decided to tell Ralph . . . eveything. That night I waited for him . . . he didn't come . . . no phone-call, nothing.' She paused. 'It was *the* night . . . that Wednesday. The next thing I heard was that you were all arrested. I knew it was him . . . McGrath . . . the bastard . . . it had to be him who put the police on to you. I never ever thought he'd do *that* . . . I mean . . . not someone like him.'

She looked at Ross. Then across at Upcott.

'I tried to see Ralph when he was on remand. I was going to tell him about McGrath.'

'That's when McGrath came for you.'

She nodded. 'Angela, Rhys's cousin, found me a place to stay down here. That's how it all started with Rhys and me.'

The room fell silent.

'Did he ever say why . . . *why* he did it?' Ross asked.

'No . . . never . . .'

'Have you got *any* idea?'

'Maybe he just wanted you out of the way. I mean he always was a vicious, ambitious bastard.'

'Too simple. There's more to it than that.'

Suddenly Upcott pushed himself off the mantelshelf and reached down to take the half full whisky glass from Ross's hand. 'Okay, Mr. Ross,' he said flatly. 'You've got your story. Now I'll be pleased if you'll go.'

Ross stood up. 'Bye, Cimmie,' he said.

'Mr. Ross . . .'

Ross paused at the open door.

'Don't forget our little talk earlier. Next time you'd be dead wrong . . .'

Ross nodded and stepped out into the farmyard.

The continuous blast of the car horn woke them from a deep,

exhausted sleep. Rhys Upcott pushed himself on to one elbow. The luminous hands of the clock showed 2.30. 'What in God's name . . .' he muttered. 'Sounds as if it's half-way down the lane.'

'Leave it,' she said. 'Just leave it, Rhys.'

He struggled out of bed and started dressing – cords, gum-boots, a thick sweater. 'Goes on like that it'll wake the boy.'

'Rhys . . . just leave it, love.'

He smiled. 'A courtin' couple. Got his backside caught on the button.'

She was wide awake now. The blast continued. 'Take your gun, love. Just in case somebody turns nasty.'

He went downstairs, picked up the gun without loading it and let himself out into the yard. There was still a heavy mist hanging over the fields but he could see clearly the white BMW with the driver's door hanging open. He reached the car and ducked his head inside. Before he could ask why Tony McGrath sat there with the palm of his hand on the horn, Pavey rose from the shadows behind him and a heavy wallstone crashed down on the back of his neck.

In the bedroom the sawing blast of the horn stopped. She heard the footsteps cross the muddy yard and the door open and close below. At that moment she heard Jimmy calling from his room. Stumbling up she picked up her dressing-gown as the footsteps came up the stairs.

She tumbled gratefully back into bed. 'Rhys,' she called. 'Go in and see Jimmy, will you?'

She heard Jimmy's door open and a muffled, puzzling gurgle from the other room. Looking up in alarm she saw John Pavey, one arm round the waist of her struggling son, the other clamped across his mouth.

She hurled herself across the bed at him but his foot came up catching her high in the chest, throwing her back.

'Now just tell me – Tony and me think you might just have had a visit from Frankie Ross . . .'

She lay on her back across the bed gasping for breath. She felt the same mix of fear and total hopelessness she had felt eight years before.

CHAPTER ELEVEN

TONY MCGRATH and Pavey sat in the white BMW on the cinder forecourt of a North Circular transport pull-up. In the cold morning air they watched a massive container lorry edge its way into the park and come to a rest between the other trucks with a shriek of air brakes. The driver jumped down, locked the cab door and moved off towards the café, his breath pluming mistily.

An old Volkswagen rattled along the road and turned on to the forecourt. In the BMW Pavey nudged McGrath. 'Eight-thirty on the button. He never changes.'

'He never changes that old banger, that's for sure,' McGrath said. 'What the hell's he do with all his money.'

'Income tax?' Pavey said and despite the early hour they both laughed.

The VW drew to a halt on the far side of the forecourt and a small man, trim, in check jacket and cavalry twill trousers got out. Locking the car door he turned and briskly crossed the cinder forecourt to the white BMW.

Inside the car Pavey leaned over the driver's seat and opened the rear door. Ex-Major George Smith slipped into the seat and closed the door behind him.

'Still driving that old kraut tank?' McGrath said.

'It does me.' Smith's voice hinted at Yorkshire.

'What do you do with your money, John and me was wondering.'

'You said it was urgent,' Smith said crisply.

McGrath smiled and took two envelopes from the glove compartment. Smith ignored the larger one and stretched out his hand for the other.

'You know the form, McGrath.'

'I should do by now.'

Mr. Smith took the smaller envelope and tore one end open. Inside was a wedge of twenty pound notes. He weighed it in his hand.

'Feels about right. Good.'

He tucked the money away in an inside pocket then took the larger envelope. Opening it he pulled out a photograph of Frank Ross. 'He looks useful,' he pursed his lips thoughtfully.

'He is . . .' Pavey said.

Smith quickly flicked through two typed pages of biographical notes on Ross.

'I warn you,' McGrath said, 'anything a bit iffey an' he'll . . .'

Smith looked at McGrath with a sort of amused contempt.

'What I mean is,' McGrath insisted, 'you don't put a notice on someone like Frank Ross every day.'

Smith said nothing. He just pocketed the envelopes, got out of the car and slammed the door.

McGrath looked at Pavey.

'You're paying for the best,' Pavey said. 'Not the most talkative.'

'True,' McGrath agreed. 'The moment he opened his envelope Frank Ross was dead.'

Chris Cottle came out of his office as he saw Ross pull the Jaguar into the yard. As Ross got out of the car Cottle crossed towards him, his arms spread wide in apology. Ross tossed him the car keys.

'What the Lord gives,' Cottle said, 'the Lord taketh away.' He grinned. 'That is if you don't keep up the payments.'

'Listen, Chris, I got a few bob. I can let you have enough to pay it off.'

Cottle shook his head. 'No way, mate, unless you want her for yourself.'

'No,' Ross said. 'I've already arranged for a much more modest set of wheels. Little MG. They should be following me round.'

'Come and wait in the office. See the fantastic business

machine rolling. Even better, come and clock my secretary's new outfit. Incidentally,' he added, 'Lucy called.'

'Yes?'

'Paul left to come round to see you at the house about half an hour ago.'

'Trouble?'

Cottle shrugged. 'Here's your new motor now. All you want is a reversed cap and goggles.'

The MG stopped in the yard and Cottle watched while Ross took over the log-book. When the business had been completed he strolled across to the car. 'Not bad. Here, if you're going back home, how about a spin in her, as they say in Chelsea.'

Ross looked at him. 'Paul and me . . . we don't need an umpire, Chris.'

'Just fancied a spin. I'm not so rushed off me feet I can't spare the time.'

Ross grinned. 'Okay, jump in. If you've got your cap and goggles with you.'

They drove over to Ross's place and pulled up outside. Chris Cottle hung back slightly as Ross went to the front door and opened it with his key. Paul was coming down the stairs.

'How the hell did you get in?' Ross said.

Paul grinned. 'Back window.'

'Great,' his father growled. 'You in some bother?'

Paul shook his head. 'I just wanted to see you.'

'How long have you been here?'

'Not that long.'

'You should have phoned first,' Ross said.

'And you would have told me not to come.'

'Sure there's nothing wrong?' Ross was aware of Cottle's agitation behind him as he walked into the kitchen.

'Why . . . does there have to be something wrong for me to want to talk to you?' Paul stood opposite him, challenging him.

'I didn't mean that, Paul.'

'Because I'll go if you don't want to . . .' the boy said.

'Calm down,' Ross snapped.

Chris Cottle moved into the arena. 'Have you two eaten yet?'

'I haven't. Paul?'

The boy shook his head.

'Fancy some Chink take-away?' Cottle asked them.

'Good idea,' Ross felt in his pocket for some money, 'there's a place on the corner. Here, grab some nosh.'

'My treat,' Cottle was already half-way out.

'Chris, get me some fags too, will you?'

'Sure.'

They heard his steps down the hall and the door slam.

As Cottle left he was far too preoccupied to notice the ancient VW cruise slowly past and continue on down the road.

In the kitchen Ross took off his coat. 'Cup of tea, son?'

'Uh, thanks.' Paul's eyes were on the black grip of a handgun sticking from his father's coat pocket.

Ross put on the kettle and turned back to Paul.

'What is it, son . . . are you worried about Thursday, going to court?'

Paul shrugged. 'Only that I don't want you to come.'

'You've got reasons?'

'None that I can explain.'

Ross leaned back against the sink. 'I think you better try, son.'

'I . . . I just don't want you there,' the boy said stubbornly.

'You'll have to do better than that.'

'I can't . . . I can't explain. Please don't come.'

'Is that what you came to say?'

'Part of it.'

'Let's have the rest then.'

Paul roamed the room picking up kitchen objects and replacing them. 'We've got to start again, Dad. You and me . . . that's if you *want* to,' he said at last in a burst of words.

'What's that supposed to mean?' Ross asked calmly.

'You may *not* want to.'

'You're not making much sense, Paul.'

'I'm just trying to be practical . . .' the boy said. 'I mean . . . maybe its better for everyone if I stayed with Keith and Lucy, I mean for good. They could adopt me.'

'Is that what you want?'

'It's what they want. Or rather what Lucy wants.'

'I didn't ask you that.'

Paul hesitated. 'I want to come back here . . .' he said at length 'to live . . . with you . . . *after Thursday*.'

Chris Cottle left the Chinese take-away and walked back towards Ross's house. Again he missed the old VW and the trim, military gentleman, polishing the windscreen as he passed.

At the house he let himself in and walked through to find Ross and Paul in the kitchen.

'Just leave me to it,' he said throwing Ross his cigarettes. 'I'll stick on some plates.'

'Thanks, Chris,' Ross turned to Paul. 'You were saying about school.'

Paul shrugged. 'I've only got a few months to go. I could transfer . . . anywhere . . . it's not important.'

'And university?'

'No way,' the boy said briskly.

'I see,' Ross handed Paul a plate of Chinese. 'Even so – just look at the place . . . it's a tip. You wouldn't want to live here.'

'I'll clean it up . . . evenings . . . weekends . . . redecorate.'

'There's washing . . . cooking . . . all the things you take for granted with Lucy.'

'There must be a launderette . . .' Paul said eagerly. 'And I can eat out . . . when you're not here.'

'No.' Ross shook his head. 'It wouldn't work.'

'At least tell the truth. You don't want me here.'

'There's a right time, Paul . . .' Ross said quietly. 'It isn't *now*. I need a while to get myself sorted out. Here, eat your Chinese.'

'I'm not hungry,' Paul said sullenly.

Turning on his heel he walked quickly from the kitchen.

'Paul,' Ross called after him. He moved to the door but Chris Cottle stepped in front of him.

'Let me, Frank,' he said.

In the street Cottle hurried after the boy. 'Paul,' he called Paul continued without turning.

'Hold up,' Chris said, touching his arm.

'If *he's* sent you to . . .'

Chris grabbed Paul and roughly turned him, forcing him to stop.

'Listen, son,' he said, 'you want some advice . . . freemans . . .' He pointed to Paul's mouth. 'You wanna stop dropping that lip.'

Paul gestured angrily. 'He doesn't understand.'

'Hang about a minute . . . has it ever occurred to you that it might be the other way round?'

'I've tried,' Paul said defiantly.

'It's not that simple, son,' Cottle said with effort. 'You've only ever known one side of your father . . . the same with Evie. How can you have any idea what it's like to be banged up for eight years . . . or what it's like when you're released.'

'He wouldn't even let me see him in prison. Explain that.'

'There were reasons,' Cottle said defensively.

'What?'

Completely on the spot Cottle shifted his feet on the pavement. 'Good reasons. You've no idea . . .'

Paul looked at him. 'Well . . . what were they?'

Chris Cottle looked up. 'Okay, Paul,' he said quietly. 'Even Frank Ross makes mistakes sometimes. Even Frank Ross deserves to be forgiven.'

'Funny,' said Paul. 'And I'd always thought you backed him all the way.'

'Come back and have something to eat.'

Paul hesitated.

'As a personal favour to me if you like,' Chris said.

Paul turned back. 'Okay.' He paused. 'Is he still in trouble, Chris?'

'Trouble?'

'He's got a gun.'

Cottle recoiled. 'How do you know . . .?'

'I saw it . . . in his coat.'

'You haven't said nothin' . . . to Frank?'

'Of course not. *Is* he in trouble, Chris?'

'It's sorta like this, Paul,' Chris Cottle said carefully, 'There are one or two people around who don't take kindly to Frank being back. I can't say no more. And don't you say nothing to him neither.'

'What *is* he going to do?' Paul asked as they reached the house.

'He'll sort it out . . . his own way.'

'He could get hurt. Is that what you're saying?'

Cottle glanced towards the house. 'He can look after himself, don't you worry. But *you* can hurt him. Just at the moment, son, he's got his hands more than full . . . he don't need no extra aggravation.'

As they entered the house George Smith watched from his VW on the other side of the street.

From the top of the office block Des Roberts commanded an uninterrupted view of the entrance to Tony McGrath's flat above the motor showroom across the street. As he shivered in the biting wind he was thinking that the mists and fogs of the last few days would have made a photograph at this distance impossible. When he had told Frank Ross that, of course he had only grinned. 'By noon, Des,' he had said, 'I promise you the fog will have lifted for me!'

And it bloody well had! Des Roberts dropped to one knee and aimed the telescopic lens at the man getting out of the car a hundred and fifty feet below. It was the tenth picture he'd taken already. He had no means of telling who were legitimate customers for the car showroom and who were visitors to Tony McGrath's flat. 'Shoot them all,' Frank Ross had said. 'I'll sort out the sheep from the wolves.'

Far below Roy Hallam entered the showroom and walked through to the stairs to McGrath's flat. Ringing the bell he waited for McGrath to open the door.

McGrath was smiling. 'Lovely morning, Roy,' he said. 'Bit of wind chased all that fog away at last.'

Hallam scowled at him. 'All right, Tony. What's the good news?'

'Here, have a drink, boy.' McGrath led him into the living-room.

'It's too bloody early for me,' Hallam said. 'Unless we've really got something to celebrate.'

'Let's see . . .' McGrath pretended to think hard. 'How about this? Cimmie Vincent is alive and well . . . and living in Wales?'

Hallam's mouth dropped open. 'Cimmie Vincent's in this country? And Frank Ross . . .'

'. . . has seen her,' McGrath said coolly.

'She told him?'

'The lot.'

'Christ!' Hallam looked at McGrath suspiciously. 'You don't seem that bothered?'

'It's sorted . . . isn't it?' McGrath said. 'Why should I be bothered?'

'Sorted? How?' Hallam said, an edge of real alarm in his voice. 'How?'

'I put a notice on him. That's how, Roy.'

Hallam rocked back. 'You what! Who?'

'Go home, Roy,' McGrath said angrily. 'It's all under guarantee.'

George Smith took his half-pint of bitter from Amy, collected his cheese sandwich and boiled egg from the girl helper behind the snack counter and crossed to a seat in the corner of the pub. From there he could just see Frank Ross and Ralph Veneker in the booth under the window. Opening his newspaper he began to study the runners at Haydock for that afternoon. George Smith was a cautious man, given to no more than the daily pound each way double. The rest of his very considerable earnings went to support his ageing mother and his three teenage daughters who were expensively acquiring upper middle class accents in one of the best known girls' schools in the country.

In the window booth Ralph Veneker was shaking his big leonine head in a gesture of utter disbelief. 'Cimmie handed the paper to Tony McGrath.'

'His boy had threatened to strip her face with acid. He'd already done an impressive little demo on her cat.'

'All the same I'll bleedin' kill 'er when I get hold of 'er,' Veneker said.

'No you won't . . . not when you know what happened. She

was going to tell you . . . everything. You were supposed to see her the night we got done.'

Veneker nodded.

'She was waiting to tell you,' Ross went on. 'She even tried to see you when you were on remand to tell you. McGrath must have found out, he went after her . . . turned her place over . . . she done a runner.'

'That geordie dreck. I'll have his eyes.'

'McGrath put us in the frame with Bryce. He knew roughly when . . . where and who.'

'But why, Frank . . . for Chrissake why? There wasn't nothin' personal between you two? Between you and McGrath?'

'A polite nod across a drinker . . . that was about the extent of our social and professional contact.'

'I could understand if he wanted in on the job we were pulling,' Veneker said. 'But then he would have come to you.'

'All I can think of,' Ross said, 'is maybe Bryce had something on him. Bryce would never take an earner, but he might deal. If it came to doing me or McGrath . . .'

'No contest,' Veneker agreed. 'Bryce wanted you so bad, Frank, you could smell it.'

'Right.'

'So . . . what are we goin' to do?' Veneker said.

'Nothing.'

Veneker's head jerked up. 'We can't just swallow it.'

Ross smiled. 'Until I know everything . . . everyone involved . . . then we'll think of something.'

In his corner seat George Smith took his boiled egg, tapped it carefully on the edge of the table and began to peel off the shell. Over his bifocals he could see that Ross had taken out a pack of photographs and was dropping them one by one on the table in front of the big man.

As Des Roberts' pictures fell in front of him Ralph Veneker shook his head. 'I'm right out of touch with the young villains, Frank. I don't know nary a one of these . Though, like you say, they might just be straights looking for a new car.'

Ross continued dropping the prints in front of him. As

Hallam's picture dropped on to the table, Veneker reacted.

'Well, well, well . . .'

'Who is he?' Ross asked.

'Filth.'

'Are you sure?'

Veneker nodded vigorously. 'He pinched me once . . . Haslam . . . Hasleigh . . . he was a D.S. then . . . Hallam . . . Hallam . . . at Vine Street nick. That's it: Hallam.'

'When was this? When did he pinch you?'

'About two years before our little business.'

'Hallam you say?'

'I'm sure that was his name. Hang about Frank . . . there's an ex-cozzer I know, got the elbow for taking it .. Danny Fitt . . . he could help.'

Frank Ross entered Danny Fitt's billiard hall wondering where exactly he had seen the old VW that had pulled over and stopped a couple of hundred yards behind him. Entering the seedy chamber with the lights hanging over the tables he was inclined to dismiss it from his mind. But the thought came back and nudged him uncomfortably. This morning surely, at the garage where he bought the MG, a very similar colour and aged VW was being filled up. Driver? A man, middle-aged. That was about all he could remember.

The man behind the counter put down his paper and strolled across to where Ross was standing just inside the entrance. 'Can I help you, mate?'

Ross looked up. 'Yuh . . . you Danny Fitt?'

The man's expression didn't change. 'Not here, guv.'

'Pity . . .' Ross said. 'I was going to put some dough his way.'

The man's face remained flat. 'Can I give him a message?' he asked.

'No . . . I don't think so.'

'Hang about. Don't I know you?' he asked suspiciously.

'You know a mate of mine . . .' Ross told him. 'Ralph Veneker. You're Fitt . . . aren't you?'

'You know how it is,' Fitt said.

'No . . . tell me how it is, Danny? My name's Ross.'

'Got it. Frank Ross.'

'Are you ready to listen?'

'Sure. You got some dosh to put my way, you said.'

'What's the S.P. on an ex-cozzer called Hallam? Big Ralph says he was a D.S. ten years ago at Vine Street.'

'Yeah . . . Hallam . . . Ray . . . no.' Fitt clicked his fingers '*Roy* Hallam.'

'You know him?'

'Used to. He put his papers in . . . D.I. then . . . going places . . . big surprise.'

'When was this?'

'About a year before I got the poke . . . seven . . . eight years back . . .' he made a near enough movement with his hand.

'Eight years.'

'That's right . . .' Fitt nodded to himself. 'Just about the time Ralph was done . . . maybe just before . . . I could find out exactly . . .'

Ross took five five-pound notes and tucked them into Fitt's jacket pocket. 'There's another pony when you've got the lot on Hallam.'

'How soon do you want this?'

'Yesterday.'

'That might come a bit more expensive,' Fitt smiled.

Ross's face was cold. He looked around the hall. 'This your place?'

'I rent it.'

'Good business?'

'It's a living.'

'How long have you known Big Ralph?'

'On and off a few years. Why?'

'Have you ever seen him when he's cross?'

'No.' Fitt looked suddenly uneasy.

'Frightening,' Ross said. 'He wrecks places. Ten minutes in here . . . chaos.'

'Okay. Point taken,' Fitt shrugged. 'Twenty-five. Where can I get hold of you . . . later on?'

The half-memory of the old VW had bugged him all through

the afternoon. He knew himself well enough, at least in this area, to know that he was prone to hyper-suspicion but the more he thought about it, the more certain he became.

Driving across Putney Heath he glanced several times in the mirror but there was nothing following. He turned right taking the near-deserted Telegraph Road. On either side of the road the trimmed hulks of elm, vandalized in Dutch Elm panic by the local council, lay like giants fallen in some monstrous battle. Quite definitely no one was following him.

He circled the heath again and came up Wildcroft Road. Then pulled to the side and killed the lights.

Frank Ross walked across the spongy heathland to the big house overlooking the summer pitch of the Putney Cricket Club. How the poor live, he thought, as he pressed the entry phone bell and heard Anne's voice.

'Frank . . .' he said.

She pressed the buzzer and he pushed the door. The staircase was carpeted warm and redolent of that special upper middle luxury that say, Chris Cottle, just missed. He reached the door of the flat.

Anne was waiting. He found that for a moment Cimmie Vincent, McGrath, trailing Volkswagens, even eight years of imprisonment were momentarily banished from his mind. She stood in the doorway, tall, slim, and somehow clean in her desire to be just with him, clear in what she wanted from this world, straight in the way he knew he could never be.

'Dinner,' she said, 'is damn nearly served.'

He closed the door behind him. 'You have such delicate ways of reminding me that I'm almost an hour late.'

'Ten minutes more and I should have been in bed.'

'Twenty minutes more and you will be,' he said. And immediately regretted saying it.

They went into the living-room and again he admired the light touch of Anne's friend. Without thinking he stopped at the leather porter's chair and ran his hand across the smooth tan leather back.

'Have you see Evie?' Anne asked, pouring him a drink.

'Of course.'

Unseen by him she raised her eyebrows at his response. 'And . . . how is she?'

He came round the chair and took the tumbler of whisky. 'I think . . .' he said slowly, 'she's incurable.' He paused. 'Or at least by the man who put her there in the first place.'

Grim-faced he lifted his glass and drank.

She watched him silently. 'And Paul?'

'We've arranged a . . . moratorium I think they call it. A truce. Or at least Chris has.'

'You want him with you.'

'Paul?'

She nodded.

'He's my *son* for Chrissake!' he exploded.

She put her own glass aside and took a cigarette. 'Isn't it time you gave up a few of the conventions?' she said evenly.

'What the hell does that mean?'

'It means time you gave up Frank Ross grassed bank robber seeks revenge . . . Frank Ross, doting father seeks unknown son . . .'

'You bitch!'

She shook her head calmly. 'No, Frank, I'm not being a bitch. I'm saying something that maybe no one else would dare to say to you. About Paul at least – if you've got something real going with Paul then for Chrissake work at it. If not – chuck it.'

'Chuck *him*?'

'*It*. The self-supporting dream. You're at the cross-roads, darling.' She paused. 'Are you hungry?'

He shook his head.

'Let's go to bed then,' she said.

He stared at her. 'Now . . .?'

'Now.'

'I haven't been to bed with a woman for eight years,' he said.

'Good.' She took his hand.

'After eight years it might not be . . .'

'Good,' she said decisively. 'When you fail, Frank, I want you to fail with me.'

He put his arms around her. 'You know what I think about you, don't you?'

'Tell me.'

'A lot.'

She dragged him towards the bedroom. 'In bed, Frank Ross,' she laughed, 'you're going to have to do a lot better than that!'

They had reached the bedroom door when the phone began to ring. She swung round, puzzled.

He crossed the room towards the phone.

'That might be for me,' he said.

She reacted instantly. 'For you. Here?'

'Important, Anne.'

Ross picked up the receiver.

'Danny Fitt . . .' the voice said on the line.

'What you got for me?' Ross glanced over his shoulder at Anne's tight face.

'Hallam put his papers in the week before you were nicked.' Fitt's voice breathed over the line. 'No one knows why. Apparently he said he had other business interests. He runs a hotel near Guildford. I've forgotten the address. And he's got a drum in town, Holland Park, mews house, paid for . . . and a tasty little bird to go with it . . .'

Anne stared at him from the bedroom door.

'Anything else?' Ross asked.

'For what it's worth,' Fitt said. 'The D.I. that nicked you, Bryce . . .'

'Yes?'

'Him and Hallam were close . . . very close. Came up together.'

Ross replaced the phone. Anne had already poured herself a large brandy. Flourishing it angrily she said. 'You gave someone this number?'

'It was important . . . I told you.'

'You *told* me . . . so that makes it all right?' she slopped brandy on the carpet.

'Jesus Christ!' he flared.

'You had no right . . . no bloody right! This place is private Frank . . . private.'

'Where are you going?'

Opening the door he glanced back at her.

'Frank . . .'

She crossed the room towards him. 'I'm sorry . . . I'm sorry, Frank . . . I didn't mean to . . . it's just this is the first time we've been alone and . . .'

'Sure.' His face was a flat mask.

'Are you coming back?'

He opened the outer door and stepped into the corridor.

'I wanted everything to be so . . .'

He hesitated. 'I think maybe it will be, Anne,' he said. And closed the door behind him.

Descending the deep carpeted stair Ross let himself out into the crisp air. The MG was parked past a clutch of trees down on the right. From some instinct or intuition he stopped and lit a cigarette, using the movements to scan the edges of the mist shrouded common. The Volkswagen was still somewhere in the back of his mind. He reached the MG, unlocked it and climbed in.

The car bucketed violently, pulling to the right. Braking he got out and inspected the tyre. As he thought the front right was flat to within an inch of the ground. There were lots of things he would have preferred to changing a tyre at that moment.

Shivering in his jacket he took the keys to the boot of the car. Goddam puncture . . . he fitted the key in the boot and turned it. Something stopped him opening it. Leaving the key in the lock he went back to the tyre and knelt down to examine it. Flicking his lighter he let the light travel round the rim. A two inch slash gaped like a wound in the rubber way above the tread. He shivered violently.

Backing from the car into the bushes he found a length of cut elm branch. The keys were still in the boot, illuminated faintly by the red rear lights. Like some French boule player he took two short paces forward and tossed the elm log in a long slow arc on to the MG's boot.

It erupted in a frightening blurt of fire and smoke that hurled him back into the bushes.

Rolling breathless among the wet undergrowth he lay there shaking. In the reassembling mist he could just see the mangled outline of the car. He found he desperately needed a cigarette. Fumbling about in his pockets, he found a packet. His hands were still shaking as he pushed open the packet and drew one out. He could feel the damp seeping through his trouser leg as he lay in the grass. A match. He felt in his pockets. Nothing. Chances were, he wheezed with silent laughter, the car lighter wouldn't work either.

He looked up at the surrealistic mass of the car. The cigarette drooped on his lip. Out of the mist a small round figure was crossing the road from the common beyond.

Frank Ross eased himself silently to his feet, his concentration totally on the figure circling the wreck of the MG not fifteen yards from him. A torchlight flicked on and probed the tangled metal. Ross moved forward.

The torch beam described a half-circle round the wreck. Then clicked off. At that second Ross's full weight hit him somewhere above the kidneys in a shoulder charge that shattered George Smith's face against the jagged metal of the MG. Lifted by the back of his jacket and hurled back into the mass of oil fumes and hot metal George Smith had no chance to regain consciousness.

He awoke with strange searing sensations around his nose and mouth ... the sweet clogging of blood in his throat ... intense pains in his shoulder and chest ... before he opened his eyes he knew he had failed.

A torch flashed over him and away. He opened his eyes. He was in the back seat of his own Volkswagen half propped against the nearside rear door. A uniformed constable was flashing a torch ... two other uniformed men were coming forward with a stretcher. His eyes focused on the steering wheel across the back of the driver's seat. Taped to it was a large white envelope. He grimaced painfully remembering that it was the envelope McGrath had given him with the photograph and biographical details of Frank Ross.

Frank Ross! The uniformed bearers were setting up the stretcher outside the car. Ross! He remembered now that he had woken up before. And Ross was wiring plastic explosive to his wrists and ankles – his own plastic 808! And he had talked.

About McGrath. About contracts he had taken from him in the past.

Blood was running freely down both sides of his face. The ambulance men were folding red blankets on the stretcher. At least for the three girls the next year's school fees were already taken care of . . .

CHAPTER TWELVE

UNSHAVEN, his clothes stained with blood and motor oil, Frank Ross stood in the doorway as the early morning secretaries clicked past on high heels towards the bus stops and tube stations that would take them to the City and the West End.

When the inconspicuous blue Ford drew up on the corner he ducked his head and saw with relief the big, slightly wild outline of Ralph Veneker's huge head. Pushing through the stream of office workers he ran across the road and climbed into the car.

Veneker side-glanced him. 'You look done in, son.'

'Yeah. I am.'

Ross reached up and took the cigarette from Veneker's mouth.

'Where to?' Veneker said.

'Just drive.'

'Chris rang . . . he's been goin' spare lookin' for you.'

Veneker produced a half bottle of Scotch from his pocket and passed it to Ross.

'McGrath put a notice on me,' Ross told him flatly.

'He what?'

'A maniac called Smith . . . wired my motor up.'

Ross unscrewed the gold cap of the Scotch bottle and took a long gulp. For a moment he let the bottle rest on his lips. Then he took another gulp. 'McGrath's used him before, he topped a face called Pullar in Newcastle three years back, and a villain called Gaunt . . .'

'Ronnie Gaunt?'

'Know him?'

Veneker shrugged. 'I know he disappeared last year. Where's this 'eadcase now? You didn't . . . Frankie, you didn't . . .'

'I turned him in . . . with all the details.'

'Thank Christ! I thought you might have buried 'im. Does McGrath know it all went bad on him?'

'If he doesn't he soon will.'

'Chris said the law were round looking for you.'

'When?'

'Early. He told me to tell you a bird called Anne's with him . . . in a bit of a state.'

Ross looked puzzled. 'You know where Chris lives?'

'The scream's on for you, Frank . . . they'll be watching it.'

'Maybe.'

Veneker glanced at Ross's haggard, unshaven face. 'Okay, mate, he said. 'Just tell me what you want me to do.'

Christie Bryce left the station and walked down the High Street. He was a man accustomed to cover even the smallest and least important of his tracks so he had already provided himself with an excuse to be walking down to the Post Office to make a phone call – he had a present to buy for his sister who lived in Scotland – and he had just remembered he had promised to phone the garage about the estimate on his car. Many professions would have considered the precaution unnecessary – but Detective Superintendent Inspectors do not often use public phone boxes twenty-five yards from their own office.

Bryce slipped into the Post Office and headed for the bank of phone boxes.

'Hullo, guv . . .' It was young Harper from his own team.

He had been right to prepare his excuse. He grimaced and looked at his watch. 'Promised I'd phone the bloody garage half an hour ago.' He opened the phone-box door.

'That's half an hour they could be working on the car.'

Harper smiled and went to the counter for his stamps. Behind him Bryce dialled and waited while the ringing tone droned on. When he heard Hallam answer he pushed ten pence hard into the slot. 'Is McGrath out of his bloody mind?' he said without introduction.

'Brycey?' Hallam's voice sounded confused.

'McGrath put a notice on Frank Ross – a man called Smith,' Bryce snapped.

'I had nothing to do with that.' In Hallam's voice confusion gave way to panic.

'You knew about it?' Bryce watched young Harper leave the stamp counter.

'I told Tony I didn't want any part of it,' Hallam protested.

'The senseless bloody moron.'

On the other side of the line Hallam lowered his voice. 'Is Ross dead?'

'Dead!' Bryce said scornfully. 'Of course he's not dead. A CI team have had this Smith for over an hour. Ross delivered him to a nick like a bag of dirty laundry. Smith's already admitted two other contract killings for that madman, McGrath.'

'Christ! What are we going to do?' Hallam croaked.

'This time you're on your own,' Bryce said.

'I swear to you . . . this is all down to McGrath.'

'If I had any sense,' Bryce said bitterly, 'I'd be making a statement upstairs right now.'

'You wouldn't do that.'

Bryce pushed another ten pence piece into the slot. 'No . . . it's too bloody late . . . eight years too late. I should have turned you in . . . I always did hate bent coppers.'

'You hated Frank Ross more.'

'There's a warrant out for McGrath's arrest,' Bryce's voice was suddenly tired. He felt weary at the muck he had to wade through to do his job as he saw it.

'Does he know?' Hallam was asking. 'Does McGrath know?'

'And Pavey,' Bryce added. 'There's a warrant for him too.'

'For Chrissake . . . have you told them?'

'I don't talk to excrement like McGrath and John Pavey.'

'If they pull Tony we're all in it.' Hallam's hand was shaking on the phone.

'You better get your tail wagging then,' Bryce said and dropped the receiver on to the phone-rest.

Veneker kept to the sidestreets, powering the car round corners, keeping a firm grip on the wheel. For some moments Ross had said nothing, slumped down, his head against the back of his seat. From time to time he lifted the whisky bottle and took a sip.

'Anything from Danny Fitt?'

Ross struggled up in his seat. 'He did his piece.'

'What did he have to say?'

'Bryce and Hallam came up through the job like Siamese twins, boys in blue together.'

Veneker frowned. 'Don't mean a thing, Frank.'

'Maybe not. But Hallam put his papers in just six days before Bryce nicked us. And now, surprise surprise, retired Detective Inspector Hallam is very close with Tony McGrath.'

'*That* looks better,' Veneker acknowledged. 'What's Hallam do now?'

Ross screwed the cap back on the whisky. 'Runs a hotel near Guildford. Bought his bird a mews house in Holland Park. He's there now.'

'So . . . it's visiting day?'

Ross nodded. 'I want to know why he resigned.'

'We goin' to ask him?' Veneker smiled. 'Nicely of course!'

In Tony McGrath's flat the phone rang. Leaning forward towards the bathroom mirror McGrath ran his razor from his sideboard down his jowl and reached out with his free hand for the bathroom extension. 'Yes, who is it?' he grunted trying to calculate the precise cut for the other sideboard.

'Tony . . .?'

McGrath recognized Hallam's voice. 'What do *you* want?'

'You alone?'

'I don't usually invite an audience to watch me shave.'

'Get out of there, Tony . . .' Hallam's voice sounded strange.

McGrath held the razor poised. 'Are you pissed?'

'They're on their way with a 'W' for you and Pavey.'

McGrath tossed aside the razor. 'Give me that again? A warrant?'

'That genius you put on Frank Ross – he wasn't up to it.'

'Where did you get this from?'

'Bryce just called me . . .' Hallam spoke fast now. 'Your man dropped it . . . Ross got hold of him, dumped him at a nick. A

CI team have been getting his life story for the past hour. He grassed on you and Johnno for two more on top of Ross.'

McGrath wiped his face with a towel. 'Get hold of Johnno ...' he said, 'go to his kennel, he never answers the phone this early. Tell him to meet me at the shop.'

'Where?'

'The *shop*.'

'Where's that?' Hallam asked.

'He knows,' McGrath snapped. 'And you bottle on me now, Roy, and the two sides of your body won't match.'

McGrath hooked up the bathroom wall phone and reaching down, grabbed up his shirt. He was pulling it on as he ran quickly into the bedroom. From a drawer he took a shoulder holster and strapped it on, pushing his shirt untidily into the waistband of his trousers.

Then he turned, snatching up a leather jacket from the back of a chair and ran into the living-room. From a safe he took three small notebooks which he shoved into his pocket. Stepping through into the kitchen he opened the freezer. From a plastic box he took a solid wad of five thousand pounds in twenty pound notes. Then he ran for the front door. The whole process had taken less than one minute.

Frank Ross left Ralph Veneker in the car and emerged from the sidestreet opposite Chris Cottle's back garden wall. Glancing quickly each way he jumped up catching the far edge of the brickwork and hauled himself over. Moving quickly down the path he reached the french windows.

In the living-room Chris Cottle and Anne heard the gentle tap-tapping. Getting up quickly Cottle entered the bedroom to see the dishevelled figure and unshaven face of Ross standing outside the window.

He slipped the latch. 'Jesus Christ,' he said. 'Do you *know* what you look like?'

Ross ignored him. 'Is Anne still here?'

Cottle nodded towards the living-room. 'In there.' He felt the anger rising inside him.

Ross entered the living-room as Anne got to her feet. She ran forward white-faced and threw her arms round him. 'Christ,' she sobbed, 'what happened? Last night I heard the explosion. I thought you were dead.'

He held her at arms' length. 'I'm okay, Anne.'

'Everything'll be all right, Anne,' Cottle leaned against the doorway, mimicking Ross's tone.

Ross turned his head angrily towards Cottle. 'What the hell's that supposed to mean?'

'What do you think, you bastard?' Cottle exploded. 'We've both been going out of our minds – your motor blown to pieces, the law banging on the door. We didn't know if you was alive or dead. You could have contacted one of us.'

'Look, I don't need a hard time from you . . .' Ross began, furious. Anne came forward between them.

'You've got to stop, Frank . . .' she was close to hysterics, 'you've got to stop before you *are* killed.'

'She's right,' Cottle said. 'Just look at you, for Chrissake!'

'I can't . . . not now . . . I'm too close,' Ross faced them, snarling.

'That's the closest you're ever going to get to finding yourself bleedin' dead. Why is the scream on for you?'

'I don't have time.' He turned to Anne. 'Go back to the flat, Anne – no one knows about it but us – I'll meet you there. Take her, Chris, stay with her.'

'What if I say no,' Cottle said. 'What if for once someone says no to Frank Ross.'

'Just *do it*, Chris!' Ross flared.

'Don't go, Frank . . . don't go,' Anne grabbed at his arm. He shook it off and walked quickly out of the room.

'Frank,' she screamed.

Cottle held her back. His face was white with anger. 'Easy, love.'

'The bastard! The selfish bastard.' She collapsed into a chair.

Chris Cottle stood looking down at her. 'Come on, love,' he said after a moment. 'Let's get you to this flat.'

Outside the motor showroom a car skidded into the

forecourt. The two salesmen polishing the already impeccable new Rover stopped open-mouthed as three men raced towards the showroom, burst through the door and made for the stairs to McGrath's flat.

Seconds later, polishing cloths still in their hands, they heard the splitting wood of a door being forced. 'Police?' one of the salesmen said to the other.

'I bleedin' well hope so,' his friend said as one of the men came racing down the stairs and out to the car waiting on the forecourt.

Inspector Gaydon reached the police car and grabbed at the RT handset. 'McGrath's blown,' he said breathlessly. 'Left in a hurry. Looks like he must have known we were on our way.'

Less than half a mile away Roy Hallam slowed his car to a halt as he approached John Pavey's block of flats. Getting out he walked quickly round the bonnet to examine his front near-side tyre. He had already seen the black car with the driver waiting outside and knowledge and instinct combined to tell him that it was police. He kicked the tyre a couple of times and shrugged. Then got back into the car and drove on.

In the third floor flat where John Pavey sat on the side of the bed in his blue underpants faced by Detective Sergeant Bell and two officers. 'At least,' he said plaintively, 'at least let me put some Jekylls on.'

'Get on with it,' Bell said. While Pavey dressed he went into the living-room and picked up the phone and dialled. After a moment he said, 'Bell here. Let the guv know we've got Pavey. No trouble, he was in kip.'

In the bedroom Pavey had pulled on a pair of trousers and a polo-necked sweater. The two officers watched him as he sat on the bed putting on his shoes.

Suddenly he propelled himself off the edge of the bed and butted one of them in the stomach. As he went down with a groan, Pavey swung the brass bedside lamp at the other officer catching him high on the side of the head. Then rolling backwards across the bed he regained his feet and dragged open the sliding glass doors to the balcony.

For a fraction of a second he hesitated at the twenty-foot

drop, then he leapt the balcony and hit the soft ground of the rose bed at the back of the flats.

Haring straight across the lawn Pavey reached the road that ran down the side of the block waving his arms at an approaching car.

The driver braked hard. 'What's the trouble?'

He had no time to react as Pavey pulled open his door, knotted his fingers in the man's hair and dragged him viciously out on to the road.

Veneker's car pulled into the neat pink and white painted mews. 'Choice,' Veneker said.

Ross nodded. 'Only to be afforded by bent coppers and bank directors.'

Veneker pulled the car to the side of the cobbled road and checked the number. 'That's the one, over there. Bijou love nest. Have it away in peace and quiet. No smell of traffic fumes – or the great unwashed.'

They got out and walked to the door. Ross lifted the fancy brass knocker and let it drop. He shrugged and Veneker closed his fist and hammered three times.

After a moment the door was opened by a good looking girl in her late twenties. She looked at Veneker then at Ross and frowned. 'Yes?'

'We want a word with Roy,' Ross said.

'Who are you?'

'Tony sent us.'

'Roy's in Guildford,' she said cautiously.

'You're telling fibs,' Veneker reached out and grabbed her arm.

'What the hell d'you think you're doing?' she spluttered as they pushed into the hall.

Ross raced up the stairs. A moment or two later he reappeared at the stairhead. 'Bring her up, Ralph. Nobody here.'

Veneker pushed her ahead of him up the stairs.

'What's your name, love,' Ross said, leaning over the banister.

She walked past him without answering. Ross followed her

into the living-room, Veneker a pace or two behind them.

'Now don't come the old acid with us,' Veneker said. 'Frank here asked your name. 'Let's have it, love, unless you want to get fitted for dentures.'

'Jean,' she said.

'Okay, Jean,' Ross took over. 'Now what time do we expect Roy back.'

'I told you – he's in Guildford.'

Below, Roy Hallam's car turned into the mews. Parking it in front of his house he got out and opened his front door. He had taken half a pace inside when a hand reached out for his coat collar and jerked him forward. Spun round and held in an armlock he was propelled up the stairs and thrust into the living-room.

'Who the hell are you two?' Before he had regained his balance Veneker twisted his arm high up his back.

'Who are you . . . what do you want?' he gasped.

'He doesn't know who we are, Ralph.'

Veneker levered Hallam's arm up further. 'Are you sure?'

'He's going to bust my bloody arm,' Hallam's face was contorted with pain.

'He tends to get a bit excited,' Ross nodded.

'Stop him, Ross,' Hallam screamed.

'He seems to know us after all, Frank.'

Ross opened the bedroom door and allowed Jean into the room. She was white-faced with fear. 'Who are they, Roy?'

'Friends and acquaintances . . .' Ross said. 'Right, Roy?'

Veneker thumped him in the back. 'Are you listening?'

'Let her go . . . she's no part of this,' Hallam said painfully.

'Part of what, Roy?' Ross lit a cigarette. 'Part of *what*?'

'Let her go,' Hallam said. 'Just let her go.'

'You animals!' Jean screamed at them, 'It takes two of you . . .'

Ross led her to an armchair and pushed gently. 'Sit down, Jean. You'll be all right. Big Ralph and I have got a problem . . . we thought Roy might be able to help us . . . it goes back a few years . . .'

'I don't know anything,' Hallam said sullenly.

'I haven't asked you anything yet.'

Again Veneker thumps him in the back. 'You're not listening again.'

'Eight years ago,' Ross said, 'you put your papers in – you resigned – what we want to know is *why*, Roy . . . why did you resign?'

'That's my business.'

Veneker chopped at the muscles of his neck. 'Wrong,' he shouted.

'Stop it for God's sake!' Jean came out of the chair.

Ross crossed to her and with one finger in her chest pressed her back again. 'Not enough money, Roy? Promotion too slow . . . not enough opportunity for someone with your – charisma?'

Hallam didn't answer. Ross fingered his expensive suède jacket.

'You like nice things . . . nice gear . . . nice wheels . . . accoutrements . . .'

Ross circled him menacingly. 'Smart little town address.' He looked at Jean. 'High class rattle. You definitely have taste.'

'I work hard for what I've got,' Hallam said.

'The hotel?'

'Yes.'

'You own it?' Ross asked.

'Not yet.'

'On a mortgage?'

'Isn't everything?' Hallam was beginning to recover from the initial shock.

'But you're doing all right?' Ross pressed him.

'I told you . . . I graft,' Hallam said.

Ross turned to Jean. Her face was covered in mascara tramlines. She was sobbing silently.

'Known him long, love?'

She took a deep breath and glanced at Hallam. 'Three years.'

'Is he going to marry you?' Ross asked lightly.

'What?' She frowned at the unexpected question.

'You know, make it legal . . . take you to see his old mum . . .

put up the banns . . . book the Co-op Hall for the knees-up . . . or is he just a muff artist?'

Jean looked appealingly towards Hallam.

'Leave her alone, Ross,' he said.

'Don't you want to marry him?' Ross persisted.

'Let her be,' Hallam shouted.

'I mean,' Ross said, 'look what you'd be getting. A lying . . . thieving . . . scheming . . . gutless douche-bag who'd sell his old mum for an ounce of burn.'

He turned to Hallam. 'Where did you get the money to even think about buying a hotel, Hallam? . . . Your police pension . . . premium bonds . . . or earners from Tony McGrath?'

'I saved it,' Hallam said.

'You couldn't save the price of a bunk-up. Why did you resign?'

'I told you . . .'

'You've been on Tony McGrath's books since you were a D.C. at Vine Street,' Ross said slowly. 'He had you straightened ten years ago.'

'No.'

'Yes, Roy. Every little number McGrath had going, he had you to give him the whisper when the law were getting too busy. You were his insurance. If anything did go wrong he had good old Roy to lay on a mug for a fitting, and your percentage came off the top.'

'You've got it all wrong, Ross.'

'How many Bank Accounts did you open, Roy . . . how many Building Societies know you under false names. How many fat brown envelopes did you find in your smother when you left a club or a restaurant?'

Hallam looked from Veneker to Ross. 'Listen . . .' he was making a massive effort, 'listen, you've got it wrong. All wrong.'

'And Bryce too,' Ross ignored him. 'Was he taking?' He looked at Hallam's face. 'No . . . not Brycey . . . he wouldn't take a bottle of cooking sherry at Christmas. But he sussed you, didn't he? . . . he found out his great mate was as bent as a butcher's hook. What did he say, Roy, when he found out you'd been on the bung from Tony McGrath ever since you put your funny hat in the bottom drawer?'

Before Hallam could answer the telephone rang. Ross turned quickly to Hallam. 'Answer it.'

'No way,' Hallam said. As he spoke his voice trailed away. Veneker had taken a knife from his pocket and pressed the blade against his neck.

Snatching up the receiver Ross held it for Hallam to speak, leaning close to listen himself.

'Hello . . .' Hallam said, aware of the knife at his throat.

'Where's Johnno?' McGrath's voice came down the line.

'I . . . I don't know.'

'What do you mean you don't know,' McGrath shouted.

'I went to his place . . . like you said . . .'

'You give him my message?' McGrath demanded.

'He . . . wasn't there.' Hallam's eyes flickered from Veneker to Ross.

'Are you trying to con me, Roy . . . I warned you what would happen.'

'Pavey's been arrested,' Hallam blurted out.

Immediately the phone clicked dead.

'They've pulled Pavey?' Ross said, taking the receiver from him. Hallam nodded.

'Where's McGrath?'

'At the shop,' Hallam said. 'That's all he told me to tell Pavey – to meet him at the shop.'

'What shop . . . where?' Veneker grabbed his arm again.

'For God's sake!' Jean screamed, 'Don't!'

'I don't know . . . I swear to you, Ross, I don't know.' The sweat was pouring down Hallam's face.

A hammering on the door below made Veneker ease off, propelling Hallam to the side of the window.

'It's Pavey,' Hallam gasped looking down.

Ross grabbed him by the lapels. 'I thought you said he'd been nicked?'

'Listen,' Hallam said, 'keep that bear off me,' he glared at Veneker, 'and listen. The police were there, at Pavey's place. He must have got clear just before they arrived.'

The hammering continued below.

'You get down there,' Ross said, 'and give him McGrath's message.'

For a moment Hallam was about to refuse then he moved quickly down the stairs and opened the door.

'You took your piggin' time,' Pavey snarled stepping past him into the hall.

'I've got a message from Tony . . .' Hallam said quickly, 'he wants you to meet him at the shop.'

'Let's have your gun,' Pavey said.

'What?'

'Get me your shooter, for Chrissake!'

Hallam ran to the top of the stairs. As he turned Ross stood on the landing, out of sight of Pavey. He covered Hallam with a gun and held out a second .38 to Hallam. Hallam took it and returned downstairs. He knew there was no time to warn Pavey and get a round in the breech before Ross could step to the head of the stairs.

'I need your car,' Pavey said, holding his hand out for Hallam's keys. With a scowl Hallam took his keys from his pocket.

Pavey took the keys from Hallam and threw his own keys to the stolen car at Hallam's feet. 'That motor outside . . . dump it.' He turned away then and paused at the mews door.

'When Tony and me get this sorted,' he said, '. . . you better not be around any more . . . that is if you don't want to end up lookin' like a butcher's shop.'

He slammed the door behind him.

From the living-room window Ross watched Pavey get into Hallam's car. Then as it began to move away he took the keys from Veneker and ran quickly out into the mews.

At the flat Anne finished her fourth cup of coffee and grimaced at Chris Cottle. 'I can't see a brandy doing me much harm at this stage. How about you, Chris?'

'I'll have a Scotch then.' He got up and paced the room. 'How long does Frank expect us to lock ourselves up here?' he exploded.

She handed him the Scotch. 'I've been thinking about it, Chris. Very carefully. Do you think he's sick?'

'He's obsessed, love. That's sick.'

She sat on the arm of a chair and swirled her brandy in the glass. 'You've tried to persuade him I suppose, Chris . . .'

Cottle nodded. 'The first day he got out we met at the house . . . I tried to reason with him then . . . but . . . he just shut off . . . shut me out.'

'I can't get near him any more either. You'd think he'd be trying to pull his life together not destroy what he has left.'

Cottle began walking the room again. 'He was shattered when he saw Evie . . . I think that finished him. He just couldn't take the responsibility for it. Men like Frank need to pass the buck. Sitting there eight years inside he passed it to whoever grassed him. If he hadn't chased him down the moment he came out it would have been like admitting what happened to Evie was his own fault.' He paused. 'Which is what it was.'

'What about Paul?' Anne asked quietly.

'The kid's all screwed up. Anyway . . . he's not a kid any more. I think Frank was expecting an eight-year-old . . . someone he could play football with on the back lawn.'

'Do you think it's too late . . . too much has happened . . . to both of them?'

'I don't know, Anne,' he said gloomily. 'I don't know what to think no more. Paul wanted to go back . . . live with Frank . . . at the house . . . the kid was desperate . . .'

'What did Frank say to him? He agreed, didn't he?'

Cottle shook his head bitterly. 'I don't even think he was listening.'

At the wheel of Veneker's Ford Ross maintained his distance behind Hallam's car. Through the Fiat's square rear window he could see the back of Pavey's shoulders. He was driving fast but not too fast to attract police attention.

As they approached an intersection, however, Pavey changed lanes, sliding left of a long articulated lorry and jumping the lights on the change.

There was no way Ross could get through. On the other

hand, he was fairly certain that Pavey had acted from the need to save time rather than because he was aware of being followed.

Jumping out of the car Ross stood straining to see through the stream of cars and trucks passing across the intersection. Through a gap between two lorries he thought he saw the green Fiat turning left about a hundred yards ahead.

The lights began to change again. Jumping back into Veneker's car Ross gunned it forward as the traffic began to move. He knew now that only luck would enable him to pick up Pavey again.

A hundred yards past the intersection he swung left and travelled the length of a dull South London street of terraced houses. At the bottom he was stopped by a railway line which gave him a choice only of right or left. A derelict bottling plant on the right seemed to give way to a large weed-covered open patch. He turned left and followed another street of terraced houses parallel to the railway line.

It was a play street, marked off and painted with an enormous jubilee hopscotch from the summer's celebrations. Tattered ends of bunting still hung from the lamp-posts. Five small black kids with crash helmets big enough to unbalance them were skate-boarding back and forth across the road.

Ross pulled up. 'Hey – d'you see a green car come along here just now? Going pretty fast!'

The answer was immediate from the biggest child, speaking from under a huge red helmet. 'Nearly had Peter off his board,' he said indignantly. 'Went down Ramsden Road.' He pointed.

Ross thanked him and put the car into gear. Sixty yards ahead he turned into a cul-de-sac. The green Fiat stood outside a long disused Sunlight laundry.

In the empty flat above the laundry Tony McGrath crouched on the floor, the phone to his ear. Forcing back the panic that rose inside him he snapped into the receiver. 'Three poxy hours! Listen, Artie, tell him there's another monkey in it for him if he can make it earlier. Ring me back as soon as you've spoken to him.'

He slammed down the phone and got to his feet. He stared

for a moment at the bare, dust-covered room, the phone wire trailing across the floor – and thought of all he had built up in the last eight years – and all that had collapsed in the last eight hours.

Downstairs he heard a step in the echoing rooms and then a voice calling his name. He took the gun from his pocket and moved quietly on to the landing. He could have sworn it was John Pavey's voice.

Then again. 'Tony – it's Johnno . . .'

McGrath felt a surge of relief. Pavey was standing at the bottom of the stairs.

'What happened for Chrissake? That lying stump Hallam said you'd been nicked.'

Pavey came up the stairs grinning. 'I was,' he said.

McGrath looked at him in admiration. 'You legged it?'

'Over the balcony. Twenty-five foot into the flower bed. I thought I was going to do myself in. Got any fags?'

McGrath gave him a cigarette and light.

'So where do we go from here, Tony,' Pavey said. 'I got a shooter and a car – and that's me bleedin' lot.'

In the old laundry below Frank Ross moved forward across the concrete floor. From the bottom of the stairs he could hear clearly the voices above.

'Artie's laying on a plan to get us to Ireland,' McGrath's voice said.

'Where from?' Pavey asked.

'Near his place in Kent . . .' McGrath said. Shouldn't take mor'n an hour.'

'Let's get moving then.'

Ross took the last stairs three at a time bursting into the room with the gun in his hand. 'Back against the wall,' he snarled.

McGrath spun on Pavey. 'Bleedin' amateur! He must have followed you here.'

'Open your jacket . . . slowly . . .' Ross said.

Both McGrath and Pavey saw his hand trembling on the gun. Neither mistook his white face and trembling hand for fear.

'The pieces come out...' Ross whispered, 'thumb and forefinger...'

'Frank, I can...' McGrath stopped. Lifting out his gun he dropped it on the floor.

'And you,' Ross hissed. Pavey took his gun and tossed it down rattling across the floor to stop beside McGrath's.

'Hands in your pockets... trouser pockets.'

'Hallam told you – right,' Pavey said.

'Right,' Ross smiled grimly.

'You should've dumped that gutless slag eight years ago.'

Pavey turned on McGrath.

'Except it wasn't that simple, was it, Tony... if Bryce had turned him in, he knew enough for you to draw ten.'

'He told you?' McGrath looked baffled. 'Hallam *told* you?'

'I knew. I put the pieces together.'

'You should've bricked that bastard Hallam up somewhere,' Pavey exploded.

'Tell him, Tony,' Ross said.

McGrath shrugged. 'We can come to some arrangement... surely, Frank.'

Ross's face set. 'Tell him or I'll blow your face off.'

Again his hand began to tremble. McGrath knew that he was within an ace of losing all control. He turned to Pavey. 'Bryce was too close... he knew the lot... if Roy so much as cut himself shaving he'd have pulled me.' He faced Ross appealing, 'It was you or me, Frank.'

'You filth,' Ross whispered.

'You know Bryce,' McGrath said desperately. 'You know what he's like... he's sick... he wanted you so bad he'd have done anything.'

'Even deal with a dreck like you.'

'What could I do? Christ Almighty, what could I do? Roy told him I knew about your job... after that what could I do?'

'You stinking grass.' The gun waved wildly in Ross's hand.

'It was Bryce not me...' McGrath backed against the wall. 'He used me... he used me, Frank, to get you.'

'I bet he really had to hard sell it to you.'

'I didn't want no part of it . . .' McGrath pleaded, 'on my mother's eyes, Frank.'

'What a chance . . . for a dog with ambition like you, Tony . . . what a stitch-up . . . walk away from a sure ten stretch *and* do up Frankie Ross . . . You couldn't resist it. And no one knew . . . all these years, no one knew *who* . . . who or *why*.' Ross thumbed back the hammer of the gun very deliberately.

'Hate.' Ross spat out. 'Hate. That's all that kept me going. Every night I dreamed about this moment.'

'Don't . . . don't . . . don't . . .' McGrath begged him. 'Don't kill me, Frank. You can have anything . . . name it . . . just name it.'

'My wife back?'

'I never knew then that it would . . .'

'My son,' Ross shouted.

'Jesus Mary,' McGrath whimpered.

'Eight years of my life,' Ross screamed in his face.

From the floor the phone rang loud in the unfurnished room. In the fraction of a second in which Ross's attention was diverted, McGrath acted, ramming his shoulder into Pavey's back, pitching him forward as Ross fired.

The explosion filled the bare room, the bullet embedding itself in the door as McGrath in a blubbering panic lashed out with his foot and sent the gun spinning from Ross's hand. Hurling himself across the floor McGrath grabbed the gun and fired wildly.

As Ross scrambled for the other gun McGrath watched in horror as his second shot hurled Pavey backwards across the room. Then stumbling to his feet he ran from the room.

The phone had stopped ringing. Ignoring Pavey's screams of pain, Ross stumbled to his feet out on to the landing. He could hear McGrath's footsteps running for the back of the shop.

Hurling himself down the bare wooden stairs he ran into one room, saw there was no exit, spun round and back into the corridor and saw the open door ahead.

Bursting through it he found himself in a narrow, dustbin-lined service alley. As he turned, McGrath's Buick, almost as wide as the alley itself, powered at him, slamming him against the wall as the wing caught his hip.

Slumped on the damp cobbles Frank Ross watched the big car scatter dustbins as it blurted down the alley and out into the street.

The dull ache in his hip was tolerable. Tolerable compared to the bitter disappointment that flooded him. He dragged himself to his feet and leaned against the door jamb. Upstairs he could hear Pavey's muffled sobbing.

Holding his hip he walked slowly back into the laundry and climbed the stairs. Pavey lay in the corner of the room, blood staining the bare floorboards and speckling the white telephone.

'For God's sake, Ross,' he gasped. 'Get an ambulance.'

Blood spilled into his mouth. He spat it out. Ross looked down coldly. 'Who's Artie?' he said.

'I'm bleeding to death, for Chrissake.'

Ross knelt down beside him. 'You will do if I don't ring three nines. Where's McGrath heading. Who's Artie?'

He lifted the phone and leaned next to Pavey's face. 'Who's Artie?'

Pavey looked up at him, his eyes glazing. 'Find out,' he said and bubbled blood across his lips.

Ross looked down at his slumped figure and dialled. 'Ambulance,' he said into the receiver as the operator's voice answered.

The ambulance nosed its way through the crowd which had gathered round the old laundry. 'For God's sake,' Detective Sergeant Bell said to one of the uniformed policemen, 'See if you can get me some elbow room.'

As the uniformed coppers began to ease the crowd back Bell addressed himself to the green Fiat parked outside the laundry. The car keys, taken from Pavey's pocket, opened the driving door. Bell turned as Inspector Gaydon approached. 'Any luck?' Gaydon asked.

'This is the one. I'll get it checked out.'

Gaydon nodded. 'Upstairs,' he said, 'as they were carting Pavey away, the phone rang.'

'Yuh . . .?'

'It was Frank Ross.'

'Ross? Haven't they pulled him yet?'

Gaydon shook his head. 'CRO are checking on a face called "Artie" – known associate of McGrath. Ross reckons he's McGrath's contact to get out of the country.'

Inspector Alec Rimmer crossed the road to his car. As he drew the keys from his pocket he was aware of another car slowing towards him. Glancing up he saw a car bonnet draw level. Frank Ross was in the driving seat. He wound down the window. 'I want a word, Rimmer.'

Rimmer walked slowly round the back of his own car and bent to Ross's level.

'You've got a bleedin' neck, Ross. Everyone's looking for you.'

'So you found me . . .' Ross said calmly. 'Get in.'

Rimmer straightened up. 'I could pull you now.'

'Don't try it, Rimmer . . .' Ross said. 'I've things to say to you.'

Rimmer stood looking down at him.

'Give me ten minutes.'

Without answering Rimmer walked round the car and climbed into the passenger seat. 'Okay,' he said as Ross pulled away. 'What is it?'

'I know who grassed on me, Rimmer,' Ross said. '. . . and I know why.'

Ross pulled the car up in an underpass, waiting for Rimmer's reaction.

'You're mad, Ross . . .' Rimmer said at length, 'insane . . . is that what all this is about. You'd get yourself blown to pieces for the name of a snout. You've got a sick wife . . . a son . . . the stink of the nick still on you and all you care about is some pathetic little hound eight years ago who grassed you for a few quid.'

Ross gave him a cigarette and lit it. Lighting his own he said, 'Is that what Bryce told you?'

'Bryce told me nothing,' Rimmer said flatly. 'Even you know him better than that.'

'You were his sergeant at the time.'

'It was his snout . . . I never asked. You know the way things work.'

'McGrath,' Ross said quietly.

'What?' Rimmer turned in his seat.

'It was Tony McGrath.'

Rimmer shook his head. The heavy traffic thundered past them.

'Are you going to listen,' Ross demanded.

'To crap like that?'

'Remember Hallam?' Ross said.

'Roy Hallam?'

'That's the one. Came up with Bryce.'

Rimmer nodded.

'Friend of Tony McGrath,' Ross said.

Rimmer smiled coldly. 'What are you trying to lay on me, Ross?'

'The truth . . . if you've got the stomach for it. Hallam had been on earners from Tony McGrath since he was at Vine Street . . . Bryce found out . . . was going to turn him in – Hallam knew enough to put McGrath away for ten. Are you listening?'

Rimmer nodded. 'I'm listening.'

'Someone had put the whisper in,' Ross continued. 'The whisper to McGrath about my arrangements. He knew that Bryce wanted me so bad he might . . . negotiate. They did a deal . . . Hallam resigned quietly, Bryce got me bang to rights.'

'Bryce wouldn't do that.'

'You know how bad he wanted me.'

'He still wouldn't deal with scum like McGrath.'

'Okay. Why do you think McGrath sent that headcase after me?'

Rimmer didn't reply.

'And who do you think got word through Hallam to McGrath that there was a "W" out on him this morning and arresting officers were on their way?'

'I don't need any more of this. Drop me off.'

'Can't take it, Rimmer!' Ross jeered.

'There's nothing to take,' Rimmer said. 'Drive.'

Ross drove forward for a few hundred yards before turning right again into the shopping centre where Rimmer had left his car. Braking, he half turned in his seat watching Rimmer's face.

'What else you got, Ross?' Rimmer asked at length.

'They've just found Pavey with a bullet in his belly . . .' Ross said quietly. 'With Hallam's gun . . . driving Hallam's car!'

Rimmer lifted his head and listened impassively with his lips pursed almost as if he was listening to a guide at an art gallery.

'Give me an hour . . . one hour,' Ross said urgently, 'with you forgetting who Bryce *was* . . . what you *thought* he was!'

He took out his hand-gun and held it out to Rimmer. 'Or pull me now and I'll take my chance with the rubber heels!'

Rimmer took the gun from him and climbed wordlessly out of the car.

At the information room New Scotland Yard the bearded officer punched out the car number which Sergeant Bell had just phoned through. As the last item of the Fiat's number was registered the television monitor filled with data.

Into his mouthpiece the officer read: 'R. G. Hallam, Sandfords Hotel, Guildford. Registration details?'

'That's fine,' Bell said and put through a call to Sandfords Hotel.

As Gaydon hurried into the room Bell was replacing the receiver.

'The car?' Gaydon asked.

Bell nodded. 'R. G. Hallam, Guildford Hotel owner. He's in London somewhere apparently.'

'Helpful. What about the gun?'

'Two sets of prints – they're checking now . . .'

'And the mysterious Artie?'

'Bingo.'

'You mean we struck lucky at something.'

'Arthur Frederick Finn. Got more form than Arkle. Owns a fibreglass pond factory in Kent. I put a call through to the local Swedes – they're on their way there now.'

Alec Rimmer watched the grey-brown water swirl through the rotting wooden piers and wondered if it had always been like that. Three hundred years ago it had been pale blue and sparkling with jumping fish and green water meadows linking its banks? He looked up at the mass of weeping nineteenth-century brickwork with disgust. Factories, chimneys, smoke, grime, villains like Frank Ross and Tony McGrath.

A man moved into his distant line of vision. Rimmer turned his head slightly to watch Detective Chief Inspector Christie Bryce hurrying along the bank towards him.

Rimmer shoved his hands miserably into his overcoat pocket and walked to meet him. 'Hullo, guv.'

'What's this all about?' Bryce stopped in front of Rimmer.

'I wanted a word . . . in private.'

Bryce looked round at the decaying factories along the river bank. 'This looks private enough.'

Rimmer nodded. 'They've got Pavey. He's in hospital. Shot . . . stomach wound.'

'What happened?'

'No one knows . . . yet . . .' Rimmer said. 'They're operating now.'

'What about McGrath?'

'Sounds like he's away.'

Bryce relaxed the tension in the muscles of his cheek.

'Someone blew in his ear,' Rimmer said flatly.

'And Ross?'

Rimmer shrugged. 'He could be anywhere.'

'I hope they bury him!'

Rimmer looked out across the river. 'Trouble is – it doesn't make sense, guv.'

'What doesn't?' There was a sharp edge in Bryce's voice.

'None of it . . . McGrath . . . Ross . . . none of it . . .'

'I thought we'd got past expecting normal human behaviour from animals like Ross and McGrath?'

'Maybe But there's something at the back of all this . . . something we missed eight years ago, guv.'

Byce looked at him suspiciously. 'You've got something on your mind, Alec?'

'Pavey made a sort of statement.'

'A *sort* of statement?'

'He was only half conscious.' Rimmer slapped at his leg with a rolled newspaper.

'What did he say?' The cold wind from the river slashed across Bryce's face. He clenched his fists in his topcoat pockets.

'I don't know exactly . . .' Rimmer said. 'But I've heard he kept on mentioning a name, kept on about . . . Hallam . . . Roy Hallam.'

Bryce was silent.

'I thought you'd like to . . . I mean I thought you'd want to know. Old mate of yours.'

'I haven't seen Roy Hallam in two years . . . over two years,' Bryce said.

'Sounds,' said Rimmer, 'as if some say . . .'

'He's involved with Pavey?' Bryce finished the sentence.

'And McGrath?'

'Involved? How . . .? . . . Hallam runs a successful hotel near Guildford. As far as I know he's never heard of Pavey.'

'Why did he resign, guv?'

'That was a long time ago, Alec.'

'He must have told you?'

Bryce leaned on the granite embankment. 'He hadn't been happy in the job for months. He didn't talk about it much but I could tell. The opportunity came up for the hotel – he saw his chance . . . took it – put his papers in . . . left quietly.'

'I remember . . . his team were a bit put out . . . Hallam didn't say much, didn't explain.'

'He was like that . . . you met him . . . he could be an awkward bugger.'

'They're going to pull him when they find him, guv.'

Bryce nodded slowly.

'This *is* private, guv . . .' Rimmer said. 'I just thought you'd want to know . . . maybe have a quiet word with him.'

'Thanks, Alec.'

'I'll keep in touch. There's a mate of mine on the CI team, he'll let me know any developments.'

'Yes . . . I'd like to know.' Bryce straightened up.

'Guv . . .'

Bryce stopped and half turned back to Rimmer. 'Something else?'

Rimmer hesitated – then shook his head.

'Sure?' Bryce was moving away.

'Sure.' Rimmer lifted his rolled newspaper in a feeble wave.

Bryce walked back to his car and stood beside it watching Rimmer's figure disappear between the huge lowering warehouses. Then he walked quickly across the road to the phone box.

In Hallam's sitting-room Veneker and Ross sat silently opposite Roy Hallam and his girl-friend. When the phone rang Hallam started slightly.

Ross got to his feet. Picking up the receiver he handed it without a word to Hallam.

Watched by the two men and the girl Roy Hallam licked his lips and ran the back of his hand across them. Lifting the receiver he said, 'Yes . . .' then in response to Ross's jabbing finger . . . 'Brycey? Is that you?'

On the table the spools of the tape recorder were already turning.

'Listen,' Bryce said, 'they've pulled Pavey . . . a bullet in his gut . . . before he went into surgery he made a statement . . . he mentioned you . . .'

Hallam said nothing.

'. . . you still there, Roy?' Bryce's voice came over the line.

'Are you sure about the statement?' Hallam pushed out the words.

'Alec Rimmer told me. They're going to pull you.'

Hallam looked up into the cold eyes of Frank Ross. Into the receiver he said: 'What do I do?'

'Get out of it.'

Ross scribbled on a pad and held it up in front of Hallam's face.

'Lose yourself for a few days.' Bryce said, 'get Jean to cover for you. I'll find out exactly what they've got. I'll contact you in a couple of days through Jean.'

Hallam read the name 'McGrath' on the pad. 'What about Tony?' he asked.

'From what Alec said it sounds like McGrath's away.'

Hallam nodded almost in tears. 'Thanks . . . thanks for the shout, Christie.'

In the phone box Christie Bryce shook with revulsion. 'I feel like I've been down a sewer,' he said, slamming down the phone.

The light plane bounced across the field and stopped near the two men standing by the American car.

'There you go then, Tony,' Artie Finn said.

McGrath nodded and began to jog-trot towards the plane. From beside the wing he yelled back at Finn. 'Dump the car for me, Artie.'

'Sure,' Finn waved as McGrath climbed into the plane. Standing in the wet field he watched it taxi into position, pause and ride in to the wind at full throttle. Within what seemed like fifty yards its tail rose and the wheel lifted from the ground.

Finn turned for the car to hear the shattering of timber across the field. Looking up he saw a police Rover bucking across the grass in a forlorn effort to prevent the take-off. A second Rover blocked any possibility of his own escape.

Inspector Alec Rimmer reached across the desk to switch off the tape recorder, pausing only to listen to Bryce's last muttered words: 'I feel like I've been down a sewer.'

Bryce sat motionless on the other side of his desk as Rimmer punched the 'off' button.

'You set me up, Alec,' he said at length.

Rimmer nodded sadly. 'I had to know, guv.'

Bryce sat silently for a few moments. 'Is Ross downstairs?'

'Interview room.'

Bryce hesitated. 'Mind if I see him?'

Rimmer shook his head. He found it difficult to speak.

Christie Bryce walked down the bare concrete staircase and through the entrance. He was vaguely aware of an attractive woman sitting on a wooden bench next to Ross's friend Chris Cottle.

'That,' Cottle whispered to her, 'is Bryce. The Man that put Frank away eight years ago.'

Bryce walked on and entered the interview room.

Frank Ross was sitting at the bare metal table smoking a cigarette. He looked up briefly as Bryce entered and dismissed the uniformed officer with a jerk of his head.

Bryce leaned against the wall. 'I'd do it again – all of it – to put you away.'

Ross looked at him. 'You're disgusting . . . do you know that . . . you nauseate me.'

Bryce snarled in contempt. 'You! You've got a bloody cheek. It's you, you and your sort that are the disease . . . a cancer . . . the only way to stop you spreading is to burn you out . . . cut you out!'

Ross laughed. 'Even when it means protecting a bent copper and a vicious slag like Tony McGrath.'

'In my book it was the only way.'

'I wonder if your guvnors will see it like that.'

Bryce pulled himself up, pride in what he was, in everything he'd done spilling out from every pore. 'Inside . . . where it counts, they will. They're police officers, not social workers . . . not gutless magistrates, not Hampstead radicals . . . they know, so does the man in the street, they know it's war . . . a different sort of morality.'

Ross lifted his head. 'Morality! How can you use that word without your teeth turning black? You're the most immoral man I've ever known. You know . . . in the nick . . . murderers . . . thieves . . . pimps . . . dopers . . . nonses . . . all the cons, all the "diseases", they all have one saving grace, a sort of common dignity, they know *what* they are, they're aware of what they've *done*, why they're away, but *you* . . you want to blame *me* for *your* corruption.'

Bryce leant towards him, theatening, menacing, hardly able to contain his loathing. 'You'll never change, you'll always be an animal, ruining other people's lives . . . your wife . . . your son . . . Billy . . . Cimmie Vincent. Everyone you touch is contaminated! You're a thief and a parasite, Ross, they'll have you away again – bank on it!' He spat out the last three words, spent, exhausted, his energy consumed by hate.

Ross looked up, almost shocked by the force of the other man's emotion, but confident that this time he was the master.

'No! Not this time, *copper*, this time it's your turn . . . you're going inside and do you know who's going to put you there? Not me, not Hallam, not McGrath, not Pavey, it won't be a face, it'll be another copper – Alec Rimmer. You see, he must have believed all that shit you pumped into him about morality.'

Silently, Bryce turned to go as Rimmer appeared in the doorway behind him and hesitated just for a moment when Ross called out, 'Open the window, Chief. I can't breathe! The air's got rather stale in here.'

Frank Ross walked out into the bleaked tiled entrance hall to see Anne rise from the bench seat. She took three steps forward and threw herself, sobbing into his arms.

'It's all right, love,' he said. 'It's going to be all right.'

Chris moved forward. 'The car's outside, mate. Come on let's get out of here.'

Outside the station Ross paused, savouring the noises, the smells, just the feeling of being free.

'Is it really all over, Frank?' Anne turned towards him, her whole body strained with fear.

'Not quite,' Frank answered quietly.

Chris jerked round. 'What do you mean?'

'They told me, Chris . . . Tony McGrath got away . . . clean out of the country.'

Chris tensed, waiting for the words he knew were coming. 'Don't worry, mate, they'll find him.'

Ross looked at both of them, realizing that in one way at least Bryce had been right. 'If they don't . . . I will!'

THE END

THE REPORTER BY PETER MAY

FIFTY OILMEN ESCAPE DEATH AS EXPLOSION DESTROYS RIG!

The headline screamed the news of the latest in a string of North Sea disasters, this one was unusual only in that nobody had died. The Government claimed they were simply unfortunate 'accidents'; but to Colin Anderson, investigative reporter for THE STANDARD, the 'accidents' turned out to be leads to one of the biggest international sabotage stories of all time – a hell-raising exclusive that was to endanger not only his life but the life of Janis Sinclair, his attractive young research assistant who'd somehow ingratiated herself into both his work and his feelings.

Based on the BBC television series 'The Standard'.
0 552 10692 5 85p

OUTSIDER IN AMSTERDAM BY JANWILLEM VAN DE WETERING

Sergeant de Gier and Adjutant Gripjstra's first adventure is a must for all fans of Maigret and Van der Valk. The author combines his background in Zen philosophy with his experience on the Amsterdam police force to create a devastatingly original and exciting plot that will keep the reader gripped all the way to its breathtaking climax.

'A strikingly original first novel . . . a couple of endearingly human policemen, an attractive murderer and a unique motive for murder.' *Daily Telegraph*

0 552 10600 3 65p

THE THIRD FORCE BY DENNIS SINCLAIR

International newsman Greg Ballard, bored with the daily routine of a desk job in New York, welcomed his new assignment in Europe . . . covering an explosive situation which could erupt into bloody civil war at any moment. When he started meeting contacts, asking questions and probing below the surface, Greg realized that a clandestine movement was at work – a 'third force' cynically bent on increasing the ever-present terror and violence to serve its own ends. . . .

Greg's journalist cover was almost perfect for the other role he was playing . . . a member of SURVIVAL – the secret international organization pledged to prevent the world from destroying itself. This particular corner of the world, Greg reckoned, was ripe for self-destruction.

0 552 10303 9 50p

DEATH AND BRIGHT WATER BY JAMES MITCHELL

THERE'S NO EASY RETIREMENT FOR A MAN LIKE CALLAN . . .

Callan's days with the Section were over, he'd had enough. But just when he'd found an escape from the killing and the violence, the mysterious Dr. Blythe appeared with a proposition – and Callan found he couldn't refuse. It looked like a simple kidnapping job – getting the beautiful Sophie Kollonaki's daughter out of Crete – but Sophie was involved with the KGB, and where they were, death was never far away. . . .

Callan and the faithful Lonely found themselves on the way to Crete before they began to suspect that there was more to this than anyone was letting on. . . .

0 552 10157 5 75p